VALERIO VARESI is a journalist with *La Repubblica*. Both *The Dark Valley* and *River of Shadows*, his first two novels in English translation, were shortlisted for the Crime Writers Association International Dagger.

JOSEPH FARRELL is professor of Italian at the University of Strathclyde. He is the translator of novels by Leonardo Sciascia and plays by the Nobel Laureate Dario Fo.

RIVER OF SHADOWS

"The narrative acumen of a master storyteller"

BARRY FORSHAW, *Independent*

"Varesi exposes a dark history that still has the power to unsettle"

JOAN SMITH, *Sunday Times*

"A heavily atmospheric narrative . . . an astute analysis of Italy's modern challenges and conflicts"

THEA LENARDUZZI, *Times Literary Supplement*

THE DARK VALLEY

"This is writing at its best and even better is surely to come"

ALASDAIR BUCHAN, *Diplomat*

"Varesi's plotting is sound, and his pacing good . . . Where he raises his game from the common ruck, however, is in his almost painterly evocation of wretchedly dark atmosphere and character. He could be the long-lost heir to Caravaggio" ROSEMARY GORING, *Sunday Herald*

"Varesi's talent for evoking place and time draws a politically and socially engaged picture of Italy's past, and the processes that have changed for ever its rural demography" *C.W.A. Judges' Comments*

Also by Valerio Varesi in English translation

River of Shadows (2010)
The Dark Valley (2012)

Valerio Varesi

GOLD, FRANKINCENSE AND DUST

*Translated from the Italian by
Joseph Farrell*

MACLEHOSE PRESS
QUERCUS·LONDON

First published in the Italian language as *Oro, Incenso e Polvere*
by Edizioni Frassinelli, Milan, in 2007
First published in Great Britain in 2013 by MacLehose Press
This paperback edition published in 2014 by

MacLehose Press
an imprint of Quercus
55 Baker Street
South Block, 7th Floor
London W1U 8EW

ISBN (PB) 978 1 906694 388
ISBN (EBOOK) 978 1 849168 687

1 3 5 7 9 8 6 4 2

Designed and typeset in Caslon by Patty Rennie
Printed and bound in England by Clays Ltd, St Ives plc

To Simona Mammano, for her valuable advice,
to Girolamo Laquaniti for having told me a lovely story
to Ilde and the "girls" at Frassinelli publishers.

Author's Note

There are two different police forces in Italy: the CARABINIERI are a military unit belonging to the Ministry of Defence; the POLIZIA are a state police force belonging to the Ministry of the Interior.

The maresciallo (carabinieri) and Commissario Soneri (polizia) can only be coordinated by the questura, otherwise they report to different ministries. As to the different hierarchies, the maresciallo is a rank below the commissario.

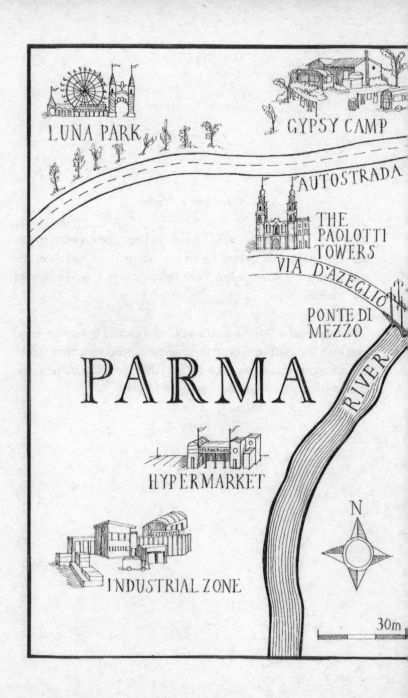

I

THE PAOLOTTI TOWERS and the bell towers of the Cathedral and San Giovanni were gradually disappearing under a blanket of mist, their outlines dissolving. It was like an evening from times gone by, before the seasons blended into one another, an evening when the city wrapped itself in a misty shell, when it seemed suddenly familiar again and the noise, bustle and frenzy died down. In the enveloping mist, Parma had stopped yelling and had taken instead to whispering, like an old lady in church.

Soneri was strolling through the streets, in the grip of a not displeasing nostalgia. Each step summoned up a litany of memories: the university, rushing along Via Saffi, and Ada, lost too soon. He stopped in Piazzale della Pace when he could no longer make out the austere lines of the Pilotta or the houses in Via Garibaldi. There was now nothing to be seen but mist, ahead, behind, beside, above. The only sure thing, and a fleeting one, was the pavement on which he walked. Then his telephone rang. Life, illusory and deceptive life, was reaching out to him.

"Am I interrupting something, sir?" Juvara said nervously.

"Not at all. Just imagine that you've grabbed me by the hair of my head a split-second before I fell down a well."

The words were so gnomic that Juvara had no idea how to respond. "So what is it?" Soneri added.

"There's one hell of a pile-up on the autostrada, a near catastrophe . . ."

"You get catastrophes in other places apart from autostradas. And you tell me it's only a *near* catastrophe . . ."

"Alright, an accident. A really nasty one. More than a hundred cars, lorries, some on fire . . ."

"O.K., so you've alerted the traffic police, no doubt?"

"No need . . . they're already on the case."

"Good. So everything's in order?"

"No, not entirely . . ." the inspector stuttered.

"What then?"

"The questore has asked if one of us could go along. Somebody's been on the telephone to say that some gypsies are wandering about among the cars, stealing things." Juvara was struggling to get the words out.

"Why doesn't he send in the flying squad?" Soneri said with some feeling, but at the same time he was aware of a need to escape from loneliness and the trap of nostalgia.

"He already has, but with the mist the way it is . . . well, the fact is, they can't find the place. There's no-one on duty who knows his way around the Lower Po Valley."

Soneri felt a threat taking form somewhere above his head, like a coiled spring about to snap. Instead, it was he who snapped as he turned in the direction of the Steccata.

"Where is this place?"

"Near the service area at Cortile San Martino. There's a road running alongside the Autostrada del Sole."

"I know the one. What about the flying squad?"

"They're driving around in circles. The questore says you're the only man who knows the roads well enough . . . the only one in Parma."

"Fetch the car and pick me up in the piazza in five minutes."

Juvara was unable to find him. The commissario had to wave his arms and jump over the chain between the columns to attract his attention.

"I'll drive," he said the moment the inspector rolled down the window. "With you at the wheel, the best we can hope for is to end up in a ditch."

Juvara did as he was told, with some relief. "I had a problem getting out of the gate at the police station," he mumbled, as he got into the passenger seat.

"That's why you never land a girlfriend. You're hopeless."

Juvara smiled awkwardly and said nothing, relaxing only when Soneri gave him an affectionate poke in the ribs as he settled behind the wheel.

The mist rose over the bonnet of the car. As they left behind the creamy light of the street lamps and moved into the narrow country roads they were plunged into a near impenetrable darkness.

"You can see why they couldn't find the place," Juvara said.

"On a night like this, everybody should stay at home, preferably in front of a roaring fire, better still with a cat on their lap. Think of all the great opportunities we miss. But, maybe it's just as well," Soneri said, thinking back to his earlier nostalgia trap.

Juvara looked at him uncomfortably, making no reply and staring tensely at the road, or at the little he could see of it, which was hardly more than two metres ahead. "Even if we do manage to find the place, with all this mist about, how are we going to catch the people we're after?"

"O.K., one thing at a time. Let's concentrate on finding the right road," the commissario said curtly. Whenever more serious subjects came up, the inspector was quickly out of his depth. It was impossible to know if it was due to indifference or shyness. Or maybe it was on account of his youth. When Soneri had been thirty, what did he care about weighing up choices or roaring fires at home?

They drew up at a fork in the road where there were no signs. Soneri was not sure which was the right way, but some instinct made him turn to the left.

"Might be this one. Who knows?" he muttered to himself.

They carried on for a few hundred metres until they heard a menacing roar in the darkness, like the despairing bellow of an animal in the slaughterhouse.

"Did you hear that?" Juvara said, sitting bolt upright as the figure of a bull came into view in the fog lights.

"Yes, and we're on the right road," Soneri said.

The animal must have weighed several hundred kilos but seemed more apprehensive than aggressive. The commissario noticed Juvara take hold of his door handle and stiffen up.

"I'm wearing red," he said.

"Relax. He's vegetarian. Even if there's a lot of good eating on you, it's of no interest to him. Be careful not to upset him, though." Soneri laughed as he flashed the lights at the bull. The beast turned lazily to face them, before lumbering off with his great scrotum swinging between his legs.

"He's well hung," the inspector said, plainly relieved.

"What did you expect? He's not like our dear Chief, Capuozzo."

They drove on in the mist from which emerged bellows and cries like the pleas of orphans at night. They caught a second bull in the headlights, its tail raised as it trotted across the road.

"A limousin. Good beef cattle."

"I thought they were less dangerous," Juvara said.

"You're thinking of limousines, and even there I'm not so

sure. Think of what happened to J.F.K., not to mention all the Cosa Nostra men who've met their end in one of them."

They came across an enormous cow, which began to moo as they drew up close. "She's going to have a memorable night of passion, with all those bulls on the loose," Soneri chuckled.

"So long as they find each other."

"They're not shy and retiring like you."

They continued on their way until the mist took on a yellowish tint.

"It's either a motorway café or a hypermarket," Soneri said.

They stopped at another fork in the road. Everything around them was the colour of moscato wine. The engine was just turning over, allowing them to hear the rhythmic strains of a primitive, metallic music, heightened by the mooing and pawing of the bulls running free in the mist. When the commissario rolled down his window to look out, the interior filled with the acrid stench of burning. "Roasted tyres on the menu," he said, swerving to the right in the direction the smell seemed to be coming from.

"We're near the accident," Juvara said.

"Smart deduction."

"What about those bulls? Where did they come from?" the inspector said, apprehensive once more.

"Am I right in thinking that you suspect that they were on a lorry which crashed into another vehicle?" Soneri said in the same ironic tone as before. "Disasters can sometimes give rise to liberation."

There were now black streaks in the mist, and the smell of burning was even more pungent. The commissario leaned forward and looked upwards through the windscreen. The sky had the appearance of a huge peroxide wig with darker patches. He turned to Juvara, who looked as amazed as a child in a fairground. Ahead of them a herd of pigs was clustered together, as though homesick for their sty. Meanwhile a horse, bringing its own aura of mystery, galloped past through the darkness which was now filled with plaintive animal cries.

"What's this? *Animal Farm*?" Juvara said.

He was answered by a neighing sound somewhere in the surrounding darkness, but almost at the same time they became aware of a flickering brightness on their left which had the colour of a good Lambrusco. The sight disconcerted the commissario, who stopped the car.

"That's carcasses burning," Juvara said.

"That's impossible. The autostrada should be on the far side." It was the only thing he seemed sure of. He remained silent for a few moments, trying to get his bearings. He was lost and floundering, overwhelmed by memories of the days when he had walked those remote roads on the plain searching for isolated spots. The past was yet again taking hold of him and this time the memories were the names of girls with whom he had long since lost all contact.

He inched forward, and rolled down his window a little. He decided to follow the smell, as do animals on heat, as the bulls were doing at that moment in pursuit of the invisible. Shortly afterwards, over to his right, patches of more intense brightness appeared. The autostrada was indeed there, a long stretch of road indifferent to its burden of tragedies.

Soneri turned onto a track running alongside it and drove towards the fires. There was a little space on the footpath and he parked there among piles of rubble, broken tiles, waste paper and used handkerchiefs. Juvara too got out, but he stayed close to the car and kept the door open.

"Now what?" Soneri asked himself as he looked at the

slope strewn with rubbish on the other side of the barrier. The inspector, continuing to look cautiously about him, made no reply.

The commissario walked a little further along the path. The flickering light of the fires, the dome of mist tinted with yellow, the bellowing of the stricken animals and music in the distance made the whole scene somewhat surreal. The countryside behind him was swarming with life not native to it, and he knew that ahead of him lay rows of crashed cars, and hanging over them was the pall of death, disturbed only by the coming and going of breakdown trucks and the sirens and flashing lights of the emergency services.

He turned back. "Call headquarters and tell them we're on the spot. Ask them what we should do next."

The inspector was only too pleased to get back to the car. "Sir, that fire . . ." he asked, leaning out the window and pointing to a bonfire on the far side.

"The gypsies, obviously," Soneri said.

"They're telling us to be patient and stay put until the police cars turn up," the inspector told him. "Can you hear the fairground?"

"What fairground?"

"The one they've put up at the shopping mall behind the service station."

"Ah, so that's where the music's coming from."

"That's right. A lot of people are going there."

At that point, the barking of a dog could be heard above the animal chorus. The mist made it difficult to tell if the sound was coming from the slope or from ditches on the far side of the barrier.

"Another lost soul," Soneri said.

"It must have been in one of the cars caught up in the crash," Juvara said.

There was a call on the radio. Pasquariello, the head of the flying squad, wanted directions to find the commissario. A sudden gust of wind made the column of smoke change direction and the stench of burning tyres came through the open window. Juvara started coughing and threw open the car door to get a breath of fresh air.

"That's how they flush out foxes," Soneri said. He saw the inspector leap back into the car with unexpected agility. He turned and became aware of a bull's head a couple of metres away. The beast's snorts made it seem like a cartoon caricature, but this effect vanished when it opened its mouth, let its tongue hang out, arched its back and gave a roar that made the mist vibrate. The commissario was unsure if it was looking for food or wanted to mark off territory of its own, but Soneri remained there rooted to the spot, while Juvara, already inside the car, shouted to him to get in.

It all seemed to him unreal, a fairground scene like the one in the distance with the blaring musical background. There he was, confronting his own Minotaur, enveloped in a mist which had taken on the improbable colours of a showground. He heard Juvara's imploring voice, but he stayed where he was, staring at the motionless beast, watching his own reflection in its large, resigned eyes. It lasted no more than a second; the bull lumbered away and vanished into the mist.

"Your shouting nearly got me gored, Juvara."

"You take too many risks. It was about to charge you for real."

"Always remember that animals are much less dangerous than human beings. A policeman is always more likely to be killed than a vet."

Meanwhile the dog went on barking, the sound growing more shrill and irritating. "He's really scared," Juvara said.

"He's afraid of the bulls, just like you." As he spoke, headlights shone out ahead of them.

"Here come the police cars," Juvara announced.

"We turned into a half dozen farmyards," one of the officers said, getting out of his car.

"You've seen nothing yet. Your real troubles will start when you try to find your way back," Soneri said, intending to be facetious but succeeding only in unsettling them.

"Where's that dog?" snapped the man who seemed to be in charge of the detachment.

The commissario made a vague gesture, raising his hand and waving it about. "There's no sign of gypsies," the officer said.

In reply, Soneri pointed to the fire on the opposite side of the road. The officer in charge mumbled something before putting a cigarette in his mouth and lighting it. The commissario did the same with his cigar. They stood facing each other in silence until a loud moo came from very close by and another stray animal appeared, this time little more than a calf, as the commissario understood from the short horns.

"Fuck me!!" The commanding officer leapt to one side, pulling his Beretta from its holster.

"No need for that. It'll do you no harm. Anyway, with this mist, there's no knowing where the bullets will end up."

The officer moved back towards the safety of his car. The bullock pawed the ground as though it was considering charging, but then changed its mind.

"If it sees you're afraid, it might be tempted to rough you up a bit."

The officer lowered his pistol only when he saw the beast trot off, but his hand was trembling as he replaced the weapon in its holster.

"Will I take the M12?" one of the policemen said,

referring to the semi-automatic they had been issued with. His superior officer said no, but he appeared badly shaken. Soneri stared at him. "First time you've seen a bull?"

The officer shook his head. He was young, one of a generation who had received all its training in a police academy. Soneri was conscious of belonging to a different age, when a peasant world still existed and a bull did not seem such an alarming, extraordinary rarity. Before he had time to feel superannuated, the headlights of the second car shone on them.

"Will someone tell me why the fuck we've been sent to this godforsaken place?" shouted the new arrival.

"Because of the gypsies, Esposito," his colleague reminded him.

"This is a jungle. We've got pigs, bulls, cows . . ."

"The world is full of pigs and cows," a policeman said.

"But not of bulls," Soneri said, cutting short the conversation.

"Commissario, can you tell me what we're supposed to do even if the gypsies *are* looting things? I can't even see the tips of my shoes," Esposito said.

"You'd better ask Capuozzo," the commissario said, plainly annoyed. "Drive up and down this road with the headlights full on, just so they know you're here."

The officer in charge was struggling to make out what was being said, because the dog was barking wildly.

"Fuck that bloody dog," Esposito cursed. A new chorus of moos struck up, muffled by the mist.

"We should continue patrolling until fresh orders come through," Soneri said.

The officers got back into their cars. In the yellow-streaked darkness, the disco music continued to blare out while the firefighters were in all probability dragging the dead and injured from the twisted metal. Soneri watched the flickering blue lamps of the police cars until they were swallowed up by the darkness. He was left on his own, a cigar in his mouth. From the direction of the autostrada he could hear a constant racket occasionally interrupted by the sound of a car accelerating away. From time to time the plain around him would come alive with some sudden agitation, animals running, chasing and perhaps facing blindly up to each other.

"Commissario!" He heard Juvara call out.

"What is it?" Soneri moved back to the car.

"I thought I heard someone running from the autostrada into the fields."

Soneri stretched out his arms. "What are we supposed to do? Unless they run into us . . ." He stopped when he saw one of the squad cars coming towards them too quickly for a routine patrol. Esposito jumped out and ran towards the commissario, waving his arms in the air. "We've found a body, a badly burned body. I think it was one of those involved in the pile-up."

Without saying a word, Soneri got into his car and followed them along the road. When he got out, the dog was barking nearby. Esposito switched on his torch and turned it onto a body, disfigured and mutilated by the flames, lying on the other side of the metal fence. There was a little Pomeranian of an indefinable colour two steps away, yelping loudly.

"Do you think he was its master?" Juvara said.

The commissario shook his head. "Normally they keep watch in silence. This one is trying to tell us something."

"The accident happened right here. He must have been thrown from the car," said one of the officers.

Soneri looked up towards the autostrada. He struggled to make out the wrecked cars, still in a long line, each one concertinaed into the one in front. A little further on, a burning tyre was giving out black smoke. "Maybe," he said, but he did not sound convinced. He took the torch from Esposito's hand and went over to the barrier, staring at that dead body whose features were now only vaguely recognisable as human.

"I don't believe he was one of the motorists. We'd better call in the forensic squad. Be careful not to trample on anything. Cordon off the area around the body."

Juvara trotted at his side as he made his way back to the car. "Do you really think . . . ?"

Soneri nodded. "That body was dumped there, but was burned somewhere else."

He took out his mobile and dialled Nanetti's number, leaving the inspector consumed with curiosity. "At the toll booth, go in the direction of the Asolana . . . you know, where Guido's *osteria* used to be. No, before you get to the grain store," he explained to his colleague, listing places which were no longer there.

When he hung up, Juvara tried to question him, but Esposito butted in. "We've taped the site off. Pasquariello is in the office and he says one car is enough if the situation is under control, but he said to check with you first."

"One will do. Apart from anything else, if there was anything to steal, they'd have gone off with it before we turned up. Besides, it's a secondary matter now," he said gravely.

Juvara remained silent, reflecting on those last words. "Are you saying we were called out on a routine matter and discovered a murder?"

"Most things are a matter of chance," Soneri said. "You ought to know that by now, seeing the number of years you've been with the force."

They went back to where the corpse was and at that

precise moment they heard a high-pitched cry, something between a scream and a groan, from a field nearby – enough to unnerve Esposito and his colleague. "Good God, what's that?" Juvara exclaimed. "Not even in the wilderness . . ."

Soneri alone remained calm. The cry caused him no anxiety but reawoke in him old experiences of farmyards, frost and horseback rides at Christmas. It was a sound he recognised from his childhood and which at that moment resurfaced from the depths of his memory as a recognition. "It's nothing to be alarmed about. There's another death, but this time it's only a pig."

Esposito and Juvara looked incredulously at each other. "So who did it?" they said, almost in chorus and in the stern tones of an interrogating policeman.

"By a process of simple deduction, I'd say it must have been the gypsies. There's no-one else in the vicinity."

"I thought they were all Muslims," Esposito said.

"The majority are one hundred per cent Italian," Soneri said in a tone of reproof. The ignorance of fellow officers on issues on which they should have been properly briefed always astonished him, but just then a car drew up to take their minds off pigs and gypsies. The forensic squad had arrived.

"One day you're going to get in touch with some good news," were Nanetti's first words as he got out his car. "You're lucky I know this zone, otherwise we'd have been looking at this corpse tomorrow morning."

"We're the only ones who know this territory," the commissario said, as though confiding in an old comrade.

"I know what you mean. We're ready to be put out to grass."

"The correct term is care home," Soneri laughed. "That's what Capuozzo calls it, and he means care of the mind."

"His," Nanetti shot back, giving him the V sign. "Anyway,

are you sure this isn't somebody who got battered about in the crash?" he asked, pointing to the autostrada.

"First a car crashes, then it catches fire. If someone is thrown onto the road, he escapes the fire, doesn't he?"

Nanetti nodded, but he could not hide a certain exasperation at the commissario's ostentatious display of logic.

"Perhaps the car went up in flames, and perhaps this poor soul tried to escape from the fire which was already engulfing him and ended up here. But in that case, he would have rolled about on the grass and there would have been some traces. Those paper hankies and those bottles, for instance, they would have been blackened or at least there would be some mark on them, no? And the grass would have been scorched, wouldn't it?"

Nanetti ran his torch up and down the slope and had to agree that there was no trace of all the things the commissario had listed. He let out a groan and said, "I'm afraid you're right. O.K., let's cut the fence and search the ground, then we can carry off the body when we get authorisation from the magistrate. The autopsy will be the real test."

"By the way, who's the on-duty magistrate?" Soneri asked.

"We're in luck: it's Dottoressa Marcotti. You know how good she is."

"Excellent. We'll not have to waste time spelling out the totally obvious." Soneri went towards his car, signalling to Juvara to follow him. The two men were walking along the autostrada barrier when they heard a deep groan, sounding as though it were produced by bronchial tubes clogged up with catarrh. The sound was accompanied by something frantically pawing the ground, and they found themselves face to face with an enormous, rotating mass topped by a majestic pair of horns. A bull and a cow were coupling on the road, almost knocking down the iron railing of a little bridge.

Juvara looked on, in part troubled and in part excited by the sight. The commissario was amused to see that Juvara was so engrossed that there was no trace of fear on his face.

"Cheers!" Soneri said to the inspector, who seemed hypnotised. He could not tear himself away even when the bull got down from the cow's back, quivering, his head lowered, his great detumescent penis dangling and almost touching the surface of the road.

"Is that the same one we saw before?" Juvara wanted to know, finally getting a grip of himself.

"Of course it is. Can't you tell from its balls?"

"Seriously?"

The commissario gave him a nudge. "How the hell should I know? It certainly doesn't look like a limousin. It lacks class."

At that moment, the cow arched its back and peed loudly on the road.

"Usually it's the male who does that afterwards." The inspector had a beatific smile on his face, as though it was he himself who had just been making love.

"So, I hope you picked up something there. Anyway, it's time to go."

The two beasts had disappeared. The mist was still all around them and Juvara seemed hopeful that another miraculous vision would emerge. On Soneri, however, that unexpected juxtaposition of past and present created in him a kind of alienation. He was in the Lower Po valley and in a familiar mist, but somehow it all seemed unreal to him, a caricature of what was imprinted on his memory.

He started up the engine and inched forward into the dense wall of mist. "And they called this road the Autostrada del Sole," muttered Juvara at his side.

2

FOR ABOUT A quarter of an hour they circled round the bonfire which was blazing in the distance like an unattainable sun.

"Where is this road?" Soneri said, growing impatient.

"You're not really planning to go to the gypsy place, are you?" Juvara said in alarm.

"Why not? Calm down, they're not as bad as the bulls."

"But there's only the two of us . . ."

"Nothing's going to happen. These are not aggressive people."

"If you say so."

"How come you're so prejudiced? You're scared of animals, but bodies burned by the roadside have no effect on you. You're afraid of gypsies and yet you hang out in discos filled with thugs with knives in their pockets, drugged to the eyeballs."

The inspector gazed at him as though the thought had never occurred to him. "I suppose it's a matter of habit . . ."

"No, it's simply that people are fearful of the unknown. Anyway, let me introduce you to them."

He drove on for a few minutes but the camp and the fire seemed to keep changing position. After a bit, he turned the car round and went back the way he had come. Thirty seconds later, the headlights lit up a white, rusting sign on which it was just possible to make out the word: DUMP.

"This has to be it," the commissario said, turning into the site.

Juvara remained silent and impassive as he watched Soneri manoeuvre the car and drive up towards some huge metal dustbins filled with rubbish. A group of children emerged and ran off in all directions. The two men drove on towards the fire, around which at least twenty people were seated, feasting. A side of pork with some meat still on the bones was hanging from a kind of trestle.

"You see now who is more dangerous?" Soneri asked iron-ically, pointing to the slaughtered animal.

Their appearance among the caravans had brought the barbecue to a halt. All eyes were trained on the commissario and inspector. An age-old distrust was evident on the faces of all those present, giving a chill to the scene. For a few seconds the only sound to be heard was the crackling of the fire, but then a middle-aged man with a floppy Borsalino cap and a tight-fitting jacket came over to them, stopping a few feet in front of Soneri and making a enquiring gesture with his chin.

"Police," Soneri said, with every appearance of calm. Juvara took up a position one step behind, watchful and wary.

"If you're here about the pig . . ." the gypsy began, but stopped as he saw the policeman shake his head.

"I couldn't care less about the pig," Soneri said. "God rest his soul," he added, smiling over at the remains attached to the hook.

"Well then?" The gypsy stretched out his arms.

"How long have you been here?"

The man turned towards the others to seek help. "Must be a couple of months now. Look, we've got nothing to do with any thefts. We killed this pig because it was already injured.

It was losing blood and would have died in any case. It was trying to force its way in everywhere, even into our caravans."

"Served it right, then," Soneri said sarcastically. "Anyway, I'm not accusing you of having stolen . . ."

"You always do. Every time something goes missing, it's always our fault."

Soneri turned and saw that a group of boys had gathered round his car. The man shouted out something in an incomprehensible dialect and they all scarpered.

"Someone was burned to death by the autostrada . . ." he began again, approaching the topic warily.

"Two people. That's what we heard. We went along to take a look, but the traffic police told us to go away. We only wanted to see if we could give a hand, but we got the usual stuff – only there to rob and steal, and all that. So they can get on with it themselves. There were other people doing the stealing," he said with a snigger.

"I wasn't talking about those who died when their cars went up in flames after the accident. There was a burned body at the side of the road, but that one had nothing to do with the pile-up."

The man turned back to the group with an expression of bewilderment. "And what does that have to do with us?"

"I don't think it has anything to do with you, but you might have seen something."

"In this mist?"

"It was light during the day."

"Yes, but if someone's going to commit murder, he's not going to do it in broad daylight."

Some of the group had started eating again, having lost interest in the conversation. Mandolin music, evoking a distant land, came from some of the caravans.

"I mean, maybe a car drew up, opened its boot and . . ." Soneri insisted.

The man stretched out his arms again. "I didn't see a thing."

"Make one more effort. Ask them all. There's always somebody who sees something, but pays no heed to the one thing that turns out to be really important for us." As he finished, the commissario stretched out his hand and gave a smile of understanding.

The gypsy leader shook hands, relieved the visit was going to be over without too many complications. "I'm Omar Manservisi," he said, but his voice was drowned in the roar of a clapped-out car shooting off at speed down the road away from the camp. All the gypsies exchanged glances which Soneri could not interpret. Manservisi too became suddenly serious, but only for a moment.

"Did you catch sight of that car?" he asked Juvara as they set off.

"I only got the first half of the number plate, AB 32. There was another figure and two letters."

"Do you know the make?"

"An old Citroen XM, at least twenty years old."

"It seemed in a hurry."

"And in this mist . . ."

They passed the bins again and turned onto a side road. The commissario took a wide turn and one wheel bumped against the kerb, making the car shudder. The inspector jumped too. "Apart from the mist, they go and build these raised roads along the side of the canals," he said uneasily.

"It's because of the flooding; it lets you move about."

"Maybe so, but it's like a rodeo."

"There're bulls there too."

"Are you sure this is the right road?" the inspector said shortly afterwards.

"No," Soneri replied with a touch of anxiety in his voice, leaving the inspector in suspense. He realised as he spoke that he was not on the road he had taken on the way there. He had made a turning to follow the wheel tracks of the car which had sped out of the camp. It was all a matter of instinct.

"So where are we going?" Juvara asked.

"Let's go on a tour of the Lower Po Valley. Is that not a lovely idea? Try to imagine there's a girl here beside you instead of me."

The inspector made no reply and for a moment Soneri was afraid he had offended him. He would rather Angela had been there. It would have been more amusing with her and he would have enjoyed needling her.

"You see that?" said the inspector, pointing ahead.

"What?"

"Someone went onto the grass and nearly ended up in a ditch."

A wavy line in the mud marked the way forward for about a hundred metres.

"Do you think it happened only recently?"

"Looks like it."

"One of those bulls was most likely involved."

The commissario said nothing, but accelerated slightly, cutting confidently through the mist. He gripped the steering wheel tightly, ready to swerve. Shortly afterwards, the flashing blue lights of a police car made him draw up.

"A police cordon," Juvara said, relieved that Soneri was forced to brake.

When they came closer, they saw a car balanced precariously between a ditch and the side of the canal. It was the Citroen from the campsite.

"An evening full of surprises," Soneri said.

The patrolman was standing beside an elderly, somewhat dishevelled man. "He's drunk," the officer said.

The commissario nodded. "I did notice," he said, referring to the skid marks he had seen further back, but leaving the officer puzzled. "Who is he?" he asked, indicating the old man but not taking his eyes off the policeman.

"We're checking him out," the officer replied, pointing to his colleague on the car radio.

The man stayed silent, prepared for the worst.

"Is this your car?" the officer said.

There was no reply. The man continued to stare ahead into the mist in the background, as though he would rather lose himself in that nothingness.

"These are false documents," reported the other police officer who had been communicating the data to the control centre. "And the car is registered in the name of one Omar Manservisi, of no fixed abode."

"Oh great! Let's get this one along to the station," the patrol leader said.

The old man's attitude was surprising. For a few moments, he stood stock still in the same position, then turned towards the policeman who had taken him by the sleeve and stared at him with the expression of a bewildered child.

"Manservisi . . . Manservisi . . . I've heard that name, but I can't remember where," said the officer.

"He's one of the travelling people camped up by the dump at Cortile San Martino," Soneri informed him.

The officer looked at him in surprise. "The ones who lit the fire?"

"The very same. Manservisi is a kind of chieftain. I believe the old guy here took the car a short while back."

"Stole it? He stole something from gypsies!" The officer's tone was incredulous.

The commissario stretched out his arms, looking again at the old man who, judging by his expression, seemed sunk in a state of drunken depression. "What about the car? We can't just leave it here in case someone crashes into it."

The patrolman raised his visor and snorted: "Suppose not . . ."

"He's coming with us. You stay here until the pick-up lorry arrives," Soneri said.

This time it was Juvara who took the old man by the arm, and as he did so the man turned towards him with the same expression as before.

"You go into the back seat with him," Soneri ordered. "He looks like the sort who could do all kinds of crazy things. Keep your wits about you."

They set off and within a quarter of an hour they saw the milk-white glow of the first lights in the city. Ten minutes later they were turning into the courtyard at the police station.

"So, how come you took the chieftain's car and were going around with forged documents?" Soneri began wearily, reflecting on the bizarre conduct of this unknown figure.

The old man looked down at a point in the centre of the desk, avoiding Soneri's gaze.

Juvara cut in. "Would it not be better for us to leave him to Musumeci? He'll be here in about twenty minutes. We've got that other business to attend to."

The commissario shrugged. "The main thing is to get him to make up his mind to talk," he said impatiently. Just then, another officer came in to take the man's fingerprints.

"Look, it's in your own interests to put an end to this, eh!" Soneri said, raising his voice in growing exasperation at the man's indifference. "Could you tell us who the fuck you are?" he went on, tossing the false identity card on the table like an ace of spades. "That way we can clear this business up. You'll be charged with possession of forged documents, car theft and drunk driving, but you'll be treated lightly."

Nothing seemed to make any impression on the man, who was now sunk in a comatose stupor. The more the interrogation dragged on, the more absurd his behaviour seemed to Soneri. He was just concluding that he had a madman on his hands when the telephone rang.

"Not making much headway here," were Nanetti's opening words.

"Not surprising, with all that mist."

"It's not a laughing matter. This burned-out stump of a human being has nothing on him to identify him. He looks as though he's been on a spit."

"Have you searched around? On the grass verge?"

"You can forget the grass verge. It's been ploughed up by the emergency services. We'll come back tomorrow and comb the slope. The torches are no good in the dark."

"Alright. We can only hope you come up with something."

He was about to resume questioning the old man when Juvara and the officer who had taken the fingerprints came in.

"Commissario, there's a warrant out for this man. His fingerprints match those of Otello Medioli. He killed his wife twenty years ago. We've been on the computer and there's no doubt."

"This is some night for coincidences," Soneri said.

He turned to face the man: the suffering appearance, the watery eyes and the weary pallor made him an improbable murderer. He looked like an ordinary old-age pensioner, but no-one was more aware than the commissario of how misleading impressions could be when dealing with criminals. It was one of the pitfalls of the trade. And in the case of Medioli, twenty years on . . .

"So, you've made up your mind?"

All of a sudden, the old man burst into life. He raised his eyes and looked rapidly around as though afraid someone was spying on him.

"It's all true," he said, with a sigh which seemed to come from deep inside him.

"At last! We've made the first step," Soneri said, with a gesture of his hand which was an invitation to Medioli to continue. Meanwhile Juvara, with perfect timing, had activated the recorder and attached a microphone to the computer.

"Commissario, I was tired of that life," Medioli said, pushing back the white hair which was hanging over his forehead.

"A life on the run?"

"With those people. In the caravans, always on the move, hiding away. What kind of life is that? If I think about it, I believe I have already served my sentence. Any way you look at it, I'd have been better off in jail."

Medioli abandoned himself to self-pity, while the commissario made an effort to imagine the man as he must have been twenty years before, still strong, sure of himself, perhaps even arrogant. When he compared him to what he was today, Soneri almost spluttered with laughter, but this, he then reflected, was the destiny of all humankind.

"You could have left sooner, couldn't you? As you did this evening. You'd have got away with it if it hadn't been for the mist, and the fact that you were drunk. After all this time . . ."

"I didn't know where to go. In the outside world, I don't

have anyone left, and in the world of the Roma travellers, I've always been a guest."

"You've no children?"

"Yes, two grown-up daughters, but they didn't want any more to do with me. I read that in the papers. I've never seen my grandchildren."

Soneri weighed him up, looking at him distrustfully. There was something about the man and his story which did not square up, and while he was trying to work him out, the officer who had taken the fingerprints brought in an old folder from the archives with the dossier on Medioli. He started flicking through it. It had been done with a typewriter and the pages were turning yellow. "Probable motive, jealousy," he read in the report.

"You stabbed her because you thought she was seeing another man, is that right?" Soneri asked abruptly, continuing to read. The man had several previous convictions for causing an affray, malicious damage to public property and resisting arrest.

Medioli nodded like an altar boy.

"But was it true?"

"I don't know. It's hard to think back after all this time. It's as though it belongs to another life."

"Yes, I can understand," murmured Soneri, thinking of his own and of other people's lives. "Unfortunately it's the same one."

The old man replied with a despairing, unresisting look. "I'm old and infirm. I've nothing to lose. All I ask is a place where I can die with dignity. Something other than a caravan, something that doesn't follow laws that are not mine. I would like a normal end – I just want to be like other people, even if that means being in jail."

"And you're telling me that's why you put on this crazy

act, this absurd flight? You must have known it was going to make us suspicious."

"A last clutch at life. If it had gone well, I'd have had a couple of hours of excitement, but it would've been even better if I'd crashed the car like the people on the autostrada. That too would have been a normal end. I heard the collisions in the dark. One after the other, a barrage, and I thought: if only that had been me . . ."

"I would hardly call that a normal end. There's a burned body on the side of the motorway in front of the camp . . . Maybe that's somebody's wife who met her end because of a husband like you."

Medioli seemed to stiffen. "What have I got to do with that business?"

"I've no idea. But I did see you make off as soon as we arrived. What do you expect me to think?"

"Commissario, I swear . . ." The man did not manage to complete the sentence. He held his head in his hands and sat hunched up as though he wanted to disappear.

"If you hadn't been as naïve as you have been . . ." Soneri said, attempting to console him. "Listen, let's do a deal: you give me another lead. You tell me all you know or have heard around the camp. Maybe, over there, someone noticed some movement, saw a car pull up . . ."

"If there was anything, the one to ask would be Omar. He checks everything and knows everything that's going on."

"You weren't on the best of terms with him?"

Medioli shrugged again. "You're O.K. over there only as long as you're useful."

"Same as everywhere else."

"Maybe so. Anyway, I was tolerated there, and if you're not one of their kind . . ."

"So how exactly were you useful?"

"I'm a mechanic. I can fix cars and engines."

"Is that all?"

"I was the odd job man. There are not many men who really work. The women and children earn their keep by begging. You understand?"

The commissario nodded.

"I was fed up doing their bidding," Medioli said bitterly. "And when I began to feel my age and get aches and pains, they started complaining that I was not pulling my weight. Some of their cars would never move even if you shoved them. I sometimes did some work for the people in the fairgrounds, and that is one hellish life."

"Are you telling me you've spent the last twenty years with the travelling people?"

"Why not? What choice did I have?" Medioli said, raising his voice slightly, seemingly on the verge of tears. "I threw it away, remember?"

"You threw it away the day you decided to murder your wife."

Medioli sighed and seemed to be once again peering into the emptiness.

"Was it really out of jealousy?" Soneri asked again.

"What does it matter?" the man whispered. "I was another person. When you grow old, you might be more forgiving and understand criminals better. You can never tell. I have been a criminal, but now I could be a policeman."

"I understand them today, don't doubt it. At least, I understand why they behave in a certain way. Then there's the law, but that's another matter."

"Perhaps my wife was not unfaithful to me," the old man murmured, sounding like a sleepwalker. "The problem is that she was vague, ambiguous. She gave me the impression that she was not thinking only of me. She kept me on tenter-hooks. That was what I really couldn't stand."

"It's the best way to make people love you," Soneri said, "but I understand it might not be easy to put up with some-body who wants to be in charge."

"That's the way it was then . . ." Medioli said, letting his hands fall on his lap in a sign of surrender, while the com-missario kept his eyes on him, thinking how grotesque, inconsistent and senseless life was.

"I still don't understand why you stayed with these people for twenty years," Soneri said, getting back into the police-man role. "Twenty years roaming about in muddy camps with people who never accepted you."

"I had no idea where to go and I hardly ever had any money. I had a half friend who worked in a fairground and I asked him to hide me until everything blew over, but the way things went, until yesterday I ended up moving from one tribe to another, running here and there, wherever there was a call for my services. I was pushed from pillar to post. It was the only way to avoid arrest. You know that a camp with travelling people is the best place to hide."

The commissario thought that observation over and it seemed to him the most logical thing that had been said in the course of that bizarre evening. Medioli's story was just one surreal piece of it. Juvara called him back to the present by going over to him discreetly. "Commissario, do you want us to make a start on checking the register of missing persons? I was wondering if . . ." he said, alluding to the body.

Soneri nodded, but was still deep in thought.

"Will we include foreigners?"

"Definitely," he replied, and as though on automatic pilot, turned back to the old man. "Were there many foreigners in the camp?"

"Not too many, but I knew a lot who tended to hang about. Up till yesterday, there was a group of Romanians at the dump. We let them be because they had been chased away from somewhere else. The spaces around the dumps are the only places where you don't get evicted."

The door opened and the same officer as before came back in. "We're ready," he announced, approaching Medioli.

"So am I," Soneri said, placing his hands on the desk in the manner of a man who has nothing more to ask. Medioli appeared disconcerted. "Are you locking me up?" he asked ingenuously.

The officer looked across at Soneri in bewilderment. "The magistrate will question you tomorrow," Soneri said.

"I was beginning to feel at ease with you," Medioli murmured, seeming overcome by despairing regret.

Soneri gestured to make him understand that this was routine and there was nothing he could do about it. The scene seemed to him, yet again, a kind of dream.

The old man stayed in his seat for a bit, and when the officer took him by the arm he had the same look of disbelief he had had at the beginning.

3

ANGELA AND THE commissario woke very early, when it was still as dark as midnight. He imagined that the previous evening's mist still lingered on outside and that everything was damp. In some way this idea enhanced the dryness and warmth of his own little corner. Angela stretched out her hand and slipped it under his pyjamas. She too was warm and her caress gave him reassurance and brought back childhood pleasures. A sense of delight mingled with unease pervaded his whole being, making him feel almost ashamed of indulging in a passivity which clashed with his normal role in life. It was as if he was letting himself go, regressing towards feelings which, however distant, were still keenly felt. As she searched more and more insistently for him, the commissario felt her body draw closer and at that moment he grasped how some men might find in a woman their lost mother, in a different way perhaps but a way which was perfectly recognisable. He understood how adulthood might well kill many things, yet without really killing them off.

Later the commissario told Angela about the evening before in the yellow mist, the animals emerging from it, the bulls, the fires burning in the night, the car speeding off and the story of Medioli.

"What is this? Euphoria? You sound drunk – on me, I hope."

"It does seem like a tale told by a drunk," he agreed. "The mistake lies in our way of thinking. We believe that everything should unfold in accordance with a predictable pattern, and when that doesn't happen, we're left baffled."

"When you start to philosophise, you're always troubled by bad thoughts," she said, putting her arms round him.

"Have you ever had any dealings with Roma travellers?"

"I have defended one or two in trials for theft. I was duty solicitor. Why?"

"Yesterday evening I ended up in a camp, the one where Medioli had been living. It's a world apart, with its own rules and regulations."

"Laws as we know them – written laws – are tied to territory, and they have none."

"And there are no written laws for them. It's all based on tradition."

They were interrupted by the ringing of the telephone.

"There's no chance of us ever getting a long lie-in even if the alarm doesn't go off," she said savagely.

"Commissario, I'm at the station," Juvara began warily, as was his wont.

"Have a good trip! You could have warned me you were off on your holidays."

"No, I mean, I'm at the bus station . . ."

"A pilgrimage to Medjugorje, is it?"

"Sir, something strange, something very unpleasant has occurred."

"What?" the commissario asked, turning serious.

"A man, quite an old man has been found dead on the coach from Bucharest."

"Was he murdered?"

"Seems not, but they called us in anyway, as a precaution. You know how it is in these cases."

"Juvara, tell me clearly what you think. Does it look like murder or not?"

"At first sight the doctor believes it was death from natural causes. Perhaps a heart attack. Date of birth 1931, so not in the first flush of youth. But there is one suspicious fact."

Soneri seriously disliked the inspector's way of delivering his report piecemeal. "What is it, dammit?"

"Death occurred many hours ago."

"You mean he made the whole journey as a dead man? No-one realised . . ."

"Worse than that. The coach travelled through the night and they were probably all asleep. But he's shut his eyes for good."

"And when they woke up, no-one stopped the coach?"

"No they didn't. No-one noticed a thing. Maybe they thought he was still resting. They were mainly childminders and carers, and when they all got off, the driver went back into his cabin to turn the bus round, without paying any attention to the old man. He says he didn't see him. I can understand that, after driving through the night."

"So, who did find him?"

"The passengers setting off for Romania this morning."

"In other words, a whole day went by and he was left on the bus parked in the station?"

"Exactly so. This morning, a woman couldn't find a seat, so the driver did a count and found he had one extra passenger. It was the old man. He was siting in the corner at the back. You know the place where the kids like to sit on a school outing? Well, they gave him a shake, but he was already rigid."

"Another surprise. O.K., I'll be there right away. In the meantime, call the police doctor."

"Commissario, there's no need for you to come. I'm here

already. It looks to me like a case which'll be solved in an hour at the most."

"No, I'd be as well to come along."

He got up and dressed hurriedly. As he was going out, Angela asked what had happened.

"I'll have another chapter in this rum tale to tell you this evening."

At the bus station, which the people in Parma familiarly call the *Pensilina*, the crowd of Romanians hoping to get away were crammed together in the waiting room. It was a huge coach with a trailer for suitcases attached. The stages of the journey and a large blue globe had been painted on the side.

"They're nearly finished, commissario," Juvara announced as the ambulance men tried to manoeuvre a steel stretcher with the corpse out of the coach. The police doctor got off after them. "I'm pretty sure it was a heart attack," he said to Soneri.

"Did he have any luggage?" Soneri wanted to know, showing little interest in the cause of death.

Juvara, the doctor and the other officers looked around in embarrassment, trying to come up with an answer.

"Check up, would you? Do we know his name?"

This time the inspector was able to step forward confidently. "He was called Igor Dondescu. He had a three-month visa."

"Get in touch with Interpol. Let's see if they can come up with anything."

Juvara looked puzzled. He could not understand why Soneri was showing such interest in the case.

"I want to know where he was born, what work he did, who his relatives were." He himself was a bit surprised at his own zeal, especially when he noticed the puzzled expressions of Juvara and the other officers. He was not sure why he was dedicating so much attention to the story of an old man from so far off, but the incident was having the same effect on him as a bullet delivered in an envelope.

Meanwhile, another policeman came up to him with a worn, shabby bag in imitation leather. "It seems it belonged to the dead man. It was under the seat."

Soneri took it. It was old and threadbare and the handles were coming off. It looked the very picture of poverty, and in it he recognised the hardship borne with dignity which had been such a feature of his childhood years. As he was examining it, a group of Romanians gathered menacingly around him.

"You let us go?" demanded a fair-haired, generously built woman.

The officer who had found the bag signalled to her to calm down, but the woman, backed by another dozen travellers, stood her ground and glowered grimly at those around her.

"That man dead, no? What you want? Once dead, dead," shouted someone else.

The commissario looked at them wearily, and detected in them all the empty swagger of life. A gratifying impetus of physical fullness was urging them to relish the moment. They were in a hurry to get back, to find themselves again, to eat, make love and sleep in the house where they had been born. These were all too human aspirations, and every lost moment could never be recovered. On the instant, he felt himself incapable of resisting that multitude of instincts.

"Alright, if the magistrate agrees, let them go," he decided, holding the bag in his hand. He turned away without saying goodbye to anyone and got into his Alfa thinking that it was somehow inhuman to die on a bus, ignored by everyone and forgotten on a seat.

"What a business!" exclaimed Juvara when they got back to the office. "Dying like a rat in a corner."

"The poor have too many problems to be upset by death and the rich are too afraid to face it."

The inspector chewed over those words, and then muttered something incomprehensible. Soneri picked up the bag, rose from his seat and emptied its contents over his desk. Juvara came over to have a look. The first thing he saw was the wallet, made of cloth and squashed into the curved form of a buttock. They opened it. Inside there were some twenty euros and a few other coins, as well as some cards, receipts, a one-way bus ticket and the identity cards of two very similar, blond-haired, bright-eyed girls. In spite of the poor quality photographs, possibly shot in a booth in a passport office, they both looked very beautiful.

Soneri turned them over in his hand for some time, trying to find the best angle of light. He then put them into an envelope which he handed to Juvara. "Get them to do some enlargements and have a few copies printed. I'd like to know who they are. Try and find out if there are any Dondescus among the Romanians in Italy."

Once Juvara had left, the commissario picked up the telephone and asked to speak to Nanetti. "You're back from Cortile San Martino," he said with no preamble.

"Another morning in the damp," his colleague complained.

"Any news?"

"Sorry. None at all. They must have used petrol judging by the state of the body. However, I think we can say it was a woman."

"That's something. How did you work it out?"

"Soneri . . . O.K., it was all burned up, but unless the fire was especially ferocious there . . . I mean there were some remains."

"What does that mean? I've known some terrible mistakes made with suppositions like that."

"We'll find out after the D.N.A. tests, alright? But that'll take some time. Anyway, I know it was a woman from other details."

"Well, out with it!"

"If I didn't know you well, I'd tell you to go and . . . Anyway, listen, the only thing that survived the fire was a half label."

"And it was from a female garment," the commissario interrupted.

"Exactly."

"How was it saved?"

"Ah, Soneri! It was a label from her knickers, and it'd got stuck between her buttocks. The fire only singed it. And I can tell you we're talking about lingerie, *very* expensive," he added with a touch of malice.

"That's the maniac in you coming out," the commissario teased him.

"What do you mean, *maniac*? Look, knickers say more about a woman than any other item of clothing, just you remember that. They're not called foundation garments for nothing."

Nanetti's extempore reflections always left Soneri bemused. They were born of repeated, obsessive observations of everything.

"You're right," Soneri admitted. Looking at his watch, he said, "To make it up to you, let me invite you to the *Milord*."

*

Nanetti took his seat slowly, with a grimace of pain. "Please, no mushrooms, eh? They'd remind me of the dampness outside."

"Take your medicine," Soneri said, pouring a glass of Gutturnio. "So, tell me all about these knickers."

"There's not much to tell. Luxury items, as I said. Deduce from that what you like."

"Someone who was well off, in other words."

"Well off . . . In my view, a woman who can afford to pay two hundred euros for a matching bra and briefs set is not doing too badly for herself."

"How do you manage to keep so well informed about female underwear?"

"What do you want me to say? I keep up to date. My marriage might have collapsed, but I didn't turn into a monk."

Alceste, notebook in hand, interrupted them. "*Tortelli a patate* and a little tripe," Soneri ordered.

"Monkfish," Nanetti sniggered, looking challengingly at the commissario with his last remark in mind.

"In that case, can I recommend a restaurant in Ravenna?" Alceste said, a little piqued.

"No, listen. It was a private joke," he said, winking at Soneri. "Give me the same as the maestro seated in front of me."

"You're right," Soneri said, in a more serious tone. "She couldn't have been short of cash. However, this makes it all more complicated."

"I agree. Circles of grandees, powerful, well-connected people . . . Just from looking at her, she could have been a well preserved forty-year old, or else a twenty-year old bimbo making a pitch for an ageing businessman. There's no question it would have been better if she'd got her knickers from Upim."

"Well, who knows? She could equally have been some poor soul who thought she'd been handed a life-changing opportunity and had splashed out on a smart outfit. Or else a prostitute. This line of work has taught me never to take anything for granted."

"What about the old man found dead on the coach?"

"Funny business," was all Soneri would say.

"It's really gnawing away at you, isn't it?"

"Yes, but only the bits I don't understand, which is to say nearly all of it. What do you make of it? Why should an old guy get on a bus in Romania and set off for Italy with only twenty euros, a bag full of odds and ends and the photographs of two girls?"

"Search me! He must've had someone here."

"That's the most logical explanation, but the point is – who?"

A couple at the table next to them got to their feet, leaving their meal half-finished. They were still arguing under their breath as they made for the door.

Alceste arrived with two steaming plates. "These'll warm your bones," Soneri guaranteed Nanetti, nodding at the *tortelli*.

"I hope so. My poor bones feel like *savoiardi* biscuits in *mascarpone*."

They began eating in silence, but halfway through the meal they became aware of a distinguished-looking gentleman with fine features who, with absolute naturalness, took a seat at the table which had been occupied by the young couple. He sat where the woman had been and absorbed himself in the financial pages, poring over the figures dealing with stocks and shares. Soneri went on eating, but kept his eye on him. After a few moments, the man turned his attention to the remains of a roast which the woman had scarcely touched. The commissario and Nanetti exchanged knowing looks, but the stranger was completely at his ease, behaving like a normal customer. His gestures, his behaviour and his relaxed way of sitting at the table gave him an aristocratic air. He poured the leftover wine into his glass, rolling it around and sniffing it like a connoisseur. Then he continued eating with some appetite, but always with an appearance of detached ennui.

"They'd have thrown it all out," Nanetti said in a whisper.

Soneri said nothing but went on peering at the man in some perplexity.

"There you go again. Now you're starting to brood. I'd be as well having a sandwich at the bar and staring at the wall. Let's at least talk about this burned corpse," Nanetti said.

"That's exactly what I'm thinking about," Soneri muttered, turning to look once more at the man beside them.

"Alright, alright." Nanetti dropped the subject.

"I was thinking," Soneri started up again, "there could be some resemblance, some connection between the woman consumed by the flames and this man here," he said, referring to the man with the newspaper.

"Well . . ." Nanetti said with some scepticism.

"I mean, someone who turns up looking well off and in a position of authority so as to conceal what he really is."

"He's hardly concealing anything."

"Yes he is, from most people here. Remember we're nearest to him and policemen into the bargain. He had a one-in-a-million chance of bumping into two men like us. And as to being in authority, I haven't the slightest doubt. He looks like a businessman."

"A good actor. But authority . . . what authority can the burned-out stump of a human being command?"

"The dead are always in authority. They belong to a world which terrifies us and that in itself inspires respect."

Nanetti stopped to think this over. Meanwhile the man at the table alongside them had finished the roast and was about to move on to the grilled vegetables which were lying untouched on a side plate. He shot a glance from time to time at the steak left more or less intact by the male companion of the woman whose place he had taken, but he did not touch it.

Nanetti had to make an effort to keep himself from laughing at the commissario's almost morbid curiosity. "What would you be like if it was a good-looking woman?"

Soneri gave him a brief look of apology, before turning his attention back to the man, who returned his glance with a smile. "Did you see the woman who was sitting here?" he asked, with complete naturalness.

The commissario nodded in surprise. He was caught off guard, as though he had been gazing too intently at a woman's cleavage.

"Would you not kiss her?" the other man continued amiably.

"Yes, perhaps."

"For me, it is as if I *were* kissing her."

Soneri shook his head while Nanetti looked on in amusement. "I don't understand."

"Regrettably, eating with her fork and drinking from her glass are not really such intimate gestures," the man sighed.

"It'd be better to have her tongue in your mouth," Nanetti let slip.

The commissario stared at him, reproaching him for what he considered unjustifiable vulgarity, but the stranger did not lose his composure. He arranged his lips into the smile required by etiquette, and went on: "If you examine the question from the point of view of hygiene, a kiss is infinitely more compromising. In any case, I would never touch a man's plate," he said, pointing at the steak opposite him.

Soneri considered the conversation a surreal postscript to the surreal events he had witnessed the previous evening. Or perhaps he was seeing things in a wholly new way. Still reeling and disconcerted, he noted that the man's jacket had fraying hems and that his newspaper was a day old.

"I can say I dine like a king and savour sniffing the perfume left by ladies on napkins. It's almost like making love. At least I lunch and dine in their company. The rest can be left to the imagination. One can indulge in fantasy, but that's exactly why the experience is so satisfying. Sex is a function of the brain."

Neither Nanetti nor Soneri spoke a word as they rose from the table, but the strange man gave a gentle wave of the hand which spoke of a natural nobility of bearing.

"You might've offered him a dessert," Nanetti said as they went to the cash desk. The commissario still did not speak.

Alceste always wanted reassurance that he had pleased his clients. "Everything alright?"

"More than alright," Nanetti smiled. "And there was some entertainment thrown in."

Alceste's expression darkened, and he looked down. "I know. I should show him the door, but I feel sorry for him."

"Let him be. I don't care how he looks, but I am curious about him."

"He's an old marchese fallen on hard times. He was born into money, but he squandered it all. He used to have three palaces in the city, but they swindled him out of the lot because his head's in the clouds."

Nanetti stretched out his arms as if to say it happens all the time.

Alceste went on. "They call him Sbarazza. He goes from restaurant to restaurant, but I think he's happier here than anywhere else. I used to offer him a lunch through there, in the kitchen, but he declined anything that smacks of charity. That's the way he is. He wants to keep up the appearance of being master of his own world. Not many people are aware he eats leftovers. He does have class. He sits there and gives the impression of having always been there. He finishes off what others leave behind, but he'll only eat from women's plates. First he observes them, then takes their place. It doesn't bother me, but some of my colleagues can't stand that kind of behaviour. They can't bear him eating dishes others have paid for. They'd prefer to throw it out, but I could feed half the city with what's left uneaten. Nobody wants it, not even for their dogs."

Soneri and Nanetti stood listening to Alceste in amazement. When they went out, they walked in silence because there was nothing to say. A sort of burning inner wound tormented them, but without their being able to identify it precisely.

"What a story! Seems unbelievable," Nanetti said finally.

The commissario shook his head. "No, it's just that poverty causes scandal and hides itself away."

4

BY THE TIME Soneri was walking across the yard at the police station, the afternoon was rapidly dying. Gusts of mist were burying the fading day and the neon lights from the offices announced the onset of darkness.

"Did you find anything in the missing persons register?" he asked Juvara.

"No. The usual names, the ones we already know. I also checked recent crime reports, but I found nothing. I'm afraid we're dealing with an illegal immigrant."

"There's a surprise!" The thought had been preying on Soneri's mind. Someone dies miles from home, no-one knows where she is and no register with information on her can be found. At least the old man on the coach had a scrap of paper in the form of a visa. That thought unleashed a torrent of associations. The image of the bus leaving the *Pensilina* passed through his mind. The dead man on it came from Romania and there had been Romanian travelling people in the encampment next to the dump at Cortile San Martino. The burned body could have been an illegal immigrant too.

Under the inspector's astonished gaze, he jumped abruptly to his feet, but his rush to the door was interrupted by the telephone. Once again it was Pasquariello, who launched straight in: "It looks as though the Lower Po Valley has become a hunting estate."

"Has the questore given orders to fire on those poor bulls?"

"Are you serious? He couldn't give a damn about the bulls. Somebody from the transport company that was taking the beasts to the slaughterhouse came here to see me, and he told us that this morning when they went to round them up they heard shots."

"Somebody could have been shooting out of fear."

"Who knows? I dispatched a couple of squads, but in this mist not even the company vets managed to make any headway."

"It would've been hard enough to catch them even in sunlight. We'll just need to be patient and let them graze."

"Whatever. I've passed on the information to you, seeing as there was that murder."

"I'm on my way now," Soneri said, looking anxiously at the wall of grey mist outside. "Picnic time again," he announced to Juvara when he hung up.

They left the city in the evening traffic. On the narrow roads of the Lower Valley they were forced to get out of the way of cars travelling too fast or to pull in behind cars travelling too slowly.

"There are some madmen on the loose," the inspector said.

"They want to escape this oppressive darkness," Soneri replied quietly.

It was the same as the night before: the mist streaked with the yellow of the lights in the service area, the hideous music from the showground and the groping search for the right road. The only novelty was the gunfire. They heard the first shot as they drove alongside the autostrada. Soneri braked and rolled down the window. He could hear the constant roar of the traffic racing by, oddly similar to the echo of the detonation hanging in the heavy air. They were about to drive off when another shot rang out.

"A shotgun," he said. "A twelve-bore hunting shotgun, I'd say."

"You obviously know what you're talking about."

"Once they used to send us to the rifle range for target practice. Now they don't even have the funds to buy the bullets."

"I'm jealous of your expertise, commissario. I don't know much about guns."

"Forget it. If you're jealous, that only means I'm getting old."

A van emerged suddenly from the mist and drew up alongside them. A man in uniform who evidently took himself very seriously leaned out and looked them up and down with a distrustful smirk: "You're either police or carabinieri."

"Police. How did you guess?" Soneri asked with a hint of irony.

"Who else would be out in this weather?" replied the man, misjudging Soneri's tone. "We're looking for the bulls, but so far we're getting nowhere. Maybe you should take a look at those gypsies," he suggested, pointing in the direction of the dump. "They're picking off the bulls."

"You sure it's them?"

"And who else would it be? As soon as it got dark, they started up with their firing practice."

"Have you managed to round up any animals?"

"One cow and three pigs, but the bulls . . . we sent out a team of marksmen and they tried to herd them against the fence alongside the autostrada, but they didn't manage it."

Another van filled with people, perhaps the marksmen, pulled up. "We're off," said one of the men. "We'll be back tomorrow morning. We can only hope there'll be some left."

Soneri switched on the ignition and set off. A few moments later he came within sight of the bonfires in the campsite, and a few hundred metres further on he saw the sign for the dump. There was a strange calm among the caravans. The side of pork had been removed and the fire had died down. The commissario sounded his horn, but the only ones who answered his call were the children, who clustered round the car. Two old women appeared between the caravans, but quickly took to their heels.

The peace was disturbed by excited shouting and a group of men came rushing in their direction, seemingly carrying a heavy weight. As they drew closer, Soneri and Juvara saw they were carrying an injured man. The commissario jumped out of his car and ran over to the small group but none of them took any notice of him. In the general agitation he was pushed aside. At the same time, two women, one elderly and the other younger, came onto the clearing and began screaming.

"Do you think he's dead?" Juvara asked quietly.

The commissario grimaced as if to say he had no idea, but then he noticed Manservisi's Borsalino.

"What's going on?"

"He's been gored by a bull."

"So you were the ones firing the shots."

"You see? You always blame us. Why don't you take a look around? There are no weapons here."

"So how come one of your men got gored?"

Manservisi shrugged. "He's drunk. Every evening he goes roaming about. When he's had something to drink, he gets the urge to go for a walk. We're not even sure it was a bull. Maybe he just fell. Once he was run over by a car and the kind gentleman didn't even bother to stop."

The women's screams changed into a keening lament. Someone threw more logs onto the fire, sending sparks flying into the air."

"Is it serious?"

"I don't think so. Mariotto's made of rubber."

"Better call an ambulance."

"No need. Once he gets over his hangover, he'll have nothing worse than a couple of bruises."

A police car drew up and Esposito, once more in charge, got out. "What did I tell you about behaving yourselves?" he started off menacingly. "Now you've taken up big-game hunting." He was about to add another threat when he noticed the commissario standing nearby. "Sorry, sir, but these people are mad."

"They say it wasn't them who fired the shots."

"Did they tell you they've got fairies at the bottom of their garden?"

"We'll get an investigation underway. As soon as the magistrate signs the order, we'll search the camp," Soneri said.

Manservisi became agitated. "I've already told you. Why don't you search the houses around here? They're all armed to the teeth."

"Don't worry, we'll treat everybody the same," Soneri said. "I'm in charge here," he continued, addressing Esposito.

As he got into his car, Esposito could not refrain from issuing a new threat. "If we hear one more shot, even from a water pistol, we'll kick your arse so hard . . ." he said, with a forceful gesture of his booted foot.

Manservisi did not look in the least intimidated. He stared at Soneri with hostile indifference. The commissario put his arm into his and led him over to the fire. Juvara understood the situation and stayed a discreet distance away from the two men.

"You realise, don't you, that if we do have to search the camp, there might be some unpleasantness."

"Who says?"

"Listen, Manservisi, you know who we are and we know who you are. And both of us know that neither of us are saints. You follow?"

The man turned proudly to Soneri, and it was clear he was prepared to do a deal, but only on terms of equality. "What do you want?"

"Information on the person whose body was burned."

Manservisi said nothing for a while. The silence was filled with music from the fairground and roars from the autostrada still shrouded in mist.

"I can only report rumours."

The mooing of a cow distracted them for a moment. "They could be helpful," Soneri said encouragingly.

"Rumours told by drunks."

The commissario's brows furrowed. "Mariotto?"

Manservisi nodded. "Are they worth anything?"

"As much as any other man's. Wine makes people talk more freely, as you well know."

"All he told me was that the night before the accident on the autostrada, he saw somebody in a black car throw something onto the embankment. This person opened the right-hand car door and hauled out a bag. Then he went along the slope a bit, perhaps to avoid being seen. He emptied the bag and made off."

"What kind of car?"

"A B.M.W. convertible. This is the one absolutely certain detail, because Mariotto is a motor car fanatic. As for all the rest . . ." His voice trailed off, betraying his scepticism.

"What was he doing there? What time was it?"

"How do I know? He was drunk, as usual. If you knew

how many times we've had to go and drag him out of a ditch before he died of exposure. When he's been drinking, he staggers off, singing dirty songs."

"Nothing else to tell me?"

"Nothing else, commissario."

Soneri turned back to his car, but as he was opening the door a shot rang out from nearby, followed by the sound of a cow mooing. He stopped to listen, but there was complete silence. He got into the car and drove off.

"Any news about where the old man found dead on the coach came from?"

"Bucharest," Juvara replied, who was more concerned about the speed at which Soneri was driving. "Wouldn't it be better to concentrate full time on the burned corpse?"

"I just don't know where to begin. Is Medioli still our guest?" he asked, as though he had only that moment stumbled on a new lead.

"I understand the investigating magistrate, Dottoressa Marcotti, is questioning him."

"I have a few questions to put to him as well."

"But he's got nothing to do with the case."

"He does. That drunk who's supposed to have been gored by a bull saw a black B.M.W. stop on the hard shoulder and tip something that might have been a corpse onto the embankment. He was there. Up to the gills in wine admittedly, but he was there."

"When did this happen?"

"The night before the accident."

"A B.M.W. Not much to go on."

"A convertible. There can't be that many around."

"Commissario, you don't spend much time nowadays in discotheques. There are more people with money to burn than you might imagine."

"Living on credit . . ."

"Can we be sure he was seeing straight? A drunk . . ."

"In this world, it's easier to find a drunk telling the truth than a sober man. And anyway, Mariotto knows all there is to know about cars. And Medioli is a mechanic."

"Do you think they might have spoken about it the following day?"

"I don't know, but I hope so. When I have nothing to hand, I follow my instincts. It's as good a method as any, isn't it?"

Juvara looked puzzled and nodded, unconvinced. Finally they reached Via Ventidue Luglio and turned into the Borgo della Posta before arriving at the police station. The inspector got out of the car with sense of liberation, as though he had landed from a spaceship.

They walked across the yard and found Nanetti standing next to the glass door.

"You were worried about us, weren't you?"

"The moment I discovered you weren't back, I got onto the telephone to the carabinieri," he said sarcastically. "I've got news."

The commissario gestured to him with his extinguished cigar, inviting him to go on.

"It's a woman," Nanetti declared with a certain solemnity. "It's been confirmed by the first tests. In my opinion, she was a streetwalker who stepped out of line and paid the price. They struck her on the head and then set her on fire. Classic underworld behaviour."

Soneri stared at his colleague for a few seconds before winking at him. "You knew that from the start."

"Intuition and experience, now confirmed by science."

The commissario groaned. "They shattered her skull?"

Nanetti nodded. "She was already dead when they set fire to her."

"Any hypotheses on the weapon employed?"

"A fractured cranium, so therefore a blunt instrument without point or blade. Might have been a club, a bar, a metal object."

"Age?"

"Not more than thirty. More probably around twenty."

"Anything else?"

"We'll continue with tests over the next couple of days. Perhaps further elements will come to light."

"I dare hope so," Soneri said.

"Do you want to know something else? They put the girl's body beside Dondescu's, the old man on the coach. With her, nobody knows her name; with him, nobody knows if he had anybody in the world. No-one has claimed him."

Soneri reflected on that detail as he walked along the corridor towards his office. In fact it struck him as very curious.

"Is Dottoressa Marcotti finished with Medioli?" he asked Juvara.

"She's finishing now. She said you could go in."

Dottoressa Marcotti was a no-nonsense woman with a still youthful face which seemed to clash with her head of soft, white hair.

"He's convinced he's had to pay too high a price, and looking at him, it's hard to disagree," she explained to Soneri, indicating the room where Medioli was detained. "He looks scared out of his wits, or maybe he regrets having run away from the gypsy camp. I wouldn't like to think they threatened him in prison."

When the commissario sat down facing Medioli, he realised the magistrate was right. His face seemed even more haggard and his body shrunken. One day in jail had been sufficient to age him ten years.

"You know Mariotto well, don't you?"

Medioli shrugged. "Is there anyone in the camp who doesn't know him?"

"Is it true he goes around at night, drunk and singing?"

"Sounds like him."

"He says that the night before the accident on the autostrada he saw a B.M.W. convertible pull up on the hard shoulder, empty out a bag with something that looked like a burned-out body, and drive off. Did he by any chance talk to you about this?"

"No, he didn't say a thing to me. But you can be sure of one thing. If Mariotto said it was a B.M.W. convertible, that's what it was. He knows everything there is to know about sports cars."

"Did he talk much about engines?"

"That was all he ever spoke about. He could recite by heart the technical details of a whole range of cars."

"Do you think he'd recognise the car again if he saw it?"

Medioli nodded. He looked embarrassed. "Of course he'd recognise it. Now that you mention it, he did once tell me, months ago, that he'd seen a black B.M.W. in the vicinity of the camp."

"The same model?"

"Who can say? The one he was talking about had alloy wheels, was low-slung, and had a picture of a small galloping horse on the left side."

Medioli seemed to have run out of energy, or else was faking so as not to have to go on. He sat hunched in the seat like a bundle of rags. "Will I get some remission of sentence?" he asked as Soneri got up to leave.

The commissario stretched out his arms. "Just maybe, if you cooperate."

"I don't know what I can do to help," he muttered, before changing the subject. "Maybe I'll get to meet my daughters again, see my grandchildren. Do you know the worst thing? Seeing things or people who belong to you change without being part of the transformation. Feeling excluded from things which should be familiar. And knowing there is no way back."

The commissario thought of the girl whose body had been burned and of Medioli's wife. At least they had been spared that painful knowledge. But these were considerations which embarrassed him and made him depressed.

"Think over what I said to you."

"What?"

"The reduced sentence for cooperating."

"I'll think about it," Medioli promised.

The commissario said goodbye abruptly and turned his attention once more to the enigma of that crime discovered by chance one misty night.

5

ANGELA WAS PLAINLY nervous. She was performing even routine tasks listlessly, as though her thoughts were elsewhere and she was going unwillingly through the motions.

"You look as though you're still in court," Soneri reproached her.

She said nothing, but surprised him with an awkward, cold embrace. The commissario drew back. "O.K., forget I said it."

They faced each other in silence, then Angela got up from the sofa and went over to take a chair from behind the table, as though to put some distance between them.

"I'm seeing another man," she announced.

Soneri felt a cold shiver inside, and for a moment it seemed as though all the mechanisms of his brain had closed down one by one. He made an effort to control himself, but he was aware he was shaking. The revelation had left him stunned.

"I take it you're fond of him," he said, with a tremble in his voice.

She gave a deep sigh. She seemed embarrassed as she looked for the words which would cause the least pain. "I haven't done it." She spoke quietly as though to mitigate the blow, but her tone was not at all reassuring.

"Are you saying you might?"

"I don't know. Perhaps not. Maybe I'm only on a journey . . . It's just that when I'm with him, I notice I get excited."

"Do I not . . . excite you anymore?"

"It's not the same." Angela was stuttering, but in those words Soneri detected only pity and concern for him. He felt everything spinning away from him, as had happened to him on the day when Ada and their son died, or on many other occasions over issues of lesser importance when he had undergone the same surgical operation, the same amputation of something he regarded as part of him. His whole life was a process of letting go, an exercise in the provisional. With Angela he had deluded himself that everything was definitive, but it was precisely this delusion which was behind their break-up. The provisional nature of the early days was the agent which had held them together and pushed them towards each other, but without fear, curiosity and desire their relationship had grown stale.

"You're always on the move. We see each other at most a couple of hours in the evening when we're both exhausted," she said.

The commissario said nothing. He could not get up from the sofa. He felt paralysed. A deep, atavistic fear, like that experienced probably only by babies on coming into the world, took hold of him. At that moment he was a baby facing a world without Angela.

She got up from her chair to go over and give him a hug. To Soneri, that seemed like the dutiful gesture of a nurse bending over a body rigid with pain, and as he looked at her he was assailed by a previously unknown mixture of attraction and rancour, a magnetic storm of emotions which cancelled every cardinal point. The face he loved was also the face of his executioner. The anguish which gripped him left him unable to move. He had never understood as he did at that moment certain acts of men, the passions that overwhelm them, the follies they commit and which he had been so often called to investigate. For a moment he understood Medioli and the mental short circuit which must have overwhelmed him.

He remained passive as Angela gave him a kiss. He was desperate to enquire about the other man, but it seemed to him puerile to drag out the usual mass of trite questions on the subject. And he was afraid of the comparison.

She took him by the hand, raised him to his feet and led him through to the bedroom. "Don't think I'm going to ditch you. It's you I want."

Soneri allowed her to proceed in her own way, but his anxiety was in no way lessened. He found himself excited but in an unhealthy way, like the hanged man's erection. It was fear which pushed him to make love, to suggest it as the only way out of that cul-de-sac, so he put his arms around Angela, clinging to her like a drowning man.

The following day he was overcome by the convalescent's weariness, and as he made his way towards the questura he had the strange feeling of being in mourning. He had asked Angela when she would see the other man, but she had merely given a shrug and said with a smile: "Don't think about it anymore." Her tone had been anything but reassuring and now that he had a long day ahead of him, he knew that doubt and anxiety would gnaw at him. As he stepped into his office, he felt such deep exhaustion come over him that he was tempted to turn and run away, but he managed to control himself.

From the moment he saw him, Juvara was conscious of the

tension etched in every line of the commissario's face. "We've had confirmation from the Bulgarian police that the dead man on the coach was from Bucharest," he informed him.

"Do we know anything else about him?"

"Nothing yet, but they've started to look for members of his family. They've haven't come up with anyone yet."

"It all went to the dogs when the regime fell," Soneri muttered to himself, but he was moved by pity for that poor unfortunate and realised that he himself had become more fragile after the blow from Angela.

"There are so many gypsy travellers there that they've reached the suburbs of Bucharest, did you know that?" Juvara said. "They move in from the countryside and take up residence on the outskirts of the city. Maybe that's why they can't find anyone."

That old man with no relatives and no-one who remembered his name moved him, and at that moment Soneri felt so close to him as almost to identify the man's destiny with his own, both of them alone in the world.

"We'll need to round up the Romanian travelling people who had set up camp near the dump at Cortile San Martino. Make some enquiries. Ask Pasquariello if he can help," Soneri said.

Before Juvara could lift the telephone, the commissario was himself in conversation with Pasquariello. "Do you by any chance know what became of those Romanians who were at Cortile San Martino?"

"They vanished into the mist, like the bulls."

"Is that possible?"

"Moving about is not a problem for them. They're not called travelling people for nothing."

"I need to find them."

"If they've crossed the provincial border, maybe our

cousins in the carabinieri could help. But if I were you, I'd call in one evening at the car park at the sports ground. The Romanians gather there a couple of times a week. We get a lot of calls from local people who say they're worried about the commotion, but they don't cause any trouble. They get together to speak their own language, do a bit of trading and send things home. These people have maintained a strong sense of community," Pasquariello said, with a hint of nostalgia in his voice.

Soneri knew what his colleague was referring to, but he did not want to go into it, preferring to focus on the place he had indicated. "Is that not the hypermarket car park?" he asked as soon as he had located it in his mind.

"It's shared. It's really big."

"I knew the Poles and the Ukrainians went there."

"Every evening it becomes an Eastern square. A Samarkand in the land of mists."

When he hung up, still pondering that image, he heard Juvara speaking English. Obviously the person on the telephone had a limited command of the language because the inspector had to repeat himself frequently, raising his voice and spelling out the words. As he put down the receiver, he said: "I asked for someone who could speak English."

"Who was it?"

"An administrator with the Bucharest police," Juvara replied, glancing at the notes he had taken.

"What did he have to say?"

"Good question. Listen to this. As far as I could understand, Dondescu has previous convictions for begging and petty theft. They also told me he was a known alcoholic. No fixed abode . . . relatives . . ." the inspector continued flicking through his notes, ". . . no, seemingly he had no relatives."

"That's it?"

"That's all I could understand. I'll try again later and hope I get someone with a broader vocabulary."

The commissario was rising to his feet when Angela came back into his mind. The sudden thought drained him of energy and made him flop back down on his chair. The telephone rang again, relentlessly.

"Excuse me if I'm bothering you, commissario . . ." Esposito began. Soneri forced himself not to grumble about that ill-timed call, but in any case Esposito went on regardless. "You know that madman? The guy that got gored or buggered or whatever."

"The singing gypsy," the commissario suggested, thinking of Mariotto.

"That's him. He's in intensive care."

"They told me it wasn't all that serious."

"Did I not tell you that lot tell fairy stories, sir? Those people are as false as Judas. That one was never gored."

"Did the doctors say that?"

"A colleague in the police office there spoke to the consultant a while ago. He had a head injury. It could have been a bull, but it's not easy to see how."

"You're right. It's not easy."

"O.K., sir. I've passed on the information. I've got my own suspicions, but it's over to you now."

This time he managed to get to his feet, put on his overcoat and leave the room without a word. He lit a cigar as he walked along the street. The city, looking as it always did, slipped past him like scenery seen through the window of a train. His distracted, slow and apathetic observations were a mark of his inability to focus on anything. Finally he arrived at the hospital, where he discovered again that the investigation acted as an anaesthetic which made him incapable of any other thought. He read the folder in the police files: wound to the head with probable internal haematoma. He made his way to the ward, where the nurse made him wait a few minutes while she tracked down the doctor. Before long a man in a green jacket with a mask hanging over his chest turned up.

"You want to know about the gypsy?" he said abruptly.

"Mariotto . . ."

"You'll get the name from the ward sister," the doctor interrupted him, without even troubling to introduce himself.

"How is he doing?"

"We got him in the nick of time. Any later and he'd have had it. They brought him in ten hours after the incident."

"In your view, what happened?"

"Surgery's my business, not policing," he said impatiently. "I don't know anymore."

"I only ask because we were told he'd been gored."

"The only bullfighting he's done is while propping up a bar." The reply was delivered with venom. "He was three times over the drink drive limit."

It registered with Soneri that he would have to put up with the man's aggression and deal with it as best he could. He felt drained. "Could you tell me if you think a bull's horn could have left him in the state he's in?" he asked calmly.

"He could only have been running for his life with the bull in hot pursuit, seeing as he got it in the neck. Not very honourable for a matador," the doctor said sarcastically.

"So it's unlikely?"

"Make up your own mind," the doctor said and turned away.

Two nurses pushing a trolley nearly bumped into Soneri. He felt like a piece of flotsam tossed about on the current. He needed to hear Angela's voice and listen to reassuring words from her, but her mobile was switched off. He left the hospital thinking that a relationship ending at the age of fifty might indicate the borderline between a living man and a resigned man, and he had no intention of descending into resignation. He had to be active, but at that moment the only way of nurturing that illusion was work.

In the hospital grounds he saw a group of the gypsy travellers, no doubt on their way to visit Mariotto, but Manservisi was not among them. He was on the point of going over to them when his telephone rang.

"You know those photographs of the girls? The ones the old man who died on the bus had in his bag?" Nanetti blurted out.

"Of course. I have them here."

"Well, they're of the same person."

"They look similar, but I assumed they were only related, sisters or something."

"I'm telling you they're the same. These are the results of the analysis carried out by the forensic squad when they scanned the faces. The only difference is the age at which the photos were taken. The first is a teenager, the second a young woman, but they are one and the same."

The commissario studied the photographs he had pulled out of his duffel coat, and gave a grunt.

"If you look closely, the younger one has no make-up and her hair hasn't been done, while the other has taken some care over her appearance. That's what's misled us."

"This could mean a lot," Soneri said, even if he was not sure exactly what.

"What it does mean is that the old man had not seen the girl for some time. If she was related to him, either she'd been in Italy for quite a while or else they had not seen a great deal of each other in Romania."

"Quite right," the commissario said, his mind elsewhere. "Is the name of the photographer on the back?"

"Dimitriescu. We found it while we were examining the photos."

"Where's he from?"

"Do you think I wouldn't have told you if it'd been written somewhere?"

The commissario made no reply. At that point, he felt like the old man who, with no more than a few coins in his pocket and the feeble clue of a couple of photographs, had been searching for the girl. The turn of events with Angela had made him hypersensitive, as though his skin had been peeled off.

"Anyway," Nanetti continued, "these are only the preliminary results. We'll do the autopsy on the roast today and we'll see if anything else emerges."

As soon as he hung up, Soneri made another attempt to call Angela, but once again she failed to reply. He felt rising inside him an anguished frustration which produced a tightening sensation, but at the same time he was aware of a renewed flow of life. He rebelled against the idea of surrender and against submitting to any sense of finality which might result from the passing years. He had no wish to give up, because that would have been similar to encountering one of the many faces of death.

On his return to the office, he found Juvara once more on the telephone speaking English, but this time with greater fluency. Soneri sat down, but immediately jumped to his feet when the mobile in his coat pocket began ringing. "I was in court," Angela said. "I see you've called me a couple of times."

He was astonished that a phrase of such banality could be of importance to him. "I needed to hear your voice," he confessed.

"You sound like a little boy who's just been told off."

"There are people here," he said by way of excuse, and in an attempt to conceal his state of mind.

"Is that what it is?" she said mischievously.

"No, I also wanted you to know . . ."

"Don't say it. There's no point. I understood everything from your voice and that's enough for me," she whispered.

"Yes, maybe it's as well if I don't talk. I've never been any good at finding the right words for moments like these. I feel ridiculous and I'll just end up ruining everything."

"Exactly. Anyway, both of us know what this telephone call is really all about."

He felt his hopes rising. He looked up to see Juvara staring at him incredulously. He smiled at him and Juvara pulled himself together. "We know a lot more about Dondescu," he told Soneri. "He worked for years as a peat digger, but he came down with something and the state gave him a sickness pension. When the regime fell, he was evicted and found lodgings for a while in some institute. He then lived without any fixed abode in various camps with travelling people, drinking too much and getting by as best he could. His pension was revoked some months ago, and it seems it was this decision which induced him to seek his fortune in Italy."

"So we have to feel nostalgic for the communist regime," Soneri said. "At least everybody had something to live on. Any relatives?"

"They told me he had a sister who was a lot younger. She was a dancer, but they've no idea what's become of her."

Soneri gave a gesture of impatience, and opened the newspaper to see a reproduction of the photographs the old man had had with him.

"Capuozzo wasted no time getting this news out."

On the opposite page there was an article about the

discovery of the body. "That was a real field day for the journalists and T.V. cameras, wasn't it?"

"If I may say so, commissario, I still don't see what connection there could be between a death by natural causes and a woman's burnt-up body," Juvara said, with some hesitation.

"I don't understand either, but I prefer to carry on believing in coincidences."

6

"THERE IS NO such a thing as coincidence. There is destiny," Sbarazza corrected Soneri. He was speaking about himself and about the particularly fortunate day he had enjoyed, and was saying it must have been written in some inscrutable horoscope of whose existence he was convinced beyond all question. On this occasion, he was seated in a place which had been occupied shortly before by a woman who emanated sensuality and good health: perhaps a bank manager. She had taken *anolini in brodo* and a little Parma ham. "It's rare for me to be able to have a first course," Sbarazza confessed. "Generally it's the main course that's left."

He was dressed elegantly and yet there was a nonchalance to his appearance, as though his clothes had been chosen carelessly from the recesses of a cupboard.

"What a woman," Sbarazza said dreamily. "The quintessence of femininity, voluptuous but with no loss of harmony, lovely hair, exquisite breasts, sensual in voice and manner. It was wonderful to make love in my imagination while her perfume floated around."

"A different one every day," Soneri smiled.

They were standing facing the church of the Steccata, under the monument to Parmigianino who was peering down on them with marmoreal irony.

"She was even kind enough to leave today's paper," Sbarazza said, showing it to Soneri, who glanced at the page with the two photographs. "Are these the two you're looking for?"

"By land and sea."

"That woman knew one of them. I heard her talking about her to the man lunching with her."

At that moment, the sun made a faint appearance through the mists and a ray of light glimmered in the sky. That too was a coincidence, or a sign of destiny, as Sbarazza would have put it.

"I must find this woman," the commissario said.

"I've no idea who she is, but if I saw her again, I'd recognise her. You can't get a woman like her out of your mind," he said, as though lost in a dream.

"Have you ever seen her before?"

"No, never. I trust she will come back here if it is written that we should meet again," he went on, still carried away by his private ecstasy.

"What happens if on that happy day she's starving and wolfs the lot?" Soneri wondered.

"Please!" Sbarazza spoke imploringly. "Spare yourself these banal thoughts. Have the courage to dream because therein alone lies our salvation. Take me. What would I be were I not able to play a part each and every day? A good policeman must know how to release the imagination and gain some insight into what might be."

"If that's what you mean, there's no shortage of people intent on making what doesn't exist appear."

"There you are mistaken," Sbarazza said reprovingly. "There's no lack of those who desire to be what does not exist, and so they prosaically imitate a model. On the other hand, the dream is life. It is a parallel universe, more noble than the world of things and of the multitudes that go about masquerading. Alceste's restaurant is always filled with such individuals. Trash . . ." he concluded with a dismissive, irreverent gesture.

"And what is your dream?"

"To be myself. I play the part of the man I was and can no longer be. I feel like a puppet abandoned at the bottom of a basket. I am poor and noble in a world of wealth and vulgarity. A splendid hoax, is it not?"

The commissario's silence implied agreement.

"Take my word for it, you will find that woman. I too long to see her again, but I'd be afraid of disappointment. It is we ourselves who make certain moments magic, not what we see. The same thing can bring either joy or sadness," he concluded with an elegant wave as he turned away.

Soneri watched him as he made his way slowly down the street which was illuminated by sickly shafts of sunlight. The commissario turned towards Alceste's restaurant, feeling like a hound in the wild on the trail of a strong scent.

"A bit late for lunch," Alceste said.

"It doesn't matter . . ."

"There's something left over . . ."

"You're taking me for Sbarazza?"

"He was up to his usual tricks again today, but with such a gentlemanly air that no-one bothered."

"It's because of him that I'm here."

Alceste became serious. "Has he done something stupid?"

Soneri shook his head. "He picked up something of great importance."

"In here?" Alceste, polishing off a plate of gnocchi, sounded amazed.

"I mean . . . the woman whose place he took."

"A real beauty."

"She knows the girl whose picture was in the paper today."

"The photograph found on the dead man in the coach?"

Soneri nodded. "I've got to find out who that client of yours was."

"I don't know her name. She comes here from time to time, but . . ."

"If she paid with a credit card, she can be traced."

"The man who was with her paid the bill."

"Makes no difference."

Alceste was drying his hands as the commissario was already on his way.

"What about the gnocchi?"

"I never say no to gnocchi. I'll have them in Sbarazza's usual place," he said, indicating the now empty restaurant.

"I've found someone who knows the girl in the photograph," Soneri announced later as he entered his office.

Juvara looked up in amazement. "How did you manage that?"

"I've already told you. I believe in coincidences. You can call it gut feeling if you like."

"I've got something to tell you."

"Fine, but first we've got to trace a certain Giuseppe Pianfarini. He was having lunch with the woman who knows the girl. He paid with his credit card, and his name is even written on the receipt."

The euphoria of his discovery had made him forget everything else – the woman whose body had been burned, his gloomy mood, and above all Angela. The moment she came back into his mind, something choked inside him and he became again prey to fear.

"Here you are, sir." Juvara surprised him with the news he

had to offer. "He lives at 15 Via Montebello and these are his various telephone numbers."

He passed a sheet of paper over to him with studied nonchalance, but in his attitude Soneri detected a trace of peevishness.

"We'll have a chat when you find the time," the inspector added.

"Yes, of course," the commissario said, as he dialled the number.

The man at the other end had the hoarse voice of a smoker.

"Commissario Soneri," he announced. "I urgently require to trace the woman you had lunch with today at the *Milord* . . . no, no, nothing very serious . . . just a bit of information . . . you know those girls whose photographs were in the paper . . . calm down, maximum discretion guaranteed."

When he rang off, he became aware that Juvara was ostentatiously displaying a lack of interest in that line of enquiry. "At least we're getting somewhere with one mystery," Soneri said, in self-justification. "I'm going to pay this Signora Robutti a visit. It seems she's a marketing director with some food company. I want to know how she got to know this girl."

"Talking about these girls," the inspector cut in, "the one who died was twenty-one or twenty-two years old and was three months pregnant."

An unpleasant sensation, like a symptom of the recurrence of a disease, assailed the commissario.

"Pregnant?" he stuttered.

"Nanetti was in touch a short time ago. He said your mobile's been turned off."

Soneri dived into his pocket for his telephone, which had indeed run out of battery, as happened often with him. He plugged it into the socket beside his desk and a few moments later a barrage of messages began to show up, accompanied by a symphony of identical notes. One was from Angela: *I see you have already forgotten everything we said . . .* He felt a second stab in the heart within a matter of seconds. The news that the girl was expecting reopened a wound that had never really healed. For him, that girl was Ada, that child his unborn son, and the burned corpse represented the irreversibility of things, like his lost youth and all that might have been but was not. He was for a moment overcome by an emotion which quickly turned to rage. He had to find who had killed her. It was the only way to exorcise his pain.

"You're right, Juvara. We must concentrate on this dead body. This must be our principal objective."

The inspector stared at Soneri in surprise as he flopped heavily into an armchair. He was so pale that he seemed on the point of fainting, but his telephone rang and brought him back to himself.

"I've been searching for you for hours," Nanetti said reproachfully.

"So Juvara has been telling me."

"I think this changes everything. Even if the fact that she was pregnant doesn't mean she couldn't have been a streetwalker, my nose tells me . . ."

"I would rule it out. Prostitutes take precautions."

"And what woman does not take precautions?"

"O.K., but it makes it less likely she was on the game. Anything else turn up?"

"Confirmation of what we suspected. She was killed by a very brutal blow, or else by a violent push. Four teeth knocked out and a broken jaw. She died instantly of a shattered skull. The body was burned and she was abandoned not more than one hour after the assault."

"So they set fire to her body not far from where she was found?"

"Somewhere in the surrounding countryside. In this temperature, her body froze quickly but not completely, because we found minuscule fragments of the bag attached to the skin."

"What about the baby?" Soneri asked, realising the absurdity of the question only when the words were out.

"Don't go there," Nanetti warned him, guessing what was going on in the commissario's mind. "You'll do yourself no good."

The commissario held back the rush of confused sensations which threatened to overcome him. "What has Marcotti decided to do?"

"The body will not be released for burial at the moment, but anyway no-one has come forward to claim it. The same with the other one, the old man. It's no accident they've been placed one beside the other."

"I might have found the girl in the photograph."

"Ah! Who is she?"

"I've still got to find that out from someone who knows her. You won't believe it, but this is all down to Sbarazza. I ran into him again, and it turned out he'd been sitting in the place of some woman who'd had the newspaper open at the right page and had been speaking about her."

"If you're so curious, why not give her a ring?" Nanetti said, but he sounded sceptical.

Instead the commissario telephoned Angela, but her mobile was switched off. Anxiety took hold of him again, but Juvara, unaware of what was going on and seeing him flare up, simply thought that colour was returning to his cheeks. Before they had time to discuss the new developments relating to the case, Musumeci appeared at the door.

"There's a woman here who wants to see you," he told Soneri.

For an instant he hoped it might be Angela, but when he went into the interview room he found himself facing a beautiful woman who answered fully to the description given by Sbarazza.

"Serena Robutti," she introduced herself, with a practised smile.

"I was going to call you," he said.

"Giuseppe told me you were looking for me, so I wanted to clear this matter up immediately."

"I was only looking for some information . . ."

"Yes, very good, but I'd like to make it clear . . ." Signora Robutti went on, with a steeliness in her voice.

Soneri gestured to her to continue.

"The girl was Romanian. Her name was Ines Iliescu, and when I first met her she was an illegal immigrant. You see what I'm getting at?"

Soneri thought this over for a moment. "You gave her work?"

The woman nodded. "As a housemaid. You know how it is. I'm always in the office, I travel a lot . . . For a while she slept at our place, but then she made other arrangements. But I assure you, I had every intention of giving her real employment. Since she was an illegal immigrant, I could not do things properly, but I was looking for some way to regularise her situation."

"You do know that's what they all say, don't you? Even on the buildings sites, as soon as someone gets killed in an accident they declare they were going to fix things up the very next day."

"I swear I would have done it, but I couldn't as long as she was not quite legal."

"So how did it all end up?"

"I'm not sure. One day, she quite simply didn't turn up. I

tried to call her on her mobile, but there was nothing . . . She just disappeared. Do you understand?"

"You are quite sure she is the one in the photograph?"

"Positive."

"What was she like?"

"She was very beautiful. The pictures don't do her justice. They're very poor quality."

"Yes, but I mean, what can you tell me about her?"

"I know she was a dancer. Folk dances, traditional Romanian dances."

"Anything else?"

"We didn't talk all that much. Apart from anything else, there was the language problem. She seemed to me a decent young woman, one who genuinely wanted to make a new life for herself, to lift herself out of poverty. Maybe a family . . ."

Soneri listened as though he had just gulped down a cup of boiling hot coffee. In every victim he found the frustrations of all human affairs, and for this reason he always felt close to them. The compassion he felt was an emotion which surpassed individual circumstances, but it was not so in this case, where there was something personal involved.

"If I knew where she was, I could offer her some assistance," the woman murmured.

"I'd like to know that too," Soneri said, leaping to his feet with one of those sudden movements of his. There were no more questions to ask, but he was left with a vague, insidious sense of foreboding.

Serena Robutti too rose quickly to her feet. "I hope what I've told you will not have implications . . . you know, for my work."

The commissario made a reassuring gesture. "All you've told me is that you don't know which clubs she frequented but she enjoyed dancing. It's something to go on."

"I don't think she went to discotheques. As I said, she did folk dancing. Gypsy dances, the gypsy tradition."

The interview ended on that note. Soneri shook her hand and watched her walk along the corridor without a backward glance. He went into his office and scribbled the name on a piece of paper which he handed to Juvara. "See if your friends in Bucharest can help."

Immediately afterwards, he dialled Angela's number but again without success. At that point, the unease he had felt shortly before changed into apprehension and then into fear – not the sort of fear which causes a surge of adrenalin, but one which burrows into the innards, like a worm under the skin. Angela was his security, the nail in the wall which keeps a person attached to life but which all of a sudden gives way. He wanted to talk to her, but had no idea where she was. The telephone in her home rang out, and after each futile attempt, the commissario felt himself gasping for breath in a hostile absence denser than water. He thought of her as though she was already far off, another possibility of life snatched away. This time, however, it was not the same as with Ada. Now he was no longer young, and starting out afresh would be much more difficult. His time was running out.

He decided to concentrate exclusively on the investigation, and left to go to the car park at the sports ground, which would already be packed with cars, vans and stalls and buzzing with unknown languages in a chorus reminiscent of a dirge or a lament. The sound seemed to him like life with its thousand faces or the many indispensable little illusions which coaxed it incessantly forward. At that point, desperate to shake off his disenchantment, he did not hesitate to plunge in head first.

7

THEY HAD TAKEN over the furthest part of the car park, making themselves almost invisible from the street. The Council turned a blind eye to the occupation because in the dead of night the foreigners did not bother anyone. Their trucks were lined up as if on a permanent campsite. One row marked the external border, closing off the area destined for the market, while inside it the various vehicles left free the passageways and a little clearing in the centre. Shrouded in mist, well away from the lamp posts in the car park, that little clandestine, extra-territorial community lived in semi-darkness. Some stalls stocked products newly arrived from Romania, while packages, perhaps even including unauthorised passengers, were loaded and unloaded from the trucks. It seemed impossible to recognise anyone in that faint light, but the whole operation was carried out as though in bright daylight. People greeted each other or shouted from a distance, and Soneri thought back to the times in the countryside where he was born when people endured the long, dark winter nights, or when in summer compassionate darkness intervened to put a stop to labour.

In the midst of the general bustle, he stopped to light his cigar. Pasquariello had been right. A sense of community was still alive there, and not only because some of the women were dressed in traditional costume and seemed to view the gathering as a sort of feast day for their patron saint. The commissario allowed himself to be carried away by the crowd swarming about him, but then quite suddenly the scene was lit up. A small stage had been erected in the centre of the market where a generator produced energy for half a dozen spotlights and for some amplifiers which were blaring out music of a vaguely eastern character. The lights in the centre and the trucks drawn up in a circle to close off the vital core of the community reminded him of the camps set up on the immense, snow-covered plains by earlier generations, arranging their wagons in a circle as defence and tending the fire to keep wolves at bay. That too represented an ancient link, never completely broken, redolent of long, silent journeys which saw fathers and sons shoulder to shoulder. On the stage, a few girls in costume were dancing, while about thirty spectators watched and applauded.

Soneri remembered that Ines had been a dancer so it seemed natural to ask about her. A man eyed him with evident distrust and without speaking a word pointed him in the direction of a corpulent figure standing on his own, keeping them under observation. The commissario went over to him. "I'm looking for Ines."

"Ines?"

"Iliescu."

"She's gone to Craiova."

"But she was here."

The man replied without looking Soneri in the face, never taking his eye off the stage. "Comes and goes. Many here like that."

"Anyone here know her well?"

"Everybody here know. All from Romania. Ask Roman. He make journeys, there and back."

-76-

The commissario moved away from that spot which was as bright as a hearth and plunged once more into the semi-darkness of the market. Roman's somewhat battered coach had seats for about forty people and he himself, in the midst of the ceaseless toing and froing all around, was engaged in negotiations with a family over a trip they wished to make. Goods from Romania were being unloaded and others – refrigerators, ovens, stoves, washing machines and packages containing various items – loaded in their place. The man overseeing the operation recorded everything in a notebook. Each item had a name and a destination, and only when it was loaded or unloaded did bargaining over the price take place. Nearby, women were queuing up at a stall selling Romanian foodstuffs.

The name Ines was known to Roman. "I took her to Craiova two weeks ago," he explained in reasonable Italian. "She stands out in my memory because she was so pretty."

"And she hasn't returned to Italy?"

"Who could say? There are so many ways to come and go. Apart from the established companies, there are lots of others. Here alone there are four. Anyway, I have not seen either her or her sister for at least two months."

"She has a sister?"

"She's pretty as well. Just one year between them."

"Ines used to dance . . ." Soneri went on, pointing over to the performance area stage behind him, nothing more than a spot of fading light.

"Yes, both did. But not in places like this," the man explained, hinting that their aims were higher.

"Where?"

The other became guarded, making the commissario realise he had gone too far with this line of questioning, and that Roman might well have previous experience of police methods. He gave a shrug, but made no reply.

"Do you get a lot of work?" Soneri asked, to change the subject.

"I don't charge a lot. The big companies take nearly twice as much. If I don't get people on board, I take goods."

The commissario looked around at indistinguishable figures moving about between the trucks, loading and unloading.

"Everything there costs less than here," the man said, before hurrying off to attend to some business and disappearing into the darkness.

Soneri lit his cigar, deeply conscious of being an outsider. It was odd to feel a stranger in your own city, and yet the names being shouted out, the pronunciation of unfamiliar diphthongs, the clothes, the faces emerging unexpectedly from the darkness communicated his non-belonging. One solitude merged with a deeper solitude, both interrupted by a signal from his mobile. It was a text from Angela which said simply: *I am interviewing*: three words conveying coolness, distance and a profound sense of alienation.

Quite suddenly, the atmosphere grew more excited. A name was passed from mouth to mouth, a name initially strange to the commissario's ears, but which gained in clarity, like an echo becoming more precise as it was repeated: "Gortan, Gortan . . ." At that moment, the headlights of a black B.M.W. shone on the vehicles and shortly afterwards a portly figure, accompanied by a woman who looked much younger than him, got out.

Soneri moved aside as lights were switched on near one of the vehicles. A decidedly suspicious looking individual, who had the look of a pimp with his favourite at his side, stepped forward. Six or so lackeys cleared a path for him, while several people hung about waiting to be received. He was plainly someone who had made his fortune, who now dispensed favours or work, and he was perhaps the most pitiless and ruthless of them all, Soneri thought, as he watched him pass in front of him, making his way towards the coach where he would receive the petitioners. The illusion of a happy community evaporated on the instant. In that area of mist he witnessed yet again all the familiar ways of mankind, but as he was falling prey to uncomfortable reflections, his telephone rang.

"Commissario, that Ines, she's not in the country now," Juvara said, with unaccustomed abruptness.

"I know. There's somebody here who says he took her back to Craiova about two months ago."

"Here where?"

"In the car park between the sports ground and the hypermarket, where the Romanians meet up once a week. They pick up some things here and send others off to their own country. They eat, dance, look for work and do deals. They reconstruct their own lives and then go their own way again. It's the destiny of all of us, isn't it?"

Not for the first time, Juvara was left baffled. "But if this Ines isn't here, who was the old man coming to look for?"

"I've been wondering that myself. Why do you think I'm taking an interest in this case?"

"Commissario, I cannot . . ." Juvara stuttered.

"For the reason that I believe in coincidences. On the one hand, a guy makes a hash of fleeing from the gypsy travellers' camp, on the other there's an old man who dies while searching . . . Behind every fact there is a certain scenario, and it's up to us to find out if the principal actors are not by some chance the same."

The inspector remained silent, so the commissario went

on: "Ines had a sister who was one year younger or older, I don't know which. The easiest thing is to believe that this sister passed herself off as Ines, and vice versa. You know how many immigrants take on multiple identities."

"I've found a colleague in Bucharest who speaks good English. I'll see if I can get him to explain this sister to me."

"Call someone in Craiova as well. The family comes from there." As Juvara was hanging up, Soneri added, "And try to trace that photographer, Dimitriescu. If he's not just a paparazzo who does snaps at weddings, maybe he can speak English as well."

The lights on the coach had been switched on, and the boss and his favourite were surrounded by people hanging around him like servants. The two were drinking calmly, while a group of people stood nearby, waiting.

The commissario turned away, his path taking him past fold-down tables placed alongside vans in which people were eating standing up and warding off the damp weather with wine. When he came to the clearing, the mist confused him and he was unable to find his bearings. He decided to follow the white lines of the car park. At intervals, a lamp post would light up a few metres around it, giving the mist a strange colour. A stronger light made him believe he was near the road, but instead of the roar of traffic he heard people talking and occasionally raising their voices. He walked across a flower bed and found himself at the back of the hypermarket, where a cluster of desperate people were rummaging in the dustbins in search of something to eat. Two had climbed inside the bins and were passing stuff out to others who added it to a pile on the ground, while others again divided it up and put it into old wheeled suitcases.

Soneri thought he made out a familiar figure standing on his own, and as he drew near he recognised Sbarazza, wearing an overcoat which was long out of fashion. "Destiny brings us face to face frequently," Sbarazza said.

"It is less elegant here than in the *Milord*."

"Undoubtedly, but here you are more sure of getting what you're looking for. Recently, the *Milord* has been very crowded and it's not easy to find the opportunity to . . . but here, there's always something to eat."

"But it's all refuse," Soneri said.

"No doubt, otherwise it would hardly be here, would it?" Sbarazza said with a little laugh. "But that is not the same as saying it's not edible. The things here are the same as products displayed on the shelves, but they have ceased to be products."

Soneri looked at him in bewilderment, drew in a deep breath but said nothing.

"Once there was no difference between food and products. Something could either be eaten or not. Not anymore. You see those tins of tuna fish with a dent in them? They are food but not products. No-one would buy them. Just as no-one would buy those packets of biscuits with a tear in the packaging, or those bags of over-ripe fruit, the blackening bananas, those lettuce leaves which would wither a little at the tips overnight, or even the confectionery past its sell-by date but still excellent. That is our good fortune," he said, pointing to the group of the destitute.

Some were already on their way, dragging their wheeled cases behind them. One came over to Sbarazza and presented him with a full holdall. He addressed him with the utmost respect: "Marchese, this is your share."

Sbarazza thanked him with a solemn gesture worthy of his ancient station. He spoke to Soneri in a whisper. "Tonight the Romanians are on the prowl, so we must move fast, otherwise they'll come and chase us off."

"You mean that they too . . ." Soneri said, indicating the dustbins.

"You can smell food a long way off when you're hungry. I had to learn quickly, but there's enough in there for everybody. You've no idea how much food is thrown away – enough to feed an army. That lot want to chase us because they'll sell off anything they can get hold of. There's no longer any solidarity among the poor. They'd cut your throat for a tin of mackerel."

Just then a shout was heard in the mist. "They're coming," he said in alarm, pushing his case aside. About twenty Romanians made for the dustbins and began emptying them.

"They'll have the night patrols down on us, and sooner or later we'll all be sent packing. The management of the hypermarket doesn't want us to take their refuse."

"Why?"

"This might surprise you, but I think we're upsetting their delicate consciences. It's a co-operative, you see. For them it's a worry to think there are people who have nothing to eat after they issued a guarantee of a full stomach for every person. They've turned into businessmen, but they still preach solidarity. In addition, they don't want to admit to themselves that they waste food, because they still remember what poverty means. Better to pretend it's all gone bad and then everybody's happy. We remind them of a mortal sin."

"You've got your share, so you've no need to go scrabbling about . . ." Soneri pointed out to him.

"I carry out other tasks. Let me put it this way: I look after the interests of these unfortunates and attend to bureaucratic procedures where knowledge, expertise and competence are indispensable. I am talking about subsidies, assistance, hospital appointments, medicines . . . They come to me and I make sure they're treated the same as everybody else. This also helps me to keep alive the memory of what I used to be. Fortunately, in the eyes of many functionaries I am still the Marchese, and my image is intact. None of them knows that I come here to rummage through rubbish and that in order to eat I employ elegant stratagems, like at the *Milord*. They see me as a philanthropist, someone who looks after his fellow man, a charitable person. That way I am taken for a wealthy man and a good Christian as well." Sbarazza gave a little laugh.

"Appearances are what counts," Soneri said. "Or rather, appearances are everything. At least you conduct yourself with class."

"These poor souls don't even have a piece of dirty floor to sleep on, ever since these foreigners turned up here. Young people with knives. For a bed in a dormitory, they wouldn't hesitate to stick it in your belly."

They were walking round the perimeter of the hypermarket, keeping close to the wall. When they reached the road they said goodnight, and Sbarazza, pulling his case behind him, disappeared in the mist.

The commissario continued towards the city centre, but even when he had reached Via d'Azeglio he had not managed to shake off the feeling of alienation which had come over him in the car park. He tried to free himself of it by telephoning Juvara. "The girl in the photograph is not Ines. It must be her sister," he said, with no preliminaries. He was following a hunch, but it was a hypothesis well-grounded in solid clues.

"I heard again from our colleague in Romania," Juvara said. "He has e-mailed the photograph to that Dimitriescu and has promised to get back to me."

"Want to bet he recognises the sister?" the commissario forecast, ending the call abruptly. At that point, a sudden recognition unleashed a rush of nostalgia which helped him shake off the feeling of alienation which had gripped him a short time previously. He was opposite *Latteria Numero 51*, one of the few of its type left in the city and once an affordable meeting place for hard-up students: *caffelatte* and politics, *malvasia* and revolution. For the last couple of days, he had been resisting the temptation to seek out that lost Neverland which had been his hope as a young man, but now in front of the latteria he gave in. From the moment he pushed open the glass door with its over-embellished handle, he felt he was back home, all the more so when he saw Jole, now very old, behind the bar, and Libero Manicardi, nicknamed "Picelli" after the historical hero of the barricades, seated at his table. An inflexible theorist who could tie even himself up in knots, Picelli represented that ideal mix of anarchism and communism which had set the city alight in the years leading up to the '70s. He had been a school friend of the commissario and they had maintained an intermittent friendship in the intervals between one journey and the next.

"Franco," he cried out on seeing him. He was one of the few who called Soneri by his Christian name.

They embraced under the delighted, tired eyes of Jole. "There's more chance of winning the pools than of bumping into you," the commissario said.

They took a seat and stared intently at each other like two lovers. Both wore a sad smile as each noticed how the other had aged. Libero was just back from a trip to Cuba, but he had abandoned all dreams of socialist paradises to come. He had moved from the revolutionary phase to oriental meditation and on to Latin American rebelliousness before ending up in a mood of cynical detachment from the world. He had no time for Castro – everything was going to the dogs.

"The only consolation is love," Picelli declared, raising his glass. "I'm with a woman who is twenty years younger than me, and it's like going back in time."

Soneri looked him up and down. The pockmarked face of a man who had lived life to the full, the long, nearly white hair still hanging down his neck, the clear eyes which shone against the leathery skin – all these things must have fascinated young women who in all likelihood saw in him a comic-strip hero.

"I am losing even that," Soneri said.

Picelli's face darkened. "That's serious, Franco. Very serious. Keep a glimmer of life open. And if something closes it down, open another one. We're not so old that we can't manage that."

"No, we're not, but at our age, after so many disappointments, maybe you don't believe in fairy tales anymore."

"When that happens, we really are old. It'd be as well to put an end to it all. What are you supposed to do in the world? Better a bullet in the head."

"I've even got a gun." Soneri laughed.

"When I think back to school days, to our scrapes with Fascists and teachers, you remember? If I had to draw up a balance sheet, I'd have to bring the books to the court. There's nothing left. Take a look at politics nowadays: two great bundles of what? Left and Right think the same way. One conformist line of thought with a ban on dissent and a mass of drivellers fucking about, looking forward to the weekend."

Soneri looked over at Jole getting on serenely with her own business: made of sterner stuff, the last generation with balls, a generation which had endured poverty and had lived during the war in close proximity to death. To people like that, even these vacuous years must seem bearable.

"And don't you dream of the weekend?"

"I have other problems. I'm in a relationship with a woman who wants to get married and have children. She's in her early thirties, she's religious and she's thinking of coming to live with me. I suppose she sees me as a conquest, not least because I've told her I'm an atheist and she wants to convert me."

"And has she?"

"I'm in love and that's more than enough. Everything else is bullshit. With her, I've at last escaped from loneliness, something I tried to do for years with my comrades, but with them I never managed to share anything that was genuinely me." Picelli got to his feet with a dramatic expression on his face. "Franco, the fact is no-one ever believed, really, deeply believed. The majority only wanted to do their own thing."

"Well, I always did mine, I always went my own way. You know how I cannot abide the herd."

"I always used to criticise you for that, and I cut you off for a while, but you were right to keep your distance."

"Anyway, here we are empty-handed, more than half our lives gone by and a sense of despair gripping us by the balls," the commissario summed up, looking out at the mist thickening in Via d'Azeglio.

Inside the latteria, he felt wrapped in a blanket as comforting as a mother's embrace. Outside, loneliness lay in wait. That was the root of his sense of alienation, and without the presence of Angela it would be total. Picelli had told him that there was nothing else: two souls seeking each other, feeling fully alive only when together in that ancient, arcane activity of striving to lose the self by clinging tightly to another person. He jumped to his feet as though galvanised by a new consciousness. He said goodbye to Picelli and did not turn back. He did not know if he would see him again. Only Jole understood it all, because she was in the habit of viewing the world and the destiny of the people in it without regret.

8

CONFIRMATION ARRIVED HALF an hour later. The girl in the photograph was not Ines but her sister Nina. "The Immigration Bureau checked the data supplied by the Ministry as well, and it turns out that more than one residence permit has been issued in the name of Ines in the last two years," Juvara called to inform him. He did not go any further, intimidated by Soneri's silence.

"Go on," the commissario said.

"In spite of having received these permits, Ines remained in Romania."

"So the old man on the bus was coming in search of Nina. But what's Ines up to?"

"From what I could gather, she works in clubs for foreigners in Bucharest. My police contact was a bit vague on this point, but you know what westerners are after in Eastern European night clubs. Ines is very pretty."

Angela came back into Soneri's mind and he felt a pang of anxiety over the time that had elapsed since he had last heard from her. He went into his pocket to find the Romanian girl's mobile number on the slip of paper Signora Robutti had given him.

"Nina doesn't use this number any more," the commissario said, in dictation mode. "I've tried several times, but the phone always rings out. See if you can find some lead from the record of calls."

He rang off and continued on his way to the courthouse. He had decided to wait for Angela to come out, but he had to be careful not to bump into some lawyer or magistrate who might recognise him, such as Dottoressa Marcotti who was in charge of the case of the girl whose body had been burned. What if Angela were to come out with the other man? Every time he thought of it, he felt unwell and keen to hear her voice, but he was irked by the telephone ringing out.

Having sent a couple of texts from which came no reply, he decided to wait a few hours under the arches or in a doorway. All the while, the mist sailed heedlessly past at walking pace. He felt ridiculous and guilty at the same time, ridiculous for harbouring the thought that at her time of life a woman like Angela could change her mind after some attempt to court her, guilty because he was shadowing her instead of dealing with the case of the dead girl. In addition, all this was taking place in the vicinity of the court to which he was answerable. Fortunately, it was nine o'clock, the city seemed asleep and everyone was free to spend their after-dinner time as they pleased.

He hung about for two hours, walking up and down the deserted lanes which were as silent as a graveyard. Towards eleven o'clock, the doors of the courthouse opened and a group of people, among whom he recognised Angela, the magistrate and a lawyer, emerged. The last two moved off in the direction of Piazzale Boito, while Angela and another man turned into Vicolo Politi, heading in the direction of Via Farini. That had to be him.

Soneri followed them until he saw them go into a wine bar. He knew he could not afford to do anything stupid since that would definitely compromise everything. He also knew he would not be able to do nothing, so his pursuit ended at that point, with him feeling so lost that he sought the protection of his own house, the only place that still had a familiar feel for him. He imagined her in bed with that man, or in the back seat of a car on a country road. He burst out laughing at himself, fearing that he was losing all his dignity, and this thought allowed impotent rage to take over from irony.

Angela appeared unexpectedly, as though ambushing him. Soneri had fallen asleep on a sofa and awoke to find her bending over him. He did not understand a word she was saying, but her voice was so gentle that the commissario forgot the scene he had witnessed. When he came round fully, he realised he was cold and ached all over.

"Come to bed," she whispered, taking him by the hand.

Soneri followed her, undressed and pulled the covers over him. She joined him almost immediately and took the initiative, almost assaulting him. The commissario's every sense was delightfully aroused, even if he still failed to understand, but when she crawled on top of him he suppressed all doubt and let himself go. Afterwards, as he relished the ardour they had shared, his eyes met those of Angela a few centimetres away on the pillow.

"Is this a wish that it would never end?" he asked, thinking more of himself than of his partner.

"Do you think it can produce these miracles?" she laughed.

"Sometimes partings can be very intense."

Angela shook her head but said nothing.

Soneri felt desperately in need of some confirmation. He wanted reassurance. He felt that something had burst inside him and was haemorrhaging, leaving him shaking with fear.

"Tell me what you want," he said finally. "Even if it will be terrible for me, I must know. I can't live with this uncertainty."

"If I were sure of what I want, I'd tell you, but I'm all mixed up. I need to understand."

"Whether to stay with me or with your other man?"

"I can't just live my life with someone as part of a settled routine. I'm trying to make out how strong the relationship between us really is, but I can only do that by questioning it. It's what you do when you're on a case and you get an idea in your head. You start to attack it, so as to understand. If it stands up, it means it's well grounded."

He knew well the methods of his woman. He had seen her too often at work in court and that made him fear the worst. "This is not a police investigation. Rationality has nothing to do with emotions. There is no way of measuring how unwell a person is, nor do I find it at all reassuring to hear that you're conducting a test."

She showed her awareness of what he meant by moving her head on the pillow. "I know. I'm asking you to live with uncertainty, to put up with my doubts, even if it's hard for you. It is for me too. After all, you ought to be used to the precarious nature of convictions, given the work you do."

"Exactly, and I've had enough of it. I'd like to have something solid in a world which is too liquid. I thought that you at least were a fixed point. Just today I met Picelli – remember him? I felt sorry for him. He's thrown everything up – him, the man who was intransigence made flesh. He's fallen in love with a thirty-something Catholic woman who wants to have children."

Angela shook her head in astonishment.

"He told me that emotions are one of the few things that matter. What's left? Every single thing that your head can think passes, but that obscure cluster of sensations that we call emotions endures. Maybe precisely because our heads can't really understand a thing about friendship, love, art . . ."

"He's not far wrong," Angela murmured.

"Maybe not, but we're running the risk of losing them," Soneri said, hoping that at that very second she would come back at him and say, no, that's not right, but she did not utter a word.

Both remained silent, thoughtful, heads on the same pillow.

The commissario broke the silence with a sudden outburst. "There's no point whining. Precariousness is the human condition. The difference is that very few people recognise it and the majority go blithely on." Anger had taken over from sadness, as it had outside the wine bar.

"But it's you I want. I am certain of this, if of nothing else," she said.

Soneri felt mildly relieved, and found the strength to go on asking questions. He was always enquiring, and for this reason it was often he who identified the villain, in police affairs as in life.

"Tell me if you've been to bed with him."

Angela did not reply. She stared at him seriously, with vacant eyes, and although not another word was spoken the commissario understood. It had never crossed his mind that she could hurt him so deeply. His phantoms took concrete shape and rubbed explosively against his subconscious and all it contained. His derailed thoughts careered off the tracks of rationality, and ran so completely out of his control as to leave him ashamed. He felt on the point of insanity. All the instruments he customarily employed to gauge things were out of kilter. Nothing could contain his pain or despair, nothing could save him from this headlong plunge into the void. All attempt at explanation, all dialogue would have been useless, and so the only partial antidote was a wordless caress from Angela. Her hand stroked his cheek, his neck, ran along his chest, washing away the pain for a few seconds.

"It has happened twice," she said after a few minutes' silence, "and perhaps will not happen again."

That "perhaps" only heightened Soneri's anguish. Angela did not dispel the ambiguity which was minute by minute eating away at him. They were engaged in an ongoing game of statement and denial and it was wreaking havoc on him.

He wandered mentally in a swamp of thoughts, then gave in. There was no point in seeking any reassurance from Angela as she herself was undecided. He looked at her without recognising her. For the first time, she appeared to him inscrutable, a stranger, and that was the most wounding sensation of all.

"You like that man, you find him attractive and perhaps he's going to be your future." Soneri sat up, yelling in fury.

She tried to keep him beside her on the pillow, but only managed to make him turn slightly to one side. "He's good-looking and clever, but you're more important. He knows nothing about the bonds between us, nor have I ever spoken about them. First and foremost there's you and me, and it will be you and I who will make any decisions," she said, with pitiless clarity.

The commissario sat with his back propped against the headboard. The investigation had reached its finale, the confession had been full and detailed, but the heaviest sentence would fall on him. He realised he had been at fault in having taken their relationship too much for granted, or perhaps, as Picelli had put it, for never having been able to get away from himself and open up to other people. He felt a lump in his throat which would not be removed by any words but only by the language of the body. He drew close to her, and they embraced, holding tightly to each other to maintain some equilibrium.

In spite of everything, he felt physically better when he left the house. He had not slept much and a multitude of thoughts were buzzing about in his head, but there was a spring in his step and in the mist which still enveloped the city he was breathing more easily. Juvara was a great believer in biorhythms, and perhaps he was right, or perhaps the body simply makes up its own mind when to respond to life and let everything else take care of itself, including the psyche.

In the police station, he found the record of the calls made by Nina. There was nothing that stood out: radio taxis, take-away pizzas, Signora Robutti, a car-hire firm and a beauty salon. The incoming calls were of greater interest. The list took up a whole page and there were some recurrent numbers.

"In great demand . . ." Soneri commented.

"They all say she was very pretty," Juvara said. "But not altogether in the clear," he added after a pause.

The commissario threw a questioning look at him.

"I've just been told she was wanted in Romania for a series of car thefts, but the impression is that she was small fry, used as cover for somebody or other."

"Have you made a fresh check on the missing persons list?" Soneri asked, changing the subject and referring to the case of the burned body.

"Nothing doing there. The forensic squad are engaged on a reconstruction of the face to produce a reliable identikit." He paused for a few moments, and then went on, "Do you know what criminologists say about bodies which have been set on fire?"

Soneri took the cigar from his mouth and shook his head.

"That normally they're people the murderer knew and with whom they had a relationship."

"A story, a love story . . ." Soneri said, accidentally plunging back into the pit of his discontent.

"Either that or a family connection."

For a moment Angela came back into his mind and he found himself overcome by feelings of rancour. He would have liked both to embrace her and get away from her. However, someone had wanted to eliminate the girl forever and destroy her with fire. Nothing had clear outlines in her case. It was a game of appearance and reality, an elusive dance of smoky figures or, better, of misty figures, since the cloak of mist was as heavy as ever and continued to weigh down on the city. Soneri paced up and down the room under the startled gaze of the inspector who seemed on the point of making some pronouncement, but after a little time the commissario wheeled round and their eyes met. It was Juvara who broke the silence. "Listen, commissario, I have a suspicion that this Nina . . ."

". . . is the woman whose body was burned." Soneri completed the sentence.

"I might be wrong. Maybe we've connected the two stories too closely and ended up with one jumbled up with the other."

The commissario shook his head, and resumed observing the coming and going of patrols in the yard. He heaved a sigh. "I don't think so. Do you understand now why I was so taken with the story of the old man who died on the coach?"

"You have a nose for . . ."

"No, it's just that I'm a bit older than you."

"If that was all . . ."

"Spending a long time with criminals makes you understand humanity. You get to a stage where you believe that evil is so familiar because it dwells inside us without us noticing."

He turned round again to find Juvara staring at him dumbfounded. "You and I too might one day become aware that it's part of our being as well, and this awareness almost always dawns when the evil manifests itself. And by then it's too late."

The commissario moved away from the window and changed the subject. "We'll find out if Nina is the girl whose body was burned when we have the identikit. It's only a matter of hours."

The telephone rang and Soneri rushed to grab it. He still hoped it might be Angela, but was surprised to hear Pasquariello's voice. "We've been interrogating that Mariotto, the gypsy."

"What did he have to say?"

"He's still saying he fell and bumped his head, but nobody believes him, even if technically it can't be ruled out."

"What do you make of it?"

"The Romanian and Italian Romas didn't get on very well. There's been a series of thefts. In my opinion, scores are being settled, but if Mariotto doesn't speak, we'll never make any headway."

The conversation with Pasquariello was interrupted by the ringing of another telephone. The head of the flying squad rang off immediately with the words, "I'll keep in touch."

Once again, it was not Angela. Nanetti, who grasped the commissario's disappointment, made a joke of it: "It could've been worse. It might have been Capuozzo."

Soneri said: "No, it's not that. It's just that . . ."

"Do you think I don't know? At least you might work something out with Angela. I've lost everything, but I'm plodding on. Meanwhile I'm getting more interested in lingerie."

"You're not becoming one of those men who make a collection of knickers?"

"Who do you think I am? Listen, colleague, do you remember the label between her buttocks that was saved from the flames? Well, there's a shop in Via Garibaldi that stocks only one brand – that very one! Do you understand me?"

"You are telling me she did her shopping there . . ."

"It's not the only outlet for that kind of underwear, but on the balance of probabilities it's likely."

"Right then. Since you've become an expert, would you like to pay them a visit?"

"Are you afraid they might take you for some kind of pansy? I don't do investigations. My job is to come up with proof."

"It was a joke."

"You're getting on my nerves, commissario. I've been there. It's the widower's syndrome, a sort of rancour that keeps you well away from anything that smacks of femininity."

"I'm already a widower," Soneri replied bitterly.

"Sorry, I've touched a raw nerve."

The commissario's mind was elsewhere, in a dreamland where the past and the present overlap, with the irreversible loss of Ada and the probable loss of Angela already a part of the landscape. That was what growing old meant – seeing parts of yourself and parts of a shared life fade away. As he forced himself to focus on the crime, memories of his dead wife and his unborn son merged with the image of the girl, producing a fresh surge of indignation inside him.

"I'm grateful for this lead. I'll go round myself," he said, cutting short the conversation.

Nina provoked a whirlwind of emotions because she brought back the trauma of the loss of Ada and the sudden disruption of his whole life. This case was running disturbingly parallel to the life he had known. He was unsettled by the realisation that people's experiences were not so very different and could be superimposed one on top of the other. Not even a solitary soul like him could claim originality.

"What idea have you formed of Nina?" he asked Juvara.

The inspector had nothing to say. The commissario envied his detachment. He was young and could dodge putting awkward questions to himself. There was time enough for that, and in the meantime it was better to let him live.

"The photographer, Dimitriescu, told me she was very shy, and she regarded her good looks as a problem," Juvara said.

"He confirmed that the photographs were his?"

"Yes. He even remembers when he took them. The first one at the end of high school and the second a couple of years later."

"They seem two different people."

"The photographer had the impression she had changed her lifestyle, but he doesn't know anything else."

Soneri contemplated the photographs in silence, but he became aware of a level of frenetic activity in the yard outside that was hard to reconcile with the rhythms of life in a sleepy town like Parma. Instinctively he thought of Nina as a naïve girl who attracted attention because of her beauty. Perhaps they had duped her and she had ended up in dubious circles. She reminded him of the fate of dogs abandoned on the motorways, acquired as fluffy toys when they were puppies and tossed aside the first time they peed on the sofa.

"What's causing all this commotion?"

"The maniac. Some serial rapist on the loose. He's been prowling after women in public gardens, in doorways, in parks. He's already raped three. They say he's a foreigner. Musumeci's in charge."

"He won't be operating during the day, will he?" Soneri said, looking at the grey skies.

"The city's completely neurotic. People are talking about nothing else. The switchboard's jammed. They're seeing maniacs everywhere," the inspector said.

Soneri was surprised he had known nothing about it, and put it down to the state he was in. "It'll be the same as with the bulls," he muttered, "but this guy knows how to keep out of sight a bit better."

9

"SEEMS LIKE THEY'VE got him," Alceste announced, as he put a plate of *anolini in brodo* in front of the commissario.

"Got who?"

"What do you mean – got who? The sex maniac, obviously. An illegal immigrant, or so they say."

"So now the witch hunt gets underway once again," he mumbled to himself as he blew away the steam from the dish. He could sense the opening of the tiresome ritual enacted so many times before: the Right railing in shrill tones against immigrants, the Left asking people not to make a mountain out of every molehill and the Fascists threatening to get their clubs down from the attic. Reality was always elsewhere, the facts denied, and he would have to deal with the consequences.

At least he could still enjoy the consolations of the table, the one pleasure left to him apart from walking in the mist and sitting at home with a book on autumn evenings. Such thoughts were running through his mind as he gazed at the rings in the soup, but they were interrupted when he found Sbarazza standing before him. His gait was so silent and discreet that it was easy to miss his approach, even for a trained eye like the commissario's.

"Thank goodness you're here, otherwise I'd have gone

hungry. There's not one free table and there's a queue of people waiting." Three women had just got up from a table next to Soneri's, and Sbarazza reached out to pick up a plate with an almost untouched chop. Another agile movement and a half-full bottle was placed in front of the commissario.

"A *dolcetto di Ovada*. Not bad," Sbarazza said

Soneri looked around in embarrassment, but no-one seemed to have noticed.

"Don't worry, commissario. The important thing is to possess the right measure of self-confidence and nonchalance. When you have these attributes, even the most crass gesture will not arouse the slightest objection, because you need a bit of pluck to make a fuss, don't you? And in this place," he added, looking around the restaurant, "who do you think has such pluck?"

The commissario thought again of the girl whose body they had found, and wondered if she had been particularly plucky. "A rare commodity," he said. "Did you fancy one of the women sitting there?" he asked.

"Each woman draws us into another world. When all's said and done, that's what seduction consists of. We're given a glimpse of the missing part of ourselves."

"Very much missing," the commissario replied in a dull voice, thinking of his own situation.

"We always lack something or other. In my case, time is running out. The man out there who is assaulting women lacks a partner, but these are all insignificant and transient passions, like a man complaining of hunger while facing a firing squad."

His reasoning was delicate and light. Listening to him, Soneri drew some consolation from his words.

Sbarazza went on. "I don't envy you, you know. For someone who considers the absurdity of our life, it must be frustrating to have to reconstruct the actions of those who steal and kill. If we were to reflect a little, we would all be forced to be good and to weigh every act, but we are such profoundly irrational creatures, governed by the passions. Our animal side always prevails. The wise man is the one who resists the pull of the passions and ensures that the brain triumphs."

"If only it were that easy . . ." Soneri muttered. "Look at you with women."

"Purely intellectual caprice, aesthetic diversion. Age is of assistance here," he said with a wink. "I can say that because it was not always thus. I was a fiery youth, and that was my ruination, yet I'd do it all again. The passions, even if they toss you about this way and that, impel you forward. It's because of them that we keep ourselves active. They move everything forward, transforming the world, perhaps into a repugnant mess, but somewhere in that shambles there'll be the spring of continual competition towards an ill-defined future." Putting his face close to Soneri's, he went on: "Wisdom is something for old men. And never believe it's a conquest of time. It's merely the decay of the body."

Inside himself, Soneri felt heartened. Any unhappiness over Angela was a sign he was still alive. Two police cars with sirens squealing passed by and he decided Sbarazza was right. The world was moved by the passions.

"Have they got him?" Sbarazza said.

"Looks like it," the commissario replied without much conviction, and before Sbarazza could ask him anything else about the maniac on the loose, the commissario got up so quickly that he seemed to be running away.

Refreshed and consoled by this conversation, Soneri set off for the lingerie shop in Via Garibaldi. En route he called Juvara. "So then, they got their sex maniac."

"If only! They arrested a Moroccan, but he was freed two hours later because he'd nothing to do with it. He was quarrelling with his girlfriend and somebody decided he was assaulting her."

"Give me some background. When did all this start?"

"Yesterday evening, a woman was attacked in Via San Leonardo, and the description of the rapist fitted one given by another woman who'd been assaulted in Via Solferino two days ago. It was probably the same man who also sexually assaulted a girl in Via Toschi."

It was true. Instincts and passions were what motivated people, and when these exploded outside the confines of law, he had to take over. He could hear sirens in the mist as the city attempted to cope with the tension created in its innermost being by an insidious virus capable of spreading and striking randomly.

The owner of the shop he went into shortly afterwards must have felt herself threatened, judging by the wary eye she cast on Soneri. She relaxed only when he introduced himself.

"Is there a Romanian girl who comes here?" he said, showing her the photograph.

"Ines. Certainly. A wonderful person."

Evidently she mistook her for her sister.

"Does she buy her underwear here?"

"She is a very faithful client. If only I had more like her."

"What kind of thing does she buy?"

"Oh, all kinds. Unlike other clients of mine, she doesn't have one definite style. One day she might purchase a very girly, matching set with lace and frills, and then two days later she would walk out with a much plainer outfit. Sometimes she would choose very sexy, see-through lingerie, but at other times she would take articles more fit for a young girl, with little angels embroidered into it. She would go from top of the range to economy items. In other words, there are no fixed rules with her."

"One of a kind, you mean," Soneri said, trying to make sense of what the woman was telling him.

"In general my clients have precise tastes and always choose the same type of article. Most times I get it right when I interpret their wants, but with Ines . . . in addition . . . such a beautiful young woman. I'm sure men go crazy over a girl like her."

"Did she ever come with a man?"

"Women never buy lingerie in the company of men, if for no other reason than not to spoil the surprise," she said flirtatiously. "However, now I think of it, I was once struck by seeing Ines get out of a dark car. There was a man at the wheel, but he stayed in the car and I didn't see his face."

"Do you remember what make of car it was?"

"I'm sorry, but I can't help you there. All I saw was a horse design on one side."

The commissario remembered Manservisi's account. It must have been the same sticker. "Do you have any idea where she lives?"

"Nearby, in Via Cavallotti, but I don't know the number. She didn't speak much about herself, and if the conversation turned to her, she would change the subject."

The commissario moved towards the door, and the woman followed him.

"Will you get him?" she asked apprehensively.

He looked at her generous figure, her enormous calves, her feet spilling out of her shoes and decided that she ran no risk of being assaulted. He shrugged and walked away.

A hundred metres further on he turned into Via Cavallotti, which in mid afternoon was deserted. He started peering at the nameplates like a postman on his first round, but there were so many names missing and those which were there belonged mainly to immigrants – Arabs, Moldovans, Russians, Albanians and Indians. Read in haste from top to bottom, the names sounded like the morning roll call in the Foreign Legion. At number 12, in a recently renovated block of flats, there were no names, only the numbers of the individual flats: 1/1, 1/2, etc. Instinctively he believed that Nina lived there, a belief suggested by the air of de luxe mystery hovering about the block and by its defensive, forbidding chestnut door with shining copper rings. He was tempted to go in, but elected first to obtain a search warrant from the magistrate Marcotti, who still knew nothing of his belief that Nina and the girl burned by the roadside were one and the same, with all that that involved.

The light was fading under the advancing front of mist enveloping one side of Via Garibaldi and wafting around the arches of the Pilotta as though a river had suddenly evaporated and was gushing down from the parapets. The sky darkened as if it had been coloured by the stroke of a brush and the whole city was plunged into shadow. He dialled Angela's number once more, but all he got was the voicemail. Seconds later, his mobile rang and he answered as quickly as a sprinter getting off the blocks.

"I've disappointed you yet again," Nanetti teased.

"Cut it out," Soneri said.

"You're waiting for a call, I know."

The commissario muttered something, but could not conceal his impatience. His colleague accompanied him along a street he had never liked. Like a tourist guide, he took note of every stage of the walk. He could not get Angela out of his mind, and still wanted her. "Anything new?" he said.

"We have the girl's identikit and she's very like the one in the photograph. I'd say there's no doubt," Nanetti said.

"I'll send Juvara to visit Signora Robutti and the haberdasher who sold Nina her underwear to see if she recognises her."

"Haberdasher! The way you speak you'd think we were still in the Fifties. The place is called Intim Shop and it sells lingerie, not underwear. And it's not even correct to call it a shop. Where have you been all these years? It's a boutique!"

"Fuck off!" Soneri said. The air all around was filled with the sound of sirens. He snapped shut the mobile without saying goodbye as he watched a police car screech to a halt under an ancient plane tree in Piazzale della Pace. Esposito jumped out as though he were in an American gangster movie and raced over the grass in the direction of the fountain and the monument to Verdi. The commissario followed him, but after a few strides he realised how seriously unfit he was. The soles of his shoes slipped on the damp grass, and he lost ground with every step he took. The extra kilos made him almost bend double as he ran, but in spite of that after a few seconds he caught up with Esposito, who was himself out of breath and panting.

"Did you see him?" Esposito managed to gasp.

"Who was I supposed to see? I was coming after you."

"The bloody bastard," Esposito swore. Other policemen emerged from the mist. "There was a call to say that the maniac had been sighted harassing some poor girl."

"Ah well, if you don't slim down a bit, the only criminals you'll catch will be the lame ones. I gave you a hundred metres' start on a three-hundred-metre stretch."

"Hey, commissario, as if this life was not shitty enough, now you want me to stop eating."

In the meantime, a multitude of the curious had gathered round but they quickly showed their disappointment. "It's time you got this dirty Moroccan," yelled a heavily made-up woman with a crocodile skin handbag. Moroccans had become the whipping boys for all misdeeds committed by incomers.

"There's a psychosis abroad, and it's spreading," Esposito was heard groaning as he walked over to his car. "Thank God I'm not on night duty. Everybody sees monsters when the lights go down."

The two men stood in silence in the thick mist, getting their breath back.

"Alright, commissario. The fun's over," Esposito said as he got into the car and switched on the engine. At that moment Soneri's mobile rang, but he was once again disappointed when Juvara's voice came on. "Have you heard about the identikit?"

"Nanetti told me. Will you go over to Signora Robutti's for an official identification?"

"O.K., but I wanted to inform you that we have the details of the calls made to Nina."

"Recognise any?"

"There are lots of them, nearly all male."

"There's a surprise!"

"I mean, they're from people who don't seem to be the same age as her, mature men."

"Does it give their ages on the printout?"

"No, but if there's a lawyer or accountant who's got his own office, he can't be all that young."

"Are they all like that?"

"One phone number belongs to a company. I looked it up on the internet and I see it's a goldsmith's. It produces and deals in top-of-the-range items."

"Leave everything on my desk. I'll be there shortly and I'll have a look."

He felt that things were starting to come together, nothing that could be proved, just impressions, feelings and affinities between tiny clues that were beginning to establish a plausible framework in his mind. His imagination and his experience in dealing with the all-too-human fact which is evil did the rest.

The mobile distracted him once again. This time he reached for it absent-mindedly, expecting a call from Capuozzo or Marcotti with a rebuke for being out of touch for days and not filing a report.

"You've been looking for me several times," Angela said, with some heat.

"Your mobile's never switched on."

"These days, I often have to keep it off. Clients call me in my office. The only ones who have my mobile number are you and a few others."

"You mean one other."

He heard a slight inhalation of breath, but it might have been a sigh. Angela changed tack. "I'd like to see you right way. Why don't you come round to my office? I'm on my own."

He felt a surge of desire for her, but the impulse was dampened by her silence about the other man. She tantalised him with a lover's flattery but wounded him by declining to give a reply which would give him reassurance or hope. Angela was keeping him on tenterhooks, in an anguished limbo of uncertainty. At times he detested her for this, and never before had Sbarazza's monologue on the prison of the passions seemed to him so profoundly true.

"You don't seem too keen," she said.

"It's not that. I've had a call from the office."

"You see? For you work is more important."

"No, if you only knew . . ."

"Well then. What's keeping you? I wouldn't like to pressurise you, or interrupt the work of a public official."

"I'm on my way," Soneri said, with unwonted ardour, snapping his mobile shut.

Angela wrapped herself around him before he even had time to take off his coat. She was aggressive, as she had been in earlier days when their passion fed off their desire to discover each other. With an equally unusual urgency which she seemed deeply to appreciate, he offered her every assistance, so there developed between them an invigorating struggle, something like the nuptial dance of insects in spring, on the divan, desk and armchairs.

Afterwards, exhausted but gratified, they flopped onto the floor, looking around in disbelief, with childlike wonder. Even in his euphoria, the moment he pondered the roots of this excessive reaction, Soneri's mood turned grim and he was again overwhelmed by the bittersweet acknowledgement of the precariousness of his condition. Their lovemaking did nothing to take away the savour of dying summer or of the final act of folly.

"You like the other guy and he excites you. It's him you want, not me," Soneri said.

"So why would I want to make love to you?"

"I'm an old habit dressed up in new attire. The other man has got you fired up and your desire is projected onto me."

"No." She shook her head, but the gesture seemed to Soneri dictated more by will power than by conviction. "In that case, I'd have gone to him, but I didn't. I came to you."

"It's fear that's keeping you tied to me. The fear of change."

"Me afraid of change?" Angela said in tones of injured pride.

"If we were angry with each other, it'd be easy for both of

us to walk away. Everything would be simpler, but the fact is we're tied to each other by a deep understanding, and maybe we believe that at our age this cannot be repeated. That's where the fear springs from," Soneri said, looking his partner straight in the eye, "but at the same time, we want the thrills we can't give each other any longer, and so we look for them somewhere else. You've found them with that guy, but the excitement you feel is like playing blind man's buff with your future, and that scares you. You come back to me all charged up, and you try to transfer onto the man who gives you security the excitement you feel with your lover. If you were younger, you wouldn't give it a second thought. You'd be off already, because you'd have plenty of time ahead of you for correcting mistakes, but as you grow older, you become more careful."

Angela made no reply and her silence wounded Soneri, who was doing all he could to wring from her some indication that she still loved him.

"He doesn't know about you."

"That goes without saying. Adultery and betrayal are based on deception."

"I've told you everything."

Angela, speaking only in staccato sentences, had a sulky expression. She too seemed to be in search of some form of reassurance which neither was able to give the other.

"You'll have to make up your mind, Angela. You'll have to choose between the exhilarating uncertainty of the new and the reassuring continuity of what you have. In each case, you are running risks."

He got up to go. Angela came with him to the door and hugged him, but said not a word.

10

HE MADE HIS way back to the office, walking quickly along the pavements of the already dark city and feeling empty inside. In quick succession, calls came from Capuozzo and Marcotti, both putting the same questions, his superior officer with overblown, plaintive pomposity and the magistrate neurotic and rapid.

"Where do we stand?" Marcotti said, straight to the point.

"The victim's name is Nina Iliescu," Soneri said.

She gave a mumbled assent, as if she knew everything already. Soneri assumed she had been talking to Juvara.

"I think I've found out where she used to live, but I'd need a warrant."

"No problem. In these cases, it's normal practice, isn't it? Was the house hers?"

"We don't know. This girl's life is a mystery that is still to be unravelled. All we have to go on at the moment are telephone printouts, an apartment we need to search and a car with the design of a horse on the side."

"A horse?"

"It's the car that dumped the body on the side of the autostrada. The same car was seen by the woman who sold the underwear to the girl, and by Manservisi, the chief of the gypsy community which set up their camp alongside the rubbish dump near the Cortile San Martino service area. That's where Mariotto comes from, the only witness that we have so far." The commissario had to stop, because the magistrate had started yelling down the telephone.

"You're making my head spin, commissario! I phoned you to get you to clear up some points and you've launched into an incomprehensible catalogue."

It had not occurred to him that he was making a summary for his own purposes rather than recounting facts to her. Until that moment, he had been accumulating sensations and unconnected fragments, and the recitation had given him the opportunity to put them all together.

"No, don't start again," Marcotti begged him. "Prepare a report and I'll read it at my leisure."

The conversation ended with that request, which seemed to him absurd. What could a report explain? The investigation was at a point which made it the equivalent of a photograph without a caption, or at least that was how it felt to him as he walked among people crowding into bars or heading home. From time to time he felt he was losing his internal balance and was under the influence of some kind of emotional anaesthetic which dulled every sense into indifference. He knew this was a means of avoiding pain. At other times he sought refuge in the past, in the years he had been living with Ada, in his unborn son whom he continually imagined as being close to him and whom he identified with some boys he ran into by chance on his long walks. When this happened, he always ended up remembering Nina. The faces of the two women superimposed themselves – one on top of the other – and their affairs ended up criss-crossing. Perhaps that was why he had taken this case so much to heart.

At the entrance to the police station he felt Angela's silence weigh heavily on him. He thought of calling her, but he was held back by the fear of getting her voicemail. He pushed open the door and made for his office.

"Commissario, there've been calls from . . ." Juvara attempted to alert him, but the commissario cut him off.

"I've spoken to them already. What I want to know is if anyone has been looking for the girl. Missing person reports, I mean."

The inspector shook his head. "No, there are none."

"With all these calls . . ." Soneri said, running his eye over the details on the printout. "When she was alive, there were plenty of them searching for her. Look at all these names." His thoughts were with those two corpses, the old man and the young woman, lying side by side in the mortuary. Two ghosts whom no-one wanted to claim and who would perhaps be tossed into a pauper's grave in some cemetery or other on the outskirts.

He drew himself up short when he realised that his curiosity was being reawakened. The world once again held some interest for him. He picked up the printout and dialled the first number at the top of the page, that of a lawyer, Federico Paglia. The telephone rang a couple of times, and then he heard a bored voice ask who was calling.

"Commissario Soneri here. I need to talk to you about Nina."

"Nina?"

"Or maybe Ines? Is that what you called her?"

The lawyer fell silent for a few seconds, then said: "Come in half an hour."

Soneri took the printout with him when he went. He was prepared for an evening listening to accounts of the girl, in the hope that this would give him the chance to learn about her from the various men who had desired, possibly even loved, her.

Paglia's premises were in the Parmigianino quarter. He saw before him a corpulent man, beginning to go to seed, with prominent, fleshy lips and the face of an ageing guardian angel.

"Why are you asking me about Ines?" he began immediately, with a slight hint of alarm in his voice.

"She was killed and her body burned," Soneri said bluntly.

For a long time, as he had done on the telephone an hour earlier, Paglia said nothing, and then: "So she was the woman . . ."

"The woman in the autostrada incident, yes," Soneri finished the sentence for him. "You called her . . ." he paused to look at the printout, "two days before she died. A seventeen minute conversation at two-twenty in the afternoon."

"We did speak," Paglia conceded gloomily. "It is not easy to forget a girl like her."

"She was your lover?"

"For nearly a year."

"It was Ines who left you?"

The man nodded. "It was hard to hold on to her. She was a girl with fire inside her, impossible to forget. I lost my head over her. That girl knew what she was about, like no other. To keep her, you had to lose your head, give your instincts free rein, indulge her desires and to hell with day-to-day living. I could not match her energy."

"So it ended?"

"I must have been mad, but at that time it was exactly what I wanted. Ines gave me everything I had ever desired from a woman."

"Did you have the impression she was exploiting you?"

"No. If she was, she was an extraordinary actress. I always felt loved," Paglia said.

The commissario thought for a minute of what exactly it

meant to be loved, but this only made Angela's silence all the harder to bear.

"I know what you mean," Paglia said. "Yes, in bed Ines was all raw passion. I never thought it was just an act. At those moments, I always believed she was committed mind and body. Unrestrained, but also attentive. I know precisely what a man of my age is looking for in a lover, but if it lasts more than a year, it can't be sex alone. I'm not short of cash for that sort of thing. I could have a different one every week."

"Did Ines ask for money?"

"Never. She wanted something different and adventurous. She wanted to travel with me. Or else, she would stand in front of a shop window, enchanted with a ring so that I would end up buying it for her. She never made direct requests."

The commissario lingered for a few moments to observe the lawyer as he spoke with great deliberation. Everything seemed to unfold in slow motion, like the clumsy movements of a sea lion. His expression had a flicker of life only when he was recalling his lover. There was something in the man that suggested an undertone of frustration. He must have had an unhappy boyhood, perhaps on account of that unattractive physique which Ines had led him to believe desirable.

"Do you think she really loved you?" Soneri said as he got up.

Paglia thought it over. "Yes," he replied, but with just a hint of uncertainty, as though he was making an effort to force himself to believe it.

When the commissario left his office, the city seemed more overcast and silent than usual. The peace of those hours when everyone was at dinner helped him recover his liking for the place, but then quite suddenly police cars started speeding by. He passed a couple of officers patrolling the back streets in the city centre, and from their radios he heard an excited exchange of voices indicating a chase. He heard mention of Via Cavestro and of a female student being pursued by a man as far as Via Mazzini. One of the two officers recognised Soneri.

"How many maniacs are there in this city?" the commissario wanted to know.

"This is the third alarm since seven o'clock," the officer said, a pretty young woman with her hair in a ponytail, the radio in her hand. "The first two were false alarms, but in this case it seems there really was an attempted assault."

Breathless voices emerged from the radio, followed by the three metallic tones that indicate a break in communication. A police car, lights blazing, raced past at top speed and screeched to a halt in the pedestrian area of Via Cavour. Under the mist, the city seemed to throb, making Soneri think of the bubbling of thermal mud.

The normal atmosphere had been shattered and not even night could restore its enchanted stillness, composed of a hissing sound from street lights, the whir of bicycle tyres on the wet roads and the drip-drip of moisture from the branches.

Soneri took the printout from his pocket and dialled the second mobile number on the list, that of one Sebastiano Goretti. Juvara had scribbled in the margin: "craftsman, manufactures domestic fittings". There was a tone of obvious embarrassment in the voice of the man who answered, perhaps because his wife was nearby. They agreed to meet in Piazza Garibaldi, at the foot of Garibaldi's statue.

Goretti was very different from Paglia. Squat and muscular, he had a somewhat aggressive expression.

"As I said on the phone, I'd like to talk about the Romanian girl, Ines," the commissario began.

He found himself facing the same bemused expression the commissario had seen on Paglia. "I've no idea who that might be."

"Nina? Anyway, the girl you used to telephone a lot," Soneri said curtly.

"Doina? Did she have other names," the man asked suspiciously

The commissario avoided the question. "We've had trouble identifying her. But you and she had a relationship, did you not?"

"A few months," the man said warily.

"And then? You split up? It's clear you carried on looking for her."

Goretti seemed embarrassed, but then his expression softened and he became more amenable. "I completely lost my head over that woman," he said, as though he were ashamed of himself.

"And you can't get her out of your mind?"

The man nodded in agreement. "Precisely because I was head over heels in love, I allowed myself to become obsessively jealous, and so she wanted to end it."

It crossed Soneri's mind that he was running the same risk. But how could he be other than jealous?

"I understand," he said, in a tone so sympathetic that Goretti was surprised.

"I have a wife and two children, as well as a business. I just couldn't keep up with her. Every time she went off, I had the suspicion that she was seeing some other man, and so I kept on calling her. I couldn't cope with . . ."

Goretti stopped, but the commissario grasped everything with a clarity he found irksome. The account given by

Goretti reawakened his own anxieties, and made him think that perhaps every man's life followed the same pattern.

"So what did you do?"

Goretti raised his head and gave him a puzzled look. The question appeared to include an accusation, and yet the tone revealed a curiosity that was far removed from the inquisitorial.

"It was she who did everything. She disappeared for a week. When we met up again, she told me she was sorry but she couldn't carry on that way."

"Did you believe she already had another man? After all, she was a hot-blooded woman and judging by what little I've picked up . . ."

"I simply don't know. She never gave me the impression of being a woman who went looking for men, and that was one of the things I liked about her. I'm the jealous type, and I could feel when the red mist was about to descend on me. I could never have a relationship with someone who made a display of herself. Doina had everything I wanted: good-looking but discreet, passive, always full of apprehensions . . ."

"With someone who was so beautiful, however . . ." the commissario objected.

"She never took the initiative, not even when we were alone, understand? I adore women who let you get on with things and who are maybe just a touch reserved. I like the idea of dominating them. No perversions, eh?" Goretti hastened to add. "Just the natural things between a man and a woman. She was my baby doll . . . my naïve baby doll."

"Did you meet her only recently? I mean, not long before they murdered her."

"Don't tell me she was the girl . . ." Goretti murmured. He was silent for a few moments, before adding, "I can't imagine who could have . . . I was furious because she'd left me, but I hadn't lost all hope."

Nor had Soneri lost all hope with Angela, but her silence seemed to suggest that the end was at hand, and that was one of the reasons why, shortly after leaving Goretti, he made another attempt to call her. Her mobile was still switched off. He tried her office but got only the voicemail, and the same with her landline at home. By now feeling highly agitated, he felt he should do something, but he had no idea what exactly, so he made for the wine bar in Via Farini. When he got there, the first thing he saw was his rival seated in the corner, munching a *piadina* as though he had just finished work and that was his supper. He was by himself, but perhaps he was waiting for someone. Soneri took a seat at a spot where he could keep an eye on him, but the other man seemed to take no interest in what was going on around him, only occasionally looking up at the bar. The commissario took out the list of callers and dialled another number. Resigned to listening to another tale of frustrated passion, he wondered if he was up to it.

Running down Juvara's printout, he saw the next name was Ernesto Greci, a company director. For him Nina was Monia, as Greci himself explained when the commissario referred vaguely to the "girl".

"It's Monia I'd like to talk to you about. I could come to your place or we could meet somewhere or other."

"No, I'll come. Where?" the man said, obviously mildly alarmed.

The commissario hesitated a moment, as long as it took to look around and glance at his rival. "I'm in the wine bar in Via Farini."

In the meantime, the smells in the bar reminded him he had not eaten, so he ordered a plate of salame and *torta fritta*, with some shavings of Parmesan and a half litre of red wine. Since he was moving in a climate of infidelity, he chose a Barbaresco rather than a local wine.

The other man was still eating, and the commissario studied him with a policeman's trained eye. He was tall, distinguished looking, took care over his appearance and had the refined features of someone whose wealth went back more than one generation. He expected Angela to walk in at any moment, and was curious to see how she would react when she saw him there. Would she greet him like an old friend or would she pretend not to notice him? It was a choice which might mark the end of their relationship, but at that moment the commissario felt nothing but anger.

Greci arrived first. He was in his fifties, with white hair, round spectacles and a bow tie. At first sight he appeared a strange individual, but when he began speaking Soneri once again found himself dealing with another predictable story of abandonment.

"Monia and I played at being husband and wife. She grasped the fact that I longed for the ordinary life I'd never had. I've travelled a lot and collected a string of short-lived relationships. Now I'd like to have a family, but maybe it's too late."

Soneri gave him a hearing, enduring again the rise of the now customary, perhaps incurable, pain. Inwardly he cursed the investigation he was carrying out, even if the ache it caused was beneficial, like a vaccine.

"And was Monia a good wife? he asked, throwing a resentful glance in the direction of his rival, two tables away.

"With her I lived the best months of my life," the man replied, as though in a dream. "Every evening I came home to find her in the kitchen, wearing an apron, and the table set. I felt happy. Sometimes we would go out to the cinema, or else we just sat on the settee watching television. On Saturday evenings we used to dine out and return home as happy as two young lovers. Monia knew how to conduct herself on all occasions. She looked like a real lady, older than her years. Even in our more intimate moments, she displayed a certain bashfulness. I adored her for that," Greci concluded, seemingly still in a dream.

The commissario listened to him and, in spite of his anguished state, he felt somewhat consoled, but when he turned towards his rival, that small dose of medicine lost its force in the face of a virus whose hold was tightening.

"How did it end?" He put the question to ward off his own troubles.

"I don't really know. One day she told me she had to return urgently to Romania because her mother had been in an accident. I phoned her many, many times but something had gone. She was cold, offhand, superficially cordial but very formal. I knew it was all over and I felt my world collapse around me. My dreams had lasted as long as a cat's leap."

Soneri was amused at this typically Parma expression.

"All dreams last that long," he declared. He would have preferred to say something like "as long as life", but he dragged himself back to the subject in hand, sticking relentlessly to the investigation. "What's your view on what happened?"

"I have no idea," Greci said dejectedly. "Maybe she found somebody else, or maybe she was fed up with me. I understand that to a young girl the routine of married life can seem deadly dull, but she did what she liked during the day and I didn't even enquire into how she passed her time. On the other hand, I knew that sooner or later . . . thirty years is quite a gulf, but I deluded myself that these girls who were born into poverty would be happy with the life of a wealthy lady. She often said to me: 'I live like a queen here. You don't know what it's like in Romania. In my village there was nothing but hovels and mud.' I thought that would be enough to keep her tied to me. After all, I denied her nothing."

"There was strong competition . . ." Soneri insinuated cynically, observing the other man closely, who continued eating calmly, with every appearance of serenity.

"I know. There's no shortage of beautiful people, all much younger than me and with plenty of money. It's a market like any other, and there's always somebody able to make a higher or better bid."

"Indeed," Soneri said, tiring of Greci's whining tone. What was really preying on his mind was the realisation that in that market he felt he was himself losing out to that distinguished, attractive, probably cultured and unquestionably wealthy individual at the other end of the room.

"But who could have killed her?"

"That's what I'm determined to find out. That's why I'm talking to everyone I know of who saw her in recent times," the commissario said, omitting any reference to the different descriptions and the myriad names that Nina went under. She was a different woman with each man. She was so many women. Perhaps that was a female characteristic and maybe Angela too concealed a different face.

"She was the object of many men's desire. You were one of many men, did you know that?"

Greci remained silent for a few minutes and then shook his head gravely. "I never wanted to know anything about her private affairs. I preferred to live happily without prying, because I was always afraid of finding out I wasn't the only one. But inside myself I had my suspicions. A woman as beautiful and as intelligent as she was . . ."

"Did you know she was pregnant?"

Greci blanched and heaved a deep sigh as he ran his finger round his shirt collar. "Do you think I might have been the father?" he stuttered.

"I don't know. I don't know enough about her life. The D.N.A. test will clear up the matter. Certainly, the dates coincide. You can't be excluded."

Another sigh. When faced with Nina, all these men were reduced to the status of motherless children, and yet in life, were they not combative animals? However, he could not conceive of that Romanian woman as being cynical and calculating. Rather she appeared to him like an impoverished girl who, with the tenacity of a starving cat, clung to life with her fingernails, unlike that man seated not far from him now. Having finished his meal, he wiped his lips with the elegant little movements etiquette demanded, and turned an Olympian glance around the room. Soneri felt a surge of detestation for him, on Nina's behalf as well as his own. Perhaps she had had her fill of men like him and of having to put up with their haughty ways.

He was distracted by Greci who moved uncomfortably in his seat. His worried expression showed that he urgently wanted to be on his way. As he got up, he betrayed signs of embarrassment, as though he were struggling to find the right way to take his leave.

"If you've no more questions," he murmured uncertainly.

Soneri remained sitting and shook his head. Greci turned and walked slowly off. At the same moment, Soneri saw that his rival too was on his feet. He stood at his table, took out a wallet and extracted a few notes, laid one beside the plate and without so much as deigning to turn to the waiter, made for the exit with studied hauteur. Soneri too got up and reverted to the role of investigator. He was tempted to follow his man, but did no more than observe him from the door of the wine bar. The exercise would have been futile in any case, since the man climbed into a Mercedes and drove away.

Back in the bar, he tried once more to contact Angela, but there was no reply. The suspicion that she had a date with that man sharpened until it became an acute pain, at which point he decided to take refuge at home, a wounded beast.

II

THE MOMENT HE woke up, he felt a sense of unease weigh heavily on him as though it were a mask on his face. He had slept very badly, tormented by nightmares. One in particular recurred: he was in hospital, stretched out on a bed in a corridor, wearing nothing but a pair of underpants and the green jacket surgeons wear, with half the city drawn by curiosity to stare at him. This dream made him restless and woke him up time after time, but when he succeeded in getting back to sleep, the dream returned and the cycle began again. After several nightmares of this type, he found himself wide awake, lying in the feeble light filtered through the shutters. He was aroused to daily life by the first ring of the telephone.

"I was looking for you yesterday evening," Angela said, materialising directly from his thoughts. "You had your mobile switched off."

"It was quite late when I switched it off, whereas yours is never on."

"I was very busy."

"With what?" he heard himself saying before he realised this was an inappropriate question.

"Shall we meet today?" she said.

"When?"

"Two o'clock? It's a quiet time."

Soneri wanted to ask why not in the evening, but this time he managed to restrain himself.

"Alright," he limited himself to saying, and it was only when he had hung up that he realised how accommodating he was being.

A few seconds later, Juvara came on the line. "Commissario, Dottoressa Marcotti's search warrant for the apartment in Via Cavallotti was delivered, but she said you hadn't given her the precise address."

It was true. He was not sure of it, since pure intuition had led him to that renovated block of flats and the board with the residents' names had only the internal numbers.

"She said she trusted you and that you could add the number later. In any case, she said, there'll be no-one in the flat so there would be no problem breaking the rule this once."

That woman was a marvel. She worked twelve hours a day and was always on top of her job. She had even managed to dispel Soneri's foul mood, so much so that now he felt himself providentially delivered from the nightmares.

"Get a joiner who can open doors to come along to 12 Via Cavallotti in an hour's time," the commissario said, happy to get into the flow of the day's work.

He trusted his instincts, as he always did. When he arrived at the appointed place, he found a police car already there. Esposito got out, plainly unamused by the inconvenience he had been put to.

"They've got me working as a taxi driver now. Next thing I'll have to stick a brush up my arse and sweep the streets when I go out on patrol," he grumbled.

Meanwhile a squat little man, toolbox in hand, climbed out of the back seat. "Unless it's one of those reinforced doors, this shouldn't take too long," he reassured the policemen.

Esposito leaned against the open roadside door and put on a mock expression of patience. "Meantime, I'll direct the traffic."

"Which apartment are we talking about?" the joiner said.

"I don't know," Soneri replied, to the man's puzzlement.

But it was not hard to find. They rang the first bell on the ground floor and an elderly, slightly intimidated, women came out.

"We're looking for a Romanian girl who lives here and . . ." Soneri began to explain, while the incredulous joiner waited two steps behind him.

The lady did not even give him time to finish the question. She pointed upwards, not vaguely but to the flat immediately above hers. They climbed the stairs and Soneri told the man to get on with it.

"Are you sure?" he said uncertainly.

Soneri nodded.

"As long as I have your authorisation . . ." The joiner pulled out an iron implement with tiny notches on the sides, stuck it into the keyhole and began manoeuvring it around in a series of slow, seemingly repetitive movements. After a few minutes of patient work, the door sprang open and Soneri went in, but only after informing Nanetti. He and his squad would do the real search.

The decor was somewhat cold and the apartment seemed not to have been much lived in. It looked more like a photograph in an architecture magazine. Glass and steel predominated. Soneri felt he was in a hotel suite, and wandered about looking for the personal touch. In the bedroom he found a wardrobe with mirrored doors, a chest of drawers and a bedside cabinet, all in an aluminium colour. He took out a handkerchief, pulled open one of the wardrobe doors and found the kind of clothes a normal young woman would wear: trousers, skirts and casual tops in bright colours. In the next compartment, he found more elegant clothes and even an evening dress alongside trouser suits, coquettish lace out- fits, miniskirts and below-the-knee pleated skirts, T-shirts that must have been tight-fitting and sober jerseys. It was as if four different women lived in the same apartment. He opened the chest of drawers and found the array of lingerie the boutique owner in Via Garibaldi had described to him. She was indeed a doll, as Goretti had defined her: she put on and took off costumes, like a doll.

Nanetti arrived while he was in the bedroom, trying to come to terms with the ambiguous, impenetrable atmosphere which hung around the house. As he came in, Nanetti gave a whistle: "What luxury!"

"I get the impression of utter misery," Soneri said.

"Don't start off on one of your bouts of moralising. Take a look around! You can't deny that girl had style."

"I don't deny it, but I can't see a single sign of real life," Soneri said, running his finger along the sideboard, leaving his prints in the dust.

"Don't touch, or else you might pollute the evidence," Nanetti said jokingly.

Soneri, lost in his own thoughts, made no reply.

"What a night it was last night," Nanetti went on. "There were at least ten rapists scampering about in the dark. A complete shambles."

"I wonder who's really attacking all those women," Soneri muttered, thinking to himself that this phantomatic person- age who appeared and disappeared in the mist had taken the place of the bulls.

"He's no fool, seeing as he always manages to get away."

"Not surprising if for the most part people report seeing ghosts."

"How many ghosts do we see, eh?"

"A lot. Or maybe the same one in different disguises," the commissario said, thinking of Nina.

Nanetti handed him an envelope from the top drawer in the chest. Soneri accepted it unthinkingly and took out a white sheet of paper folded in four. There was one sentence, in capital letters scrawled in black ink by a broad nib. SHITTY ROMANIAN, COW, BLOODY WHORE. BREAK OFF WITH HIM OR YOU WILL COME TO A NASTY END.

"Whoever wrote this was not a particularly nice human being," Soneri said, showing the page to Nanetti.

"Especially not with foreigners."

Soneri put the paper in his pocket and stood in silence as officers from the forensic squad passed him on both sides as though he were an island in a dual carriageway. Nanetti moved off to organise the search, and Soneri realised that he had no more business in a house which made him feel like he was in a pharmacy.

"Can I go then?" the joiner said.

The commissario nodded and went out with the man following him. Esposito was on his telephone in front of the block of flats. "I'm on duty in Via Cavallotti. I can't go chasing after the maniac with this man in my car." Pasquariello had probably asked him to check a report but had forgotten about the joiner.

"Commissario, they've all gone mad here. People are calling the emergency number every time they see a man peeing against a wall. They're all scared stiff."

He helped the man into the car and set off with tyres screeching. Soneri walked off in the direction of the questura, along Via Garibaldi as far as Piazza della Pace, then past the Glauco Lombardi museum, the Regio, the Steccata, the Parmigianino, before turning into the portico in Via Mazzini, a monstrosity of post-war reconstruction in stern, geometric cementwork. As he was wondering how he could accustom himself to such ugliness, he ran into Angela with the other man. She seemed decidedly nervous, but she stopped to say hello. The man, however, drew aside to look in a shop window.

"We're going for a coffee. Want to join us?" she said.

"I'm busy," Soneri said, shaking his head and stepping back. "But I see you are too."

"You're wrong," Angela said, sounding disappointed. "Anyway, we've got to talk."

"As soon as we can find the time," Soneri said, turning away. He did not know what had come over him at that moment – a mixture of anger, frustration, regret and that sense of emptiness which he had felt obliged to placate with a flourish of ill-tempered pride. As he crossed the piazza, listening to the clock on the Palazzo del Governatore strike eleven, he had to admit to himself that there was more to it than mere jealousy. The truth was that compared to that man he felt inferior in every way – less imposing, less well-off, less good-looking and even ridiculous in his duffel coat as against the other's designer suit. Why would Angela choose him?

When he got to the office, Juvara noticed the foul mood etched on his face and avoided attempting to engage him in conversation.

"Any news?" Soneri asked after a while.

"Dottoressa Marcotti wants to know the precise address of the apartment you searched. And she has also decided to have genetic tests carried out on the foetus."

"Do we know the sex?" the commissario said. His discomfort had once again brought back unwelcome memories.

"No, but perhaps the police doctor . . ."

Soneri made a shrug and said it did not matter. He was

already floundering with various thoughts in his mind when his mobile vibrated. *You were a shit just now. Come at two.* The text read like an order, and the commissario wondered whether to put his pride first and turn down the invitation, or to accept and show how reasonable he was being. Eventually he settled for the second option.

To take his mind off the encounter, he set to work. He wrote down the names of Nina's ex-lovers he had spoken to the night before and handed the paper to the inspector. "See if you can find out anything more about these three," he told him. "You could maybe work on it with Musumeci. They've all got an alibi for the night of the murder, but you never know."

He remembered there was another number he should check, one belonging to a firm of goldsmiths. "What's the company name?" he asked Juvara.

"Golden," came the reply. "They're at Lemignano di Collecchio."

"Is there anything more about them?"

"The owner is called Giulia Martini, and her daughter, Micaela, is a partner."

"What do they do? Make jewellery?"

"Commissario, this might surprise you, but they do a lot of work for some diocesan curias. They make sacred objects in gold and silver. There are samples of their work in a catalogue. If you want, you can see it online. Just type in www—"

Soneri interrupted him at once. Nothing seemed to him more absurd than hours spent glued to a screen which substituted imitations for reality. He was convinced it was one of the many forms of hypocrisy which were becoming more and more widespread in the world: the incapacity to look at things as they really were, even when they were disconcerting. The commissario found the whole phenomenon stomach-churning.

"I'll drop by tomorrow. This Martini, is she married or divorced?"

"I told you, she works for the priests. She has a lawfully wedded husband, name of Roberto Soncini, the father of Micaela, but he's not on the board. He travels and is in charge of the sales."

The conversation was disturbed by a commotion in the courtyard. Half a dozen police cars came in one after another, followed by other unmarked vehicles. They all parked under the fir trees. Two officers, one on either side of a foreign-looking figure whose arms they were holding tightly, emerged from the mêlée of slammed doors, shouts and curses. Only when the first flashbulb lit up the grey of the courtyard did Soneri realise that with remarkable perfection of timing the press had also arrived.

"So they've finally got him," Juvara said.

The rapist who had been terrifying the city for two days had ended up in a police trap, meaning that Parma could go back to considering itself the best of all possible worlds.

"That's one case solved," the inspector said.

"We've still a long way to go with ours, and it seems to me even more serious."

"Commissario, people care most about the immediate threat. Do you expect them to care about one murdered Romanian girl? There are many who would like to see all foreigners burned alive. Did you find anything of interest in the apartment?"

"A death threat, not much else. This Nina is an elusive figure, everything about her is mysterious. I can't make head nor tail of it all."

Soneri got up and went out. Juvara watched from the

window as he made his way through a group of excited officers. His calm stood out in the midst of all the euphoria.

He bumped into Sbarazza outside the *Milord*. "Nothing doing today." He shook his head and indicated the crowded restaurant. "There's an exhibition of Parmigianino's works on, but at this time of day the stomach takes priority over culture."

"That's very human," Soneri smiled. "Can I invite you for some salame and *torta fritta* at the wine bar down the street?"

As they walked towards it, the commissario was struck by the thought that this bar, a modern imitation of an old-style osteria, was becoming an obsession for him and he was continually on the lookout for excuses to go there. On this occasion there was no sign of the person he feared meeting, so he was able to relax. Sbarazza was a man who exuded good humour.

"You are one of the few who knows I am a tramp," he said, with the air of a man sharing a confidence. "I am known in this city as the 'Marchese'. Everyone respects me and they even raise their hats to me. If they knew how I really live, they wouldn't give me a second glance. They would despise me because here where everything is supposed to sparkle, they've no time for losers. But I haven't lost, on the contrary! They're the losers. I have won."

Soneri looked at him with a smile. Sbarazza seemed to him sincere as only those who have attained a high level of indifference to convention can be. "I imagine you feel extremely free – much more than previously, I mean."

"I am afraid of nothing. I am a true revolutionary. I try to live the life the priests preach, and since they avoid practising themselves, I do it for them. If you think about it, Christ was the greatest revolutionary who has ever appeared on this earth. A scandalous, unbearable creature, much more so than the communists, don't you think?"

"Do you suppose that's why they put him on a cross?"

"If we set theology aside, that's exactly why, no question about it. Just imagine what they'd do with him today. They'd call him an extremist, a fanatic, a troublemaker, and they'd use crueller means than nails to crucify him. They'd treat him like a madman, sneer at his preaching and ignore him. And that's what they'd do to me too if I didn't have this veneer of nobility to fool them. If I were a poor man I wouldn't be granted a permit to live in this town, but I am the 'Marchese'. It's like the label on certain products. They are valueless, deplorable, but they have the brand name and so they cost a lot. Or rather, they do have a value. That's the whole difference – in other words, nothing."

He spoke with no rancour and with an offhand casualness which revealed an enviable serenity.

"They all struggle for this nothing," Soneri said, looking around him at the tables of office-workers, lawyers and accountants, all in jacket and tie, all as indistinguishable from each other as pieces of macaroni churned out from the same processor.

"This is what we've become. You could be a stinking cesspit of a person, but the important thing is to keep up appearances." Sbarazza chuckled, making the commissario wonder whether appearances, the paradoxical appearances of life, amused him as much as any operetta. "And then this city, full of unreconstructed vermin strolling about bedecked in clothes worth a king's ransom, all to cover up their own vulgarity."

Soneri entertained the malicious thought that his rival

belonged to that caste. "You've got to make allowances. Their fathers shovelled shit in stables and they look on this past with shame. They do all they can to live it down."

"A big 4×4 with leather interior is the best remedy against the nightmares of the past, preferably with a bull bar, presumably to ensure defence against cows and their shit. I who had a father who was never short of money or women have been less fortunate," Sbarazza added, in another of his paradoxes. "I have discovered that what others envied in us was in reality the sentence we were serving. It is bad not to have wishes. The poor people I work with have many very human wishes: food, shelter, protection from the cold, surviving the slings and arrows. Everything ties them to the things which are of real importance, and sweeps away all that is superfluous. In this context, it does not take long to rediscover what is real in life. It has happened to me and each time I seem to be reborn. I look at all these people and laugh," he declared with a sweeping gesture, "because I behave like a mask and live on what they throw away. Then I turn up at the clubs with my aristocratic manners and enchant them as much as the pied piper. Believe me, that is real enjoyment – a fancy-dress ball, nothingness."

Soneri found this speech tragic. Unlike Sbarazza, he could not find anything exhilarating in the frivolity of life.

"There's no easy way out," Sbarazza went on. "You're either a believer, and in that case this world and all that's in it is short-term and of little importance, or else you're a non-believer and you'll arrive at the same conclusion, because nothing has any sense. Know what I've decided? To be a non-believing, good Christian. If there is someone up there, I'll take my chance on grace being doled out. It's better than being a hypocrite."

"You're not short of practical sense. You've been given a thorough grounding in prudence by poor people."

"That's not all. Finding a purpose in other people is the only way to have a role in life and to feel yourself loved. When all's said and done, is that not what we all want, to feel loved, ever since we were babies and screamed for our mother's breast and the soothing consolations of her embrace? It doesn't really matter if there are people out there who dispense love out of self-interest: all that's needed is one person who's sincere."

The commissario's instinct told him that Sbarazza was right. All he wanted was to have Angela near him. He looked at his watch and saw it was a quarter to two. He got up feeling reassured. Each time he spoke to Sbarazza was like a breath of fresh air. All in all, it was good to know there was someone who kept the lamp of hope burning, and he hoped the light was not the flicker of a funeral candle.

"Tomorrow I go to see the Chair of the Committee for Social Services," the old man said as Soneri was leaving. "I've convinced him to open another dormitory and a refectory. I'm a great actor!" And he executed a tango step and a half-pirouette.

Soneri too did a kind of pirouette when Angela seized him by the arm and pulled him to her as soon as he set foot in her office, and when they were face to face, he was thankful to see that her expression was not hostile.

"You were a complete shit," she said, but in a gentle voice.

"What was I supposed to do? Express approval?"

"It was only a coffee."

"And the rest."

She kissed him to cut off further discussion, but he was

waiting for a denial which did not come. There were no more words. They eased effortlessly towards that communication by gesture, touch and expression which characterises the boundless, soundless, shapeless world of the emotions. It was like a canal cutting through that chaos of fear and joy that bubbles inside each one of us, and is nearly always betrayed by words. In that way, it was possible for them to cling closely to each other even without having dispelled the rancour of betrayal, like two tigers making love while still biting at each other.

"Where are you with the case of the Romanian girl?" Angela asked him later when they had dressed

Soneri said only: "I had lunch with Sbarazza."

"Ah, the missionary," she commented.

"And an optimist, one who holds on to belief. I like his freedom of outlook in this world of rigid mindsets."

"And I like you when you get hot under the collar," she replied, taking him again in her arms.

The commissario remained passive. "Is that all you like me for?"

"I've been at work on your behalf these last few days," Angela said, pulling away from him. "I have a certain number of Romanian women among my clients, mainly young women assigned to me when I'm on duty in court. Some of them knew Nina and they all speak highly of her. They say she was a good person and that many men fell passionately in love with her because she was so beautiful, but she never took advantage of this to run off with their money. She wanted to marry an Italian and settle here, have children . . . in other words a normal life after all she'd suffered. She worked as a cleaner in several houses to put aside some money. A really nice girl."

The commissario heard her out and grew increasingly

frustrated over his inability to make headway in the case. He owed it to that Romanian girl, all the more so because she reminded him of his wife. "Maybe she was even sending some money home . . ."

"A nice girl undoubtedly, but don't go making a heroine out of her," Angela said quietly. "Your desire to rise above the vileness you deal with on a daily basis makes you idealise some things and some people too much."

"Criminals are sometimes better than a lot of the phoney people with their noses in the air that go about this city. The poor people Sbarazza meets show more solidarity. The Romanians who meet at the sports ground still have a sense of community, they help each other . . ."

"They help each other and they knife each other," Angela reminded him. "Because they're poor they need the protection of the clan. As soon as they become rich, they'll forget all that, even as many of us have. Affluence corrupts and there are not many who resist. Just a few, like Sbarazza, and they've had too much of everything so they can afford the luxury of living a grim life with perfect tranquility."

"Now it's your turn to overdo it with your dose of realism."

"Let me bring you back to earth. I told you I like you because you can still get indignant and angry. Affluence has done you no harm. You're still the wild thing you were when I first met you. There's something solid inside you, in spite of all your insecurities, something everybody always notices."

"O.K., you've brought me down to earth. In fact you've floored me."

She shook her head in good-humoured reproach. "There you go exaggerating again. It's not like that," she said, but she did not go on, leaving him once more without a full explanation. "See you tomorrow?" she said a moment later, another rapid change of mood.

The commissario gave a nod, but inside himself he felt disappointed. He was finding life trivial, elusive, anchored to the most fragile of intentions. A nothingness, as Sbarazza had put it.

I2

AS HE TRAVELLED along the Cisa road, the bulls at Cortile San Martino came back into his mind. He wondered if they were still wandering loose in the Po Valley or if someone had managed to round them up. He hoped that instinct had driven them towards the woods on the Apennines and that they were living there in the company of the wild boars. He was still thinking of his own sun-baked mountains as he turned into the artisan district of Lemignano, with its workshops, warehouses and little villas. Suddenly, he caught sight of an oval bronze nameplate with the word GOLDEN in elegant italics. The atmosphere was typical of areas reserved for the prosperous. He rang and saw a light go on in the intercom. A woman's voice asked, "Who is it?" but she was drowned out by a chorus of dogs barking in a yard nearby. The C.C.T.V. cameras, the guard dogs and the reinforced doors all added to a sense of tension in the atmosphere, which would have been like that in the trenches in time of war, had it not been for the workers in overalls inside the workshops and the coming and going of vans.

The interior was welcoming: rugs, heavy wooden furniture and a pleasing scent of rosehip perfume. Soneri introduced himself to a secretary with a serious and sad demeanour.

Giulia Martini, who must have been in her mid-forties,

had the ascetic look of a mother superior. She was thin, short and sharp-featured.

"May I know why you are here?" she demanded.

"A Romanian girl has been murdered. You may have read in the newspapers . . ."

"What of it?"

Before replying, the commissario ran his eyes along the wall behind the woman, dominated by a portrait of the Pope. "Her mobile phone shows that there were some calls made from another mobile registered in the name of this company."

If the woman were at all disconcerted, she had no difficulty in dissembling. She paused only a few seconds for reflection.

"We did have a Romanian employee some while ago. She used to come in after six o'clock in the evening to clean the offices."

"Was her name Ines Iliescu?"

"Yes."

"Her real name was Nina. She was murdered and her body burned."

The woman did not betray the least sign of discomposure. She kept her thoughts to herself and said nothing.

"Don't you think you have some explaining to do? When did she come here?"

"She came until a few weeks ago."

"And then?"

"We neither saw nor heard anything further from her. She simply disappeared."

"The telephone calls continued until a week ago," Soneri said.

"We carried on trying to reach her. She was very good and it's not easy to find reliable people nowadays."

Soneri gave a smile which was more of a smirk as he looked at the samples of sacred vessels arrayed inside display cabinets.

"Whoever was trying to reach her did find her," he snapped. "Twenty-one minutes of doing their best to convince her."

The woman was growing impatient. She adjusted a plait behind her ear and glowered at the commissario.

"When I dialled that number, a Roberto Soncini replied," Soneri said calmly. "Is your husband responsible for personnel matters?"

"My husband takes no part in running the business. He's good at selling, and that's his field," Giulia Martini said.

"You mean he does the round of the curias, the bishop's palaces . . ."

"We don't sell only sacred objects. We deal in jewellery as well. Look, commissario," she cut him short, "I can tell you for a fact that we have nothing to do with the death of this girl. You ask me for explanations, and I accept that that is your job, but I assure you that any explanations relate exclusively to the personal sphere. Do you understand me?"

"Perfectly. This girl was, or used to be at one time, your husband's lover," the commissario said.

Signora Martini looked at him coldly, leaving Soneri unable to decide if that look was meant to convey hatred or merely expressed the need to work out a strategy.

"You are well versed in the ways of the world," she began again, by way of resuming control of the conversation. "My husband often conducts himself with great superficiality," she said, never taking her eyes off him.

The commissario got the impression that she had already written him off. He looked hard at the woman and thought that Soncini was not entirely to be blamed for turning his attention elsewhere. Apart from anything else, she must have limited interest in the emotional sphere of life, but at that moment declaring herself a woman betrayed got her out of a tight corner. She seemed to be challenging him: yes, my husband has a lover, and so what? Should that bother me?

"Did you know about this affair?"

"She wasn't the first and she won't be the last," she replied, with conspicuous irony and detachment.

"With the cleaning lady . . . a bit vulgar, don't you think?"

"Men are pigs," she stated in a fatalistic tone, gazing at the commissario as if to make it clear that she included him in that judgment.

"Did you sack her? In such cases, that's generally the outcome . . ."

"Not at all!" she said, shaking her head. "I've told you. She disappeared. Anyway, as far as work went, she always performed well. Her defect was to be very pretty and I believe that if she stopped turning up, it was to avoid distressing consequences."

"Your husband has no hand in running this business, do I understand correctly?

"No. He's one of our employees," she stated firmly. Just then, with remarkable timing, a door opened behind her and there appeared a slender girl with long chestnut hair and a dark dress reaching below the knees. She too had a severe appearance. She approached Soneri, holding out her hand coldly. "Micaela Soncini."

Perhaps because the walls were lined with sacred objects, Soneri thought that there was something nun-like about the girl.

"Micaela, the commissario is here about the death of the Romanian girl who worked here for a time," Signora Martini said, throwing her daughter a look of complicity and then proceeding swiftly to change the subject.

"I was explaining that my daughter and I are the sole owners of the company."

The girl had gone over to the armchair where her mother was seated and had placed her arm on the back of the chair, taking up a fashion magazine photo shoot pose. "I am responsible for the day-to-day running of the business and for customer relations," Signora Martini explained. "My daughter deals with the economic and financial side of things. She studied at Bocconi University."

"And your husband does the sales . . ." the commissario butted in, attempting to bring the conversation back to where he wanted it to be.

"Exactly," the woman confirmed, raising her voice.

"He gets a fixed salary and commission, I suppose."

"He spends money like water." This time it was the daughter who spoke. "My mother . . ." she said, glancing at her before going on, "will no doubt have explained to you that if it'd been left to him, the company would have gone bankrupt long ago."

"The mobile from which the calls were made to Ines Iliescu is for your husband's use alone?" the commissario asked, turning back to her mother.

"Yes, but for that phone we have a pay-as-you-go contract," she said.

"Now if there's nothing more we can do for you . . ." Micaela interrupted.

Soneri got up, aware of the full force of their hostility. He had the feeling of being somewhere between the crypt and the sacristy, and this made him uneasy. Even the rows of workshops and villas facing him as he came out seemed more welcoming. He climbed into his car and turned back towards the city. On the way, he tried to contact Angela, but without success. He got her voicemail both at her office and on her mobile.

"Do a bit of research on these two," he told Juvara when he got to his office. He handed him a sheet of paper with the names of the mother and daughter, the joint owners of Golden. He then asked: "Has all the fuss over the arrest of the monster died down?"

"They're interrogating him. If you ask me, Musumeci will be completely insane by midnight."

"And he might end up raping Capuozzo," Soneri said, riled by Angela's silence.

"Listen, commissario, I'd do anything I could to help you, but I can't make head nor tail of this entire business."

Soneri almost felt a surge of tenderness. Every so often, with the impetuous spontaneity of a young hunting dog, Juvara surprised him with one of these generous outbursts.

"Neither can I," he replied with a smile. "We need a stroke of luck. In this case, coincidences have been important, and maybe there'll be one more. When all's said and done, Parma is a small city, isn't it? Sooner or later, you bump into everybody."

"Well," Juvara muttered, "I've been around for a while, but I still haven't found what I'm looking for."

"That too is a matter of coincidence, you know. However hard we try to construct our lives for ourselves, there's not much we can do against chance. This poor Romanian girl was pursued by men because she was exceedingly pretty. She could have had a good life if she'd given herself to the highest bidder, but she wanted to build her own future, even if that meant breaking her back cleaning toilets and offices. She wanted an ordinary life, a husband, children . . . and along comes some madman who murders her."

"Are you certain that's how it went?"

"What else?" Soneri raised his voice. "Do you think a woman takes on work as a servant light-heartedly? Washing underpants, making beds and changing pillowcases?"

"I meant to say that sometimes . . . in other words, in certain cases, I've had occasion to see things change so quickly that I was left dumbfounded."

"I know, but for the moment I see it in those terms, and that's what makes me so furious with myself for not yet getting my hands on whoever killed her."

The inspector stared at him, partly intimidated and partly sympathetic. After a while, he said: "You're forgetting about the text."

"What text?"

"The one here in the printout. Didn't you see it?"

There were several texts, all except one with the numbers of Nina's ex-partners. He had not read the list thoroughly enough, and had taken too much for granted. He immediately attempted to make a call, but the reply was the usual recorded reply. "Do you know whose phone this is?" he asked.

"I've written it out for you underneath," Juvara said. "It seems to have been stolen about a fortnight ago from a certain Giorgio Pagni during a burglary at his house. He'd left the mobile in a drawer when he went to the seaside for a couple of days and he only noticed the theft when he got back, so there was a delay in blocking the account. It's all set out in the statement I got the people in the crime report office to forward to me."

"And in those two days, only one text was sent."

"Just the one you see."

"Yes . . ."

"Come, everything's prepared," Soneri read aloud. Then he added: "What mast is the phone connected to?"

"You were talking about coincidences, so here's the funny thing. The text was sent from a telephone transmitted by the mast at Cortile San Martino."

"This really and truly is a step forward," Soneri exclaimed.

"I wouldn't be too sure," Juvara cautioned. "All the conversations from a good stretch of the autostrada and from a huge swathe of the Po Valley, not to mention the local hypermarket, go via that relay station. And remember the fairground was operating at that period and the text was sent at half past six on a Saturday evening."

Soneri groaned and his enthusiasm drained away. As though by magic, what had seemed a promising lead turned out to be a dead end. The same dead end as before. Once again, anguish overwhelmed him. It had been dark for some two hours, the days were slipping past and the investigation was making no progress. He took out his mobile and dialled Soncini's number. He should have done so earlier, he realised, when the other answered, in no way put out by the call he was receiving.

"I know you've already seen my wife and daughter."

Soneri noted with alarm he was losing his touch. He had not paid heed to that different number in the printout, he had failed to read Juvara's notes and now he realised that Soncini had already been alerted by the two women to the possibility of an interrogation. In all probability they had agreed on their stories so as to ward off suspicion. His mind was not focused, as the magistrate Marcotti had gently suggested.

"I need to talk to you," the commissario said. "Could we meet at the wine bar in Via Farini in an hour?"

"Alright," Soncini agreed. He showed a surprising degree of compliance. Only when he had rung off did Soneri realise that he had fixed the meeting for dinner time. Out of scruple, he tried to call Angela. He very much wanted to go round to her place but would have preferred to receive an invitation from her. The mobile was switched off, but the office phone rang. Just as he was beginning to fear hearing the recorded message, she picked up the receiver. "You got me by pure chance. I was on the way to the prison."

"Can we meet later?"

Angela hesitated a few moments before answering. Soneri detected an embarrassment which was now becoming all too familiar.

"I think I'm going to be tied up for a bit, and I'm already feeling very tired."

He did not know whether to believe her or to view her reply as a diplomatic lie. It would have been easy to check up since each had the keys of the other's house, but he had no wish to go snooping and he was in any case afraid of what he might discover.

He was about to ask her what she was doing in the prison when she said: "Anything new on the Nina story?"

Now it was his turn to remain silent for a few moments. He wanted to talk only about the two of them, but he felt so low that he launched into an account of his visit to Golden.

"It can't have been nice talking to those two harpies," Angela said.

"Do you know them?"

"Signora Martini found making money her only raison d'être after her husband's many betrayals. She takes revenge on him by making him aware he's nothing more than a hired hand."

"Why doesn't she dump him?"

"You must be joking! They're a deeply Catholic family and she works with priests. If she was separated or divorced, she could kiss goodbye to her dealings with the bishop. She cares more about her business than anything else. She's turned her daughter's wedding into a commercial deal."

"Why? Who's she marrying?"

"The eldest boy in the Dall'Argine family. You know, the ones who manufacture engines and hydraulic pumps."

"Ah!" Soneri said distractedly. He did not understand why they were talking about weddings.

"I see my information fails to interest you," Angela said. "I don't know when I'll get back but send me a text before you go to bed."

"I wanted to talk about us," the commissario mumbled. "We should be making decisions, shouldn't we? How long do you intend to keep me dangling?"

"I am not keeping you dangling."

"You're still seeing that other man. You can't make up your mind."

He heard a snort from the other end of the line. "Listen, we'll talk about this later. I'm not up to it at the moment."

As the conversation ended, the commissario felt short of breath and experienced the now customary agitation which made him feel he needed air. He left the office to seek relief from that state of quasi-asphyxiation but found his lungs filling with the dead miasma of the mist.

He dragged himself to the wine bar where he had arranged to meet Soncini, but he noticed his rival's Mercedes parked with two wheels on the pavement, and when he approached the door of the bar he made out, in the half light of the portico, a tall, trim figure. The other man slowed down, but when he saw Soneri turn the door handle to go in he changed direction slightly, with the gentle movement of a boat in a regatta, and walked on towards the far end of the road.

The commissario was sure that he had been making for the wine bar, and that his being there had made him change his mind. Perhaps that was where he was to meet Angela and he preferred to avoid unpleasant encounters. Soneri watched him move off, speaking into his mobile phone. Suspicion prompted the idea that he was calling Angela to change their rendezvous.

He had no more time to think about it before Soncini arrived. He recognised him instantly even though he had never seen him before. The idea he had formed of him corresponded perfectly to the man he now found standing before him – long hair, greying, smoothed down with gel, dark moustache, tall, lean, slightly stooped, skin suggesting exposure to a multiplicity of tanning lamps, all combining to give the impression of fragility, like a crumbling tower. He told him he had once been employed as a model and had worked on the catwalks in Milan. Perhaps it was there he had met his wife, a woman with money and anxious to show if off.

"Were you recently Nina's lover?" Soneri adopted the inquisitorial tone from the outset.

"Our relationship had been ongoing for some time, with ups and downs," Soncini replied, with irritating detachment. "We separated several times but always got back together again."

"Did you get to know her when she was working at Golden or earlier?"

"No," he said with an ironic smile. "Earlier. It was she who wanted me to find her a job. Ines was very keen on her independence and wanted a normal life. She spoke a lot about marriage and children."

"You were in no position to guarantee her these things."

"No," he said, shaking his head. "But she was young and she had time on her side. And we were very close. She went off with other men, but in reality we never separated from each other."

"Indeed," the commissario murmured, thinking of his own situation. "In the last few weeks, had you got back together?"

"Yes. She said she'd never have hesitated about getting married to me if I'd been free. She didn't care about the difference in age. Believe me, we were very much in love."

"Why was Ines not with you on the night of the crime?"

"I was busy. I was with a lawyer friend. There was a problem over an order for some goldsmith's work. Then we went to a bar on Lake Como. I don't know what Ines was doing that evening. She told me she'd be going out with some Romanian friends I didn't know."

"What's the name of your lawyer friend?"

"What's going on? Do you want verification?" Soncini sounded astonished. "Look, I'm not telling you lies. But you can call him, he's Arnaldo Razzini. Check with him."

"It's my job to double-check."

"Then go ahead," Soncini declared brazenly. "I'm an entrepreneur. I don't go around assaulting women the way these foreigners do. Ines told me all about what goes on in Romania."

"You say you are an entrepreneur, but your wife might take a different view," Soneri said maliciously. "She tells me an employee paid by commission . . ."

Soncini glowered at Soneri with deep resentment, but he could not hold that look for long. He was obviously a spineless human being, a man of straw.

"Well then, say that I'm a manager, will that do? I'm a good salesman, and nobody can take that away from me. Not even my wife." He spoke of her as though she had the right of life and death over him.

The commissario stared at him and thought of Giulia Martini. A couple who hated each other but were held together by business interest, exactly like members of a board of management. She kept him in exchange for being able to sell to bishops and cardinals the outward display of married life, while he moved from one bed to the next, deceiving young foreign girls. The commissario delighted in the opportunity to disrupt their minuet and cause trouble. "Your wife and your daughter tell me you spend money like water . . ."

Soncini gave the slightest of shrugs, as though bored. "My daughter used to love me a lot, but she's come under her mother's control."

The distance between them seemed to bother him a great deal, but everything in Soncini appeared improbable. He was a man who must have dabbled in everything, but who had so completely wasted everything life had offered him that he was incapable of even one authentic emotion. The commissario looked hard at a face that could in another age have been Casanova's, and had the displeasing impression of seeing in front of him a man embittered, exhausted and dissatisfied, let down by his body and by age. Quite suddenly, Soncini was transformed into a ghost.

"I've nothing more to ask you," Soneri said, anxious to be free of the man.

Soncini rose slowly to his feet. He had maintained a kind of fading, early autumnal attractiveness, and his walk as he left the bar had the slow deliberateness of an elderly gentleman.

Soon after, Soneri too went out. The discussion with Soncini added nothing to what he had already known, but did leave him with some impressions he could not yet manage to decode. And no-one knew better than him how important impressions were when everything appeared inexplicable.

13

THE NIGHT WAS a time of peace for the commissario, when the inexplicable ceased to torment him. The darkness of the *borghi* in the old town set itself up as a natural obstacle to anxiety, leaving it no option but to slink off. Momentarily washing his hands of his problems offered great relief and gave Soneri, as he strolled about in the mist, a break from his nightmares.

It did not last long. Once more the sirens blared out in the labyrinth of streets around the Duomo. Excitement exploded and transformed itself into a mob. An ambulance raced by, pursued by the curious on foot. They made for the Vicolo del Vescovado, but the entrance was blocked by a pair of police cars. In the midst of things, he made out the figure of Musumeci and immediately afterwards saw a flushed woman being taken by the arm by Esposito.

"We've made a cock-up of the whole thing," Esposito shouted.

"You mean it wasn't him," the commissario said, meaning the Moroccan now being crucified as the Brute of Parma.

"No, no way. Oh, don't get carried away. He was no saint, eh! He did try to hassle that girl."

"Him and how many others, Esposito? There are

thousands of potential rapists, especially among respectable, apparently innocent fathers of families."

"Maybe so, commissario, but this is one weird human being," he concluded with an eloquent gesture of his finger.

Musumeci was conducting interrogations and a number of people were lined up along the wall of the Bishop's Palace. There was something blasphemous or even perhaps deliberately provocative in raping a woman in that place. A symbolic coincidence, and Soneri had a continuing interest in both coincidences and symbols. A new piece of information crackled out on a radio held by one of Esposito's colleagues. A man whose description fitted the rapist had been seen under the Portici del Grano at the City Hall. After a challenge to the spiritual power, it was the turn of the temporal power. Two cars sped off with tyres screeching. The commissario followed them on foot. A few metres on, some boys went racing past him, and he too broke into a run, abandoning himself to a puerile excitement that reawoke memories of leaping from stone to stone in furrows created by water or by tractors, and of boyhood competitions on sun-soaked paths lined by poplar trees, and at the same time contemplating how pitiless is time in burning us up.

Soneri stopped in Via Repubblica, in front of the police station, unable to decide if his breathlessness was due to emotion or exertion. He had the impression that, quite suddenly, that night he had begun to make some headway. Something must have been happening under the mist which seemed to be continually rolling over the city, even if to all appearances everything was returning to its customary stillness and to the subdued sounds of the night-time hours. He walked along Via Mazzini, and observed the faint lights on the far side of the river pierce the darkness, while the bells of the Duomo rang a quarter to midnight. He leaned on the parapet of the Mezzo bridge and looked over at the river only a few metres below but almost silent. He was finally floating with a lightness he had been experiencing for some time, nothing more than a bubble released from the graceful hand of a child, rising without wind, tossed slowly about before bursting, forgotten.

The ringing of his mobile brought him back to earth. "Commissario," the voice of Pasquariello's deputy came booming out, "we've got the car you described to us, the black B.M.W. Remember?"

"The one with the horse on the side? Of course I remember."

"Well, you won't see much of the horse, because there's a scrape on the side of the car, but we think this is the one you're after."

"Where is it now?"

"Here with us."

"Who was driving?"

"Two Romanians. We've checked with the vehicle registration office, and it turns out the car's stolen."

Soneri muttered something incomprehensible. "When?"

"Couple of months ago. But that's not all. The pair who were in the car are underage. The guy who was driving is seventeen and the other one's sixteen."

"How did you apprehend them?"

"They crashed into another car at the Crocetta and ran off. A squad car gave chase until they turned into a cul-de-sac. There may have been a third person who got away."

"Don't let anybody touch the car, and first thing tomorrow morning call in the forensic squad. I want that car examined," Soneri ordered.

Shortly afterwards, he was at the police station. On the way he tried to get through to Angela, but without success.

He sent her an ambiguous text: *I don't know if I'll go to bed tonight. What about you?* He saw the B.M.W. parked in the courtyard, not the most recent model, but one still in vogue. It had a long scratch on one side, but the galloping horse could clearly be made out.

"Where are the two you've arrested?"

A custody officer escorted him to the interrogation room, but before they went in he warned him: "I think you're wasting your time. They won't open their mouths."

They were young, but they had the look of having been through a lot.

"You stole the wrong car," the commissario began. "Anyone in possession of it is in deep trouble, facing much more than a straightforward charge of car theft."

The two remained impassive. They seemed not to have understood what was being said to them. Soneri turned back to the officer.

"Do these two understand Italian?"

"They understand perfectly well. They're bluffing."

"It'd be better for you to come clean, much better," the commissario threatened. Not a muscle on the face of either man moved.

"Even if you are underage, a murder charge is no trivial matter," the commissario said.

Only at that point did the two exchange a brief glance, but still did not say a word. They gave the impression of being in a waiting room rather than a police station, and the idea of ending up in jail seemed not to have crossed their minds. They stared straight ahead impassively, with an inexpressive, almost obtuse look on their faces. The commissario wondered how they could maintain that pose except by anaesthetising the brain, leaving it dulled during the hours and hours of waiting, with no other aim than to let time pass. He would have liked to punch the pair of them and shake them out of a silence he found deeply irritating.

"Where are you from?"

No reply. Soneri looked questioningly at the officer.

"They had no papers on them, commissario. We're making enquiries with the immigration office."

He peered at the two young men impotently. Although in a fury, he did no more than take a seat opposite them, attempting to intercept any glance they exchanged. Their clear eyes darted about like lizards', but when they were still they had the fixed vacuity of a pane of glass.

"I don't understand why you're so keen to make trouble for yourselves! Ruining your lives before they've really begun." Addressing the officer, he added, "The car was the one used in the Iliescu murder."

He hoped to make some impact on the boys, to shake them out of their apathy, but they were plainly hard cases. Or simply two lads who had been trained in a code of blind obedience to the clan, imposed by beating after beating. Or else they were terrified. Only once did the younger of the two display a sign of concern, throwing his mate a glance which the commissario read as a willingness to yield, but immediately afterwards everything settled back as before: the same apathy, the same immobility, the same lizard-like looks.

The commissario cut short the interrogation. "O.K. You'll be spending the night in the cells."

He got up and walked slowly to the door. As he squeezed past the custody officer, he stopped and turned round for a last look at the two Romanians staring into the void, as impassive as ever.

In the corridor he bumped into Pasquariello, who had the grim expression on his face of a man dragged out of bed in the middle of the night.

"So? Where are these two little shits?"

Soneri nodded in the direction of the room he had just left. "It's a waste of time going in. They're like two statues."

They both went into the office of the head of the flying squad. There were three officers at work on the case, but at that moment the commissario felt the absence of Juvara and his computer skills.

"The car was stolen from some firm," one of the policemen announced.

"Which firm?" asked Pasquariello.

"It's called Golden. It's a goldsmith's firm based in Lemignano."

Something clicked in Soneri's mind, even if he would not have been able to identify the connection which was suggested. Unquestionably he was facing another coincidence: he had just been talking to the irreproachable family which held the reins in that firm.

"Do you know it?" Pasquariello said.

The commissario nodded. "Nina Iliescu worked there for a while and then she became the lover of the owner's husband."

The chief of the flying squad gave a malicious grunt. "So the skin trade was part of it after all. Who would have guessed it? What about these two Romanians? Can we put a name to them?" Pasquariello asked the officers.

"No. Either they're illegals or else we're going to have to do lengthy research. Meantime, we've taken their fingerprints."

"Have a look in the camps of the Roma travellers. It's likely they come from there," Soneri suggested, remembering Medioli's ill-fated flight.

Pasquariello agreed. "Maybe you're right. Running off with a car with no licence is typical of them. It wouldn't be the first time."

"There were some Romanian Romas at Cortile San Martino in the clearing near the rubbish dump. They left a couple of days ago and who knows where they've ended up? I requested help to trace them, but we'd need the collaboration of our cousins," the commissario said, referring to the carabinieri.

"Is there no way to get them to talk?" Pasquariello asked.

"No, and even if they did, they'd give a false name. Who knows how many aliases they have," Soneri said.

"And how many expulsion orders . . ." added one of the officers, his eyes still glued to the computer screen.

"Anything found in the car?" the chief of the flying squad said.

"A quick search didn't reveal anything, but maybe tomorrow Nanetti will come up with something," Soneri said, as he left with Pasquariello.

"Do you think these two clowns have anything to do with the murder?" Pasquariello asked.

Soneri shook his head. "I don't believe so, but who knows? They could set us on the right track."

He turned away without saying goodbye. As he walked under the archway which led to the Borgo della Posta, he heard the bell on the Duomo strike one. Immediately after, the mobile in his pocket vibrated. *Perhaps I won't either*, he read on the screen. He knew she meant she would not go to bed that night any more than he would. A state of agitation once again overcame him. These few words could indicate either that she had complex work in hand or that she would not be going home.

He felt the need for some slices of Parmesan and a good, dark Lambrusco, always the best remedy at moments like these. He was about to head home but had to jump aside to avoid a squad car arriving at top speed. The car stopped in the archway, lights flashing and sirens blaring, until the officer raised the barrier. Two other cars also arriving at high speed came in behind the first.

Soneri rushed back into the courtyard. In the absence of Parmesan and Lambrusco, throwing himself into the thick of the action could well be the best way to keep worried thoughts at bay.

"We got him! This time we caught him with the mouse in his mouth," shouted Esposito, hauling out a man of distinguished appearance but plainly distraught.

Soneri watched him go past, ashen-faced, head bowed, dressed like an executive: jacket and tie, finely fashioned knee-length overcoat, English shoes, elegant trousers with flares. The commissario followed the short procession into the offices and it occurred to him that this was the night of the reckoning. He left to his colleagues the satisfaction of the first interrogation and went off to pour himself a coffee from the machine. At that instant, he felt once again refreshed. All the clamour around him seemed to him a vacuous, grotesque pantomime and for that reason, with that coolness which follows disappointment and disengagement from spent passion, he succeeded in seeing the world in a wholly new light.

Pasquariello appeared at his side. "Why don't you come in as well? We're going to interrogate him."

The man was called Vincenzo Candiani, a professor fairly well known in the city. Soneri tried to imagine the reaction of Parma's *bien pensant* society when they discovered that the Brute was not a foreigner, nor even some poor addict, but a respected professor of Law. Observing him now, seated on a plywood seat in the police station, leaning forward on his elbows like an ancient elm tree blown over by the wind, made him an almost pitiful figure. The commissario saw reflected in the man all the instability of humanity. Only the most shadowy of boundaries separated the professor revered in the lecture halls from the depraved, rapist ogre. "A nothingness," as Sbarazza had said in support of his view that everything cohabited in every man in a turmoil continually churned up by circumstances.

Esposito whispered into Soneri's ear. "He was in a doorway in Borgo Scacchini, with his prick in his hand, ready for use. We were phoned by an old woman of ninety-odd years, the most alert in the building. At first we couldn't believe it. A professor like him. Just imagine, we've seen him so often in court."

"We're not sure of anything yet, Esposito. Human beings can take as many forms as the mist," the commissario said.

Esposito looked at him without seeming to understand a word. He said nothing then turned away to give orders to his men.

"Professor, what are we to make of this?" Pasquariello began in a menacing tone.

"I lost my head . . ." Candiani kept on repeating. He had opened his coat and loosened his collar because of the heat, making him look like a man who had fallen asleep fully dressed on the settee after lunch. He looked around at the policemen with a kind of candour, as though he wanted to apologise for what he had done, but did not really think he had done anything particularly serious.

"You could have had any woman you wanted," Pasquariello continued. "What's going on?" he said incredulously, shaking his clasped hands back and forth.

"I lost my head," Candiani repeated again, but this time he added, "It was all because of one woman. It all began there . . ."

It all seemed unbelievable, and yet that man seemed genuinely possessed by an obsession, a toad lurking deep in his guts. His eyes were sparkling brightly and his face seemed to be twitching like a bird's. He was in the grip of a febrile agitation which would calm momentarily before flaring up again as he faced the questions put by Pasquariello and Musumeci. He gave every impression of having surrendered completely and even of being happy to be free of a weight, as had been the case with Medioli in that same room days earlier.

"Have you any questions for him?" Pasquariello asked Soneri, leaving Candiani in the custody of Musumeci until the magistrate arrived.

"Not now. I don't know if he has anything to do with my investigations, even if Parma's a small town and everything links up."

He had thought of contacting Angela to ask her about the professor, but he would not have been able to cope with a switched-off phone and the conlusions which that would have provoked. All his fears and conjectures merged into the one image of his beloved making love to that other man, with all that might be obscene or noble in lovemaking.

He went out to light a cigar, and in the still, heavy air of the courtyard he rediscovered some peace. The whirlwind of arrest after arrest had disturbed him, causing him to feel the need to let his impressions settle and pass through the sieve of his memory. This he could do only by drawing apart a little from the throb of the action, and looking on from a distance.

As he was going over all that had happened that night, he heard footsteps behind him. He turned and saw Juvara approach with his stumbling walk. He had a scarf round his neck and the dreamy air of someone who has overindulged.

"You look as though you're just out of a discotheque," Soneri greeted him.

"I was at a party," the inspector said in self-justification. "There was such a racket I couldn't hear the phone."

"You can go to bed. Nothing's going to happen as regards our investigation before tomorrow morning."

"What's been going on? There's such a frenzy . . ."

"They've picked up the rapist and it turns out he's a well-known university professor. But what matters for us is that they've arrested two teenagers driving the car from which Mariotto was seen dumping the body of Nina alongside the autostrada. We're not going to find out much more until tomorrow. We'll have to wait until Nanetti looks it over."

"Was it them?"

"I doubt it. They're just boys, and the car was stolen two months ago at Golden. That's the most intriguing aspect."

Juvara nodded. "And this rapist?"

"He says he lost his head over a woman and from then on he went haywire. Want to bet it was Nina?"

"She was well capable of it. He obviously wouldn't have been the first."

"It wasn't her fault if men went running after her, nor if they lost their heads over her. All they wanted was to screw her, but then they got in deeper than they expected, and that's all there was to it. Was that her fault? She was looking for a man to marry, but the ones she found wanted her as a toy. They ended up whimpering when she moved on."

"No, I just meant . . ." Juvara, stung by the commissario's exasperated response, stuttered incoherently. Each time Nina's name came up, a conditioned reflex provoked him into an outburst.

"Get to bed. That's what I'm going to do," Soneri said, calming down. "I've got nothing more to do, not this evening anyway."

He watched the inspector turn away before he moved off himself. He wanted to be on his own, perhaps at a table in an *osteria* with a half litre of wine in front of him, but there was nothing open at that time. Night life was reduced to a series of squalid clubs and no-one was out after dark anymore, perhaps because it was too hard to put up with the silence.

The silence was broken in Via Saffi by his mobile ringing, producing the same effect on the commissario as an alarm clock on someone fast asleep.

"Are you still awake?" Angela said.

"I'm not even home yet."

"Who did you go out with?"

"Are you kidding? It was you who went out, not me."

"If that's what you think, you're off the mark. Let me warn you it doesn't seem to me the ideal way to make a fresh start."

"But I never finished! I still don't understand why you wanted to put me through all this. It's hard to bear when your most ferocious torturer is the person you love. I don't know what to make of you, you're tormenting me . . ."

He realised that for the first time he had let himself go, speaking out without caution or discretion, and it seemed that Angela was deeply moved by this fact. Soneri had overcome the reserve ingrained into men from the mountains where he was born. It had dissolved in the slow heat of the passions bubbling in his soul. "But perhaps you've finished with me," he said, his voice breaking slightly.

"No, that's not the way it is," Angela contradicted him with sudden gentleness. "I was at the prison for an interrogation until half an hour ago. I didn't go out with anyone."

"But you might have done."

"I could have," she said drily.

"And it was only work that stopped you?"

"That had a lot to do with it." Her reply was delphic, keeping him on tenterhooks.

Soneri could no longer put up with her frankness. He was thinking he would have preferred a merciful lie when it occurred to him that this desire for security was absurd.

"I'm going to bed. It's nearly three o'clock," he said, after waiting a few seconds in vain for her to speak.

"If it weren't so late . . . Come tomorrow to my office," Angela proposed.

"So we're not meeting any more in the evening?"

She deflected the question. "I like our encounters over the lunch break. They're less predictable."

"What have you got on in the evening?"

He heard an impatient snort from the other end of the line. "Is that you off again, the interrogating policeman act?" Angela raised her voice. "You know it's the wrong approach."

"What do you want me to do? Keep my mouth shut while you're being unfaithful?"

"Oh God, unfaithful! That's the way people spoke half a century ago."

"You can use any term you like, but I prefer to speak plainly."

"Come round tomorrow," Angela invited him once more, this time in a more wheedling tone of voice.

"I'll tell you all about Professor Candiani."

"What has our great academic done?"

"He's been raping women."

"Him! There were some rumours about a female student. When did you pick him up?"

"An hour ago. In flagrante. In Borgo Scacchini."

"He's an advisor to the court and a friend of a lot of lawyers."

"Including Paglia?"

"I think so. They meet in an equestrian club in the hills, near Traversetolo. I believe it's called Cerreto."

The mention of horses touched a chord in Soneri's memory.

"A police patrol unit stopped the car used to dump Nina's body in the ditch," he said.

"So you're home and dry," Angela exclaimed.

"Not quite dry, but we're on the home run," Soneri said, as Angela repeated her invitation to lunch the following day.

14

HE AWOKE ABRUPTLY and sat bolt upright in bed. His bedroom seemed to hold on to the darkness of the night, and he searched vaguely around until his eyes located the phosphorescence of the alarm clock. Nearly nine o'clock. He groped on his bedside table for his mobile phone, but then saw something shining on the floor. He could not remember putting his mobile on vibrate, but the pulsating movement must have caused it to fall off.

"I've been looking for you since seven," Nanetti grumbled.

"I was up till three," the commissario said.

"Good sign. It means you're coming back to life."

"Go to hell. I was working. They'll have told you what happened while you were asleep or reading crime fiction."

"I've never read any such thing in all my life. I know real detectives like you . . . ."

"Do you want me to tell you again to go to hell?"

"It'd be better than being where I am now. There's a stench in this car that would make a python throw up. They must have been using it for the delivery of take-away fry-ups."

"Oh God, the smells are getting to you now! Have you found anything worthwhile?"

"Not so far. The fingerprints belong to the two boys, as

well as to an army of other people. No trace of Nina's, if that's what you want to know."

"And that's all?"

"There's a till receipt," Nanetti said off-handedly. "I don't think it's got anything to do with the Romanians. They'd rather take things without going near any till."

"What kind of receipt is it?"

"A computer shop, called Elettronica Sauro, in Borgo Regale."

"Did they spend much?"

"No, two hundred euros. Maybe an accessory, who knows?"

"Is there a date?"

"Six months ago. It must have fallen and ended up under the seat. Anyway, I'll stick it in an envelope and attach it to my report. There's nothing else of any interest."

Soneri dressed hurriedly and grabbed hold of his mobile. There were seven unanswered calls. Juvara, Nanetti, Musumeci and Angela had all called, but the only one he was interested in calling back was Angela. When he was greeted by the familiar voicemail, he went into a rage which almost drove him to smash the mobile against the wall. He left the house and set off for the police station with the unpleasant feeling of not being abreast of developments.

The first person he met was Musumeci, who looked weary but euphoric. "I've had compliments from Capuozzo," he said.

"Let me add mine," Soneri said with a tired voice. The opinions of the chief of police were of no interest to him.

"The newspapers have only managed to get it into 'late news', but you've no idea the uproar it's caused!"

"That way the good people of Parma will learn to consider themselves as living in the best of all possible worlds," Soneri

-168-

said. "What extenuating circumstances has our professor of Law given?" he asked, realising only as he asked the question just how extraordinary it was that the holder of a Chair of Law should break the law so outrageously.

"Commissario," the inspector began, drawing closer to Soneri with an air of complicity, "he's up to his eyeballs in cocaine. We found some in his house, and since it was a fair amount he's facing a charge of drug pushing as well."

"Who would have believed it, eh?" Soneri exclaimed sarcastically. "He said he lost his head over a woman. Did he say who she was?"

"A Romanian woman," Musumeci said. "He said her name is Doina, and that she dumped him without any warning, and I think I can understand why."

The commissario lit a cigar and as he inhaled, he saw the inspector standing silent and embarrassed before him.

"And?"

"These are unconfirmed stories," Musumeci said, in an attempt to play things down. "We've heard from a couple of the professor's ex-girlfriends and, you see . . . it seems his tastes were a bit on the perverted side, if you get my meaning."

"Seeing what he was up to, he could hardly be called normal, could he?"

"Certainly not," Musumeci said quickly. "It all fits. I just couldn't find the right words," he went on, his embarrassment increasing while Soneri struggled not to laugh out loud. He had frequently heard the inspector use scurrilous language when speaking to the men in his division, and here he was almost blushing in front of him. A question of rank, no doubt, but Soneri also knew that yet again age was a factor.

"You don't need to go into details. I can imagine them for myself."

He thought it was perfectly reasonable of Nina/Doina to leave him. She seemed to meet only men who wanted to keep her as a toy, or a doll, in Goretti's words, but one so beautiful as to make grown men, seemingly sure of themselves, lose their heads.

These thoughts were in his mind as he made his way along the corridor leading to the office of the road patrol.

The moment he saw him, Juvara gave a start as though he had been caught in the act of committing some crime. "There you are at last! Dottoressa Marcotti has called several times. She needs to talk to you."

"About what?"

"The carabinieri have caught up with the Romanian Romas who were camped at Cortile San Martino."

"Where are they now?"

"At Suzzara. That's why Marcotti was looking for you, but in the end she had to decide for herself. I explained to her that you were running late and that . . ."

The commissario cut him short with a wave of the hand. "Get over there as soon as you can. With Musumeci. He's half gypsy and he'll take no nonsense from these people."

"Yes, but Marcotti also ordered the carabinieri to identify the two car thieves."

"We'll see if the Romas will talk. There's no way of knowing if this pair belong to the same group. And who cares anyway? This is our investigation and the bold boys in the carabinieri have no idea what's behind it all."

Juvara got up, a picture of confusion. Soneri was already on the way out and took no notice.

The inspector called him back. "One thing, sir. I've found out who owns the flat in Via Cavallotti."

The commissario gave him a quizzical look.

"It's an accountant, name of Gino Aimi."

"The name doesn't mean anything to me."

"Nor to me, at first, but then I checked up Traversetolo on the company list at the Chamber of Commerce and discovered he's chairman."

"You see where coincidences lead?"

"There are getting to be a lot of them," the inspector said. "That's a good sign."

A moment later he was in his Alfa and heading for Golden. He needed to speak to Soncini, and more so to his wife.

The countryside around the city looked strangely like a black and white photograph. Even the wheat, which was past time for harvesting, was so soaked by the rain that it had a grey cast. The plane trees lining Via Spezia seemed turned upside down, with the bare branches dissolving into the mist and looking more like roots exposed by running water. The last trace of colour vanished totally when he turned into the street leading to the industrial zone of the city. Every time he ended up in one of those places, he wondered how it had been possible so totally to eliminate every hint of beauty.

The sight of the pyxes, chalices and crucifixes in the offices of Golden did nothing to raise his spirits after such ugliness, particularly since he also found himself confronted by Signora Martini's decidedly unwelcoming expression. However, the woman herself was too conformist to allow herself to voice her displeasure. She restricted herself to coldness and to that blank expression she must have put on in response to setbacks in a dull life.

"I trust you are not the bearer of bad news," she said with a scowl. "Policemen . . ."

"Good news. We've found your car. A bit scraped but intact."

She showed no emotion other than a forced smile. "Where was it?" was all she wanted to know.

"It was being driven by two teenagers: two of the Roma community."

As had happened on the previous occasion, the daughter came in and took up position alongside her mother in a prearranged pose under the portrait of the Pope.

"Who had the use of that car?" Soneri said.

"My husband. He's the one who does the travelling. My daughter and I have smaller cars."

"Is your husband available?"

"Micaela, go and call your father." Signora Martini gave orders in the tone of one accustomed to being obeyed.

"We'll get rid of that car," she said. "The lease was nearly up and we'd have changed it in any case."

At that moment Soncini came in, followed by his daughter, meaning the whole family was now lined up in front of the commissario. Each one wore a different expression, as though they were passengers thrown together by chance on a tram. Soncini looked nervous and bereft of the *bon viveur* self-certainty he had previously displayed, his wife gave the impression of keeping the situation under control while waiting patiently, and the daughter glowered at the commissario with unconcealed malevolence.

"I've read the witness statements about the B.M.W. It was stolen from Via Cavallotti some time after ten o'clock at night. At that hour I presume that it was not there for reasons connected with work . . ." Soneri began.

"You presume? My clients do not necessarily see people during office hours."

"Priests go to bed after Vespers, or else are at their prayers," Soneri said.

Soncini was about to reply when his wife interrupted him.

"He was with his lover." She cut him short so peremptorily that there followed a few moments of silence which no-one dared to break. "That's what you were getting at, weren't you, commissario?" she went on. "They already know the Romanian girl had a flat in that street," she said, throwing a reproachful look at her husband.

Soncini said nothing. He seemed relieved to let his wife take the initiative.

"You didn't report the theft until ten o'clock the following morning," Soneri continued, in an inquisitorial tone.

Giulia Martini turned to her husband with what seemed like a challenge. She appeared to be inviting him to get himself out of trouble.

"I only noticed the following morning when I went to pick it up," Soncini said.

"Commissario," his wife intervened with her customary brusqueness, "it seems to me that we have cleared this matter up, don't you think? The car was stolen two months ago, and what happened thereafter is no concern of ours."

She was in charge, as was evident from the subservient expressions of husband and daughter. It was her task to defend the family, the business, the veneer of respectability.

"Do you know Gino Aimi well?"

"Of course," Soncini replied. "He's a good friend. I don't see what . . ."

"Was it through him that you found the house for Iliescu?"

The man was at once embarrassed and his wife looked on, savouring the spectacle.

"It's logical to turn to friends . . ."

The woman gave a devious smile, but her attitude upset Soneri more than it did her husband. It announced that she feared nothing and that his questions in no way unsettled her.

He, on the other hand, was aware of having no other weapons in his armoury.

"The good old-fashioned male complicity," she remarked sardonically.

The commissario ignored her. "However, it's very curious that your lover was tossed into a ditch after being hauled out of a car similar to yours."

Signora Martini's face darkened slightly.

"You did say 'similar'," Micaela intervened determinedly. "We're hardly the only ones in this city who have a B.M.W."

Soncini stopped her going any further. "Commissario, there's something important I haven't told you. Nina was burning her bridges with her relatives. She wanted a life of her own, where she wouldn't have to be accountable to any family members. Do you understand me? One side of the family was mixed up with the Roma people, and I don't have to tell you what that means. They never leave you alone. They're always trying to screw cash out of you. Over and above that, they were trying to decide her future for her, arrange a marriage. She rebelled, and they made her pay. They tried so many times. To them, I was a thief, someone who took the community's women away. For that clan, Nina was a licence to print money. Like her sister."

What left Soneri most dumbfounded was observing Soncini's wife listen impassively to her husband's account as though it involved a complete stranger. Micaela likewise betrayed no emotion. They were the real clan, untouchable, calculating, hardened to a state of indifference. Thinking of his own anguish over Angela's betrayal, Soneri envied that tough-minded woman.

"Commissario," Soncini's voice interrupted his reflections, "I have no way of proving it, but I am pretty sure that those Romanians tried to frame me too. What could be better than to steal my car and then use it to murder the woman with whom I'd been having an affair? Maybe they wanted to do it immediately after the theft but had to put it off because . . ."

"How could they know you wouldn't report the theft?"

"They've managed to put me under suspicion. Proof of that is your presence here."

"You have a poor opinion of us, but our sins are not a matter for criminal law," Giulia Martini said, once again throwing an accusatory glance at her husband.

"As for your sins, you can attend to them yourselves." Soneri was curt because he was tired of the conversation. The whole range of Golden's sacred objects lying nearby made the room look like a sacristy. He felt nauseous as he rose to his feet and observed the triumphant expression on Micaela's face. As before, when he went out he felt the mist to be a comforting and friendly presence. It was good not to see too far ahead and to lose himself in it as though in sleep.

He drove back to the city with a vague, troublesome ill humour weighing down on him. En route, he received a phone call from the prosecutor Marcotti to inform him that the two Romanians arrested for car theft were still taking advantage of their right to remain silent. As for the camp they came from, she was still waiting for the report from the carabinieri. In due course, he would receive fresh news from Juvara and Musumeci, who had gone to Suzzara to find them in their new campsite.

When he got to the office, he found the membership list of the equestrian club at Traversetolo left for him by Juvara. It included the majority of the people most involved in the case, and Nina seemed to be the focal point around which the whole lovers' comedy rotated. The slightest change of perspective could give a new slant to the whole story, which was itself as changeable as its participants, who in their turn differed every time in their continual denial of their role.

There was no knowing what angle would be revealed by that receipt for Elettronica Sauro found in the B.M.W. by Nanetti. He had decided to stop at the shop when he noticed that it was gone one o'clock. Getting up late meant drifting through the day, as his father had always warned him. Right on cue, the mobile rang.

"So, are you coming or have you had second thoughts?" Angela took him by surprise.

"You're like a cat. You decide when to purr."

"Do hurry."

It was yet another very intense encounter, and Soneri abandoned himself to it with the bitter conviction that the ardour was not really aroused by him. But soon all thought faded away and everything was transformed into pure instinct and desire, with all rationality irrelevant. Sex could have the same narcotic effect as sleep, with the difference that it did not last as long.

Then the reawakening, followed by the return of the familiar spectres. It was no doubt the same for someone coming round after taking drugs: the same withdrawal symptoms after the injection-induced high.

"Angela, have you made up your mind about us?"

He heard a brief snort at his side. "Why must you always ruin every beautiful moment?"

"I have a need for certainty, an absolute need."

"You know there can't be certainties, don't you?"

"I would be happy with the illusion."

"Even if I spoke reassuring words, even if I were to tell you that I'll stay with you always, you would still leave here as doubtful as ever," Angela whispered to him. "One moment later, you'd have forgotten what I said. And you know that's true, you're sure of it, so I don't understand why you go on like this. I don't want to deceive you and show contempt for what you are and have always been. Your own rationality rebels against yourself. Haven't you always claimed that you detest people who allow themselves to be dominated by instinct? Haven't you always said you'd never let yourself go that way?"

"Goddammit, Angela, I only want to know if you want to stay with me or would rather go off with the other guy. I'm not asking for an everlasting pledge!"

"You know perfectly well that things have to be constructed day by day."

"Constructed day by day? What drivel is that! Everything has fallen apart, Angela. Everything I believed in since I was a boy – my profession, my marriage, the son I never saw, my dreams . . . and now you and I are going to pieces as well. I'm broken up inside, and I can't take it any more."

Angela gave him a hug, but in that gesture he thought there was more tenderness than real feeling.

"If we feel all this, it means we have still a lot to give each other," she murmured in his ear, all the while holding him tightly and communicating a pleasing sense of warmth.

"At least I'm happy about one thing," Soneri said. "There's no sign of that pity for the other that sometimes comes out with two people who have been together a long time."

Angela pulled back to look at him more closely and more intensely, then said simply, "No, no pity." Somehow a phrase which could have been wounding sounded, on the contrary, gentle.

Shortly afterwards, as he was on the doorstep, the commissario felt a moment's confusion. "You were supposed to talk to me about Candiani," he said.

"I can ask about him if you like, but maybe you'd rather not."

"Why not?"

"The other man," she said with evident embarrassment, "he's a great friend of his. If you want, I'll call him and try to ask him . . . He wouldn't refuse."

"Forget it. I'll see to it myself," Soneri said, before dashing down the stairs to escape the anguish which threatened to overwhelm him yet again.

15

ELETTRONICA SAURO OCCUPIED some thirty square metres, divided between display space and workshop. Giorgio Sauro, the young man in his thirties who was manager, seemed to have wagered everything on it. He was plainly a courageous individual since, apart from anything else, he had not given his shop an English name. This was enough to make Soneri take to him immediately.

"I do know Signor Soncini. He's been here a couple of times and I've added his name to our client list. I keep him up to date by e-mail."

The commissario produced the till receipt which Nanetti had given him. "Could you identify what this referred to?"

Sauro examined the date and the amount. He opened a drawer and pulled out a sort of ledger. He was exceedingly punctilious, and it crossed Soneri's mind that he and Juvara would get on well.

"It's to do with the repair of a laptop, a Sony. He had problems accessing the internet from it."

"Would that be Signor Soncini's own laptop?"

"That I couldn't say. If it was his, he must have another one seeing as he's never come back to collect it."

"Have you still got it?"

"Yes. He paid me and then said that a friend of his, a girl, would come and pick it up, but she never turned up. I called him a couple of times and he always said she'd be along soon. As you can see, I'm a bit short of space and I can't keep too many things."

"Has Soncini been here on other occasions?"

"A couple of times in the last few months," Sauro replied after consulting his ledger. "The last time was a few days ago."

"What was he here for?"

"Problems with the hard disk on his office computer."

Soneri registered this information without having any idea what it might mean, and when Sauro tried to explain, he said: "Save yourself the time. I won't understand the first thing."

"I thought the police . . ."

"Not all of them, not the older ones, not me."

"It's all a question of familiarity. I've got a customer in the police force who could teach me a thing or two."

"Is his name Juvara?" Soneri said, with no doubt in his mind.

"You see? You guessed right away. You might not understand much about computers, but you've got a feel for things."

"It's very famous, that feel," Soneri said as he was leaving.

In the short time he had been in the shop, the afternoon light had faded. Darkness was advancing between the houses of the *borghi*, but there was still the bustle of daytime. Soneri turned into Via Farini and came out on Piazza Garibaldi. The clock on the Palazzo del Governatore showed ten past four, but the lights in the windows on Via Repubblica had already been switched on. The gathering dusk strengthened his sense both of the importance of his investigation and his remorse towards Nina, due to more than the desire to find the truth. At certain moments, the thought of this young woman

– pregnant, murdered and consumed by fire – moved him deeply, and each time the thought came back to him it set his nerves jangling. Something similar had been happening in the city since the papers had screamed out the news of Candiani's arrest. Parma, a hive of gossip and rumour at the best of times, was already beginning to take the development on board, partly relieved that the Monster had been identified and partly already exorcising the memory by picturing Candiani as a deranged outsider in an upright, hard-working community.

The city was digesting everything with a smile and a satisfied belch, he thought to himself as he walked through the door of the police station. Juvara, however, had the expression of a man whose lunch was lying heavily on his stomach. "Were there bulls running free at Suzzara as well?" Soneri enquired.

"Commissario, those Romas are not the most friendly of people. There were two of us against seventy of them."

"I didn't expect you to challenge them to a pitched battle."

"They don't like us! They'd rather see a herd of bulls than have a visit from us."

"Who does like us? We get sour looks even from people who come whimpering to us when their pockets have been picked. The Left accuses us of being too right-wing, and the Right accuses us of being too soft."

The inspector made a resigned gesture. "Well, the upshot is that we didn't find out very much."

"Still, it was worth trying."

"The carabinieri went one stage further. They searched the camp. Maybe that's why the Romas were so pissed off."

"What did they come up with?"

"Gold. They're specialists in thefts of gold."

"That's hardly news."

"Not true. Thieves today go in for copper. The price has gone through the roof, and it's not hard to find – building sites, warehouses and even electrical wires. I saw some statistics on the internet . . ."

The commissario silenced him with a wave of his hand. "Find anything else?"

"That they hated Iliescu."

"Hated her?"

"The moment we mentioned her name, they went berserk and started spitting on the ground. 'Whore' was the mildest epithet they used."

It all fitted in with Soncini's story. Nina must indeed have been lonely and desperate in her effort to defend herself, fought over by her various lovers and by a ruthless community, but for precisely that reason the girl seemed to him all the more admirable. For him the investigation was breaking down more and more barriers and becoming more than a simple act of duty.

"Listen, Juvara," Soneri said, changing the subject. "What's this Sauro like, the guy with the computer shop? I know you're one of his clients."

"I've only been there a couple of times," the inspector said.

"Juvara! You're a policeman! You've no need to be so defensive. If anything, it's your job to put the questions other people have to answer."

"I thought for a moment he'd been up to some funny business."

"Not at all. One of his other customers is Soncini, who's been to him a few times with some problem with his laptop and with something else I couldn't understand. Anyway, he never went back for the laptop. He told the guy that a female friend would be along for it, but she never turned up. It might be Nina, but you can't be sure with a man like Soncini."

"You see now that computers can be excellent leads?"

"Don't kid yourself. If there'd been anything compromising on that laptop, do you really think they'd have left it with your friend?"

"He's not a friend, but he's good at his job. And I believe he's honest into the bargain."

"O.K., could you work on him a bit? You know, one expert to another? By the way, I liked him too."

Just then the telephone on his desk rang.

"Commissario, at long last." It was Dottoressa Marcotti.

He was about to defend himself but the investigating magistrate came straight to the point. She was a woman with no time for small talk and invariably in a hurry, another reason why she and Soneri got on so well.

"I have requested authorisation to tap the phones of all of Iliescu's lovers. I hope the judge will agree in all cases. Meanwhile, your colleagues have sent me an account of the C.C.T.V. footage shot near where our car thieves were operating. Not much help, I have to admit. The only worthwhile thing is that the older one turns to the younger and says they'd been set up. It's a sentence that could mean everything or nothing."

The commissario gave a groan and nodded, but before he could say anything, she put him on the spot: "Tell me, have you by now come up with a theory about what's been going on here?"

He did not know what to say. Each time he began to develop a hypothesis it was overturned a moment later, and he had failed to translate that complex of impressions continually whirling about in his head into anything coherent. "Not yet," was all he said.

He heard a laugh at the other end of the line. "We're doing a great job! Neither one of us has a clue!"

"It won't be like this for long," he said.

"I do hope not," Marcotti said. "With every case, you have to go through a period of darkness when you don't know which way to turn, but we've cast so many nets that sooner or later some fish will get tangled up in them, you'll see." The prosecutor was an incurable optimist.

At that very moment, Soneri would have happily asked her to marry him. Having a woman like that at your side was the equivalent of a transfusion of ginseng. Angela was made of the same stuff, and that was one of the things he liked about her – always assuming she chose not to leave him.

He lit a cigar and decided to go out. It was rush hour, the time when employees left their offices, the admin staff and managers all dressed in the standard, starched-and-scented uniforms. He felt a pang of nostalgia for the sight of house-wives carrying shopping and shouting in dialect to each other from opposite sides of the road, or workmen with cloth coats thrown over their overalls as they cycled home from factories still located inside the city and not ten kilometres into the hinterland, like Golden.

His mind was still on the squalor of those lots out at Lemignano, where the asphalt and the factory buildings had devastated fields and vineyards, when he came across a noisy procession of cars decked out in white ribbons. He watched the parade as it turned into Via Cavour, opened specially. He was going in the same direction, as far as the junction with Strada al Duomo. Just ahead, he saw the square overflowing with vintage cars and the cathedral precinct crowded with people done up in all their finery. Security guards manning the barriers prevented onlookers from drawing too close to the festivities. Official cars and company limousines swarmed busily about, as though the Duomo were the Grand Hotel.

The mystery was solved when a woman's voice squealed

out: "It's the wedding of the eldest of the Dall'Argine family."

That name clarified everything. The eldest of the Dall'-Argine line was marrying Soncini's daughter. The wily, emerging dynasty was forming a union with a scion of the patriciate, thereby ennobling their line. Soneri moved off, in search of fresher air he could breathe in solitude. Never till that moment had he felt himself so proudly anarchist, with a will for freedom and the purity of a young wolf.

He wandered about aimlessly until hunger and curiosity brought him back to the wine bar. He went into the dining room and looked from table to table, simultaneously fearful and hopeful of spying his rival, but Sbarazza was already seated at the table where he had last seen him. He got up and with an elegant gesture invited Soneri to sit beside him.

"So now you're laying on receptions," the commissario said.

"It's getting harder and harder at the *Milord*. Too busy. I have to adapt. This evening I had no appetite for tinned tuna," he whispered confidentially.

"No problems here?" Soneri said, pointing to the bar.

"Bruno knows me. A good man, like Alceste."

"But they're nearly all men here."

"Not so. There were several couples."

"Was there a couple sitting here?"

"Yes, having a light meal."

"Do you mind if I ask what they looked like?"

Sbarazza stared at him, clearly taken aback. "You want a description? He was tall, distinguished-looking, well turned out. She seemed very lively, not exactly beautiful but with character, if you get my meaning."

Soneri hesitated for a moment, and as he was about to answer he became aware of Sbarazza's baffled expression fixed on him.

"What is it? Does that correspond to the identikit of two suspects?"

"No, not at all. I was just thinking how vulnerable we all are."

"Ah," Sbarazza smiled. "We are eggs with fragile shells, or better, we are fragile, full stop. We don't even have a shell."

"Rather than having no shell, right now I feel as if I have no gravity," Soneri said.

"That might be an advantage."

"Like being in water without fins or in the air without wings."

"Don't be such a pessimist. The mistake we make is to be always engaged in a search for certainties. We need certainties, we demand them, we never resign ourselves to being what we are. If we were to face up to our condition we'd be more serene and might even see opportunities rather than frustrations."

"Facing up to what we are is itself a certainty, is it not?"

"Alright, I grant you that, but it's the only one: the certainty of not having certainties. That has to be our starting point."

"That's very much the reasoning of a police officer, you know. They teach exactly that to beginners: given a case, never start out with a preconceived idea. But in fact a commissario has the facts in front of him."

"You know better than me that facts are never objective! Take history. What we are convinced of today will have no value tomorrow, and the day after that something different will come along. We die each evening and wake up afresh the following morning, and so the world renews itself minute by minute. The essence of our being is changeability, not stability, and every man who aims at coherence is nothing but a self-deluding fool. The point is to accept what we are and open ourselves to the great flourishing of possibilities which time continually offers us. The acceptance of the world, that's the secret. Do you remember Nietzsche?"

Fortunately Bruno came over to the table at that moment. "What can I get you, Commissario?"

"I'll have some *culaccia* and Parmesan shavings."

"Marchese, would you like something else?" the waiter asked with absolute seriousness.

"I'll borrow something from the commissario. He's the only man with whom I would share a plate."

"And bring us some red Lambrusco," Soneri said. He needed a drop of strong wine to wash away his thoughts. As he was being served, he raised a slice of *culaccia* to his mouth as though officiating at some rite. "These are my certainties," he announced, his tone doleful.

"I see you've understood. Life is like a game of cards: you must always wait for something good to emerge from the pack. Look at me. I once had a mansion and a family endowed with coats of arms and emblems evoking battles won and honours received. The most absurd thing is to imagine you can actually leave something behind you. They drummed this into me ever since I was a boy by showing me portraits of my forefathers in the corridors of our ancestral home. The genealogical tree is a load of bollocks."

Sbarazza seemed to be on the edge of delirium, but Soneri could not dispute the force of his logic. His thoughts went back to Angela and those passionate lunchtime rendezvous, but for the moment he had drawn from the pack the card he had, and to ask for anything else for the future was futile.

He poured himself a glass of Lambrusco the colour of black pudding. "That couple, the one that was here . . ." he began hesitantly, with the unpleasant feeling of possibly occupying the seat recently occupied by his rival.

"You haven't got it, have you?" Sbarazza interrupted him with good-natured authority. "You're still after the confirmation I do not wish to give you. What does it matter to you if you know or don't know? All it would do is poison your evening. Have you any idea how many things are happening at this moment in your favour or to your disadvantage? Dozens, but you don't know. We live in a constant state of unawareness, and this is both our salvation and our damnation. It leaves open the doors of our emotions but makes us as volatile as an alcoholic scent."

The mention of alcohol made Soneri throw back a glass of Lambrusco in one gulp, looking for that mild euphoria which would keep him afloat. "It may be destiny that I have some very unforthcoming witnesses," he said.

"I think I understand your situation. It's one I've been in many times myself." Sbarazza had assumed a more serious tone. "If the person you're fond of has already decided to leave you, there's nothing you can do to convince her otherwise. If on the other hand she is unsure, the only thing you can do is be gracious. The only salvation lies in graciousness towards your neighbour because what all humans, even the most atrocious criminals, seek is to be loved. We are all orphans, after all, are we not?"

Soneri nodded thoughtfully, going over in his mind the criminals it had been his lot to encounter in his work as commissario. Yet again, Sbarazza was not wide of the mark.

"It may seem not worth much to you that all we can do is exchange feelings of unhappiness. I'm aware it's a bad deal, but that's all there is. Unless . . ." Sbarazza broke off abruptly.

"Unless what?"

"Unless you turn to God."

"That's a different matter altogether," Soneri said. "In any case, He does not seem to take much interest in human affairs."

"Please! Don't come out with bar-room arguments. I expect better of you."

"It's just that not even by having recourse to God do I find any sense in things."

"You are an incurable rationalist. You search for meaning in things so as to draw some reassurance, but God is beyond the boundaries of our reason. We dance on the edge of a waterfall, waiting to be finally washed away, ignorant of where we'll end up. We can't choose: life overwhelms us. Others have written the script and if it's a question of God, then it all comes back to what I was saying a moment ago. Listen, pick a card from the pack and resign yourself to your choice. At the end of the day, we'll all get the same pay-off."

"I'm playing more than one game," Soneri said.

"I understand. One is that girl whose body was burned, is it not?"

"I've been drawing cards from the pack for some time now, but I never get the right one."

"Sooner or later you will. You'll see. My advice is still the same. Let events follow their own course and take every opportunity as it presents itself. All you have to do is recognise the opportunity when it comes."

The commissario heaved a deep sigh and again sought refuge in wine. It would have been good to end the evening on that note, with the right flavours in his mouth, but he knew that any time now the bar would fill with noise and laughter loud enough to exasperate him. In addition, Sbarazza had not entirely endeared himself to him for the reticence he had shown earlier. He still had a lingering doubt over whether Angela and the other man had really been there, but the descriptions fitted. Here too his policeman's frame of mind was becoming a burden. Events were getting on top of him in spite of his obstinate determination to put them in order.

"I must go and see my old ladies and gentlemen. It's dinner time at the hostel, and that will be followed by a bit of socialising," Sbarazza said, with that light irony which marked his detachment from the world.

"You're not going to the wedding feast then?" Soneri asked, referring to the Dall'Argine–Soncini ceremony.

"Money provides no remedy against vulgarity," commented the old man with a smile of kindly commiseration.

16

THERE WAS SOMETHING profoundly vulgar about the profanation of the night which had transformed Piazza Duomo into an *haute couture* bonanza. In clothes alone, the wedding must have cost thousands of euros, before taking jewellery and limousines and vintage cars into account. The chatter among Benedetto Antelami's marble sculptures clashed with the notes of the organ as they swelled out through the wide-open doors of the Cathedral. Perhaps the chalice used to give communion to the newly-weds had been manufactured by Golden.

Soneri detested solemn ceremonies. He found them phoney and was always afraid of laughing out loud when faced with such pantomimes, but what he saw unfolding before his eyes outdid anything he had ever previously seen. It verged on being a display of ostentatious marketing, degenerating into a senseless replay of society functions of the sort recorded in glossy magazines in a hairdresser's salon. In spite of that, he stood there, leaning against the wall of the old Fiaccadori bookshop, staring, glued to the spot, incapable of dragging himself away. He was, as Sbarazza had advised, letting events take their course.

And events did indeed take their course. As the couple emerged to a flurry of rice and flashbulbs, the noise rose in volume, the cheers bounced off the noble stones of the Duomo rising in a crescendo until they deafened the golden angel on the cusp of the belfry somewhere beyond the curtain of the mist, and even awoke Correggio's little *putti* in the neighbouring church of St John. But then in a sudden diminuendo the piazza fell silent and the commissario was aware of the shudder which precedes movement, as when a train is about to depart. He realised that something must have happened to change the evening's programme, and he felt no displeasure at seeing that exhibition disrupted.

Pasquariello's voice on the mobile brought him up to date with what had happened. "A bomb has gone off at Golden."

"Was anyone hurt?"

"No, it wasn't a big bomb, but if it had gone off when the workers were around . . ."

"Yet another problem!"

"Two idiots. The carabinieri picked them up in the vicinity. They're Romanian."

Soneri could not help thinking that this was another point in favour of Soncini's hypothesis. The Romanians really were out to take revenge on him.

"How did they find them?"

"The idiots didn't notice the security guards doing their first round. The guards heard the explosion and raised the alarm, and our two lads ran straight into a carabiniere patrol."

The piazza was emptying. With the occasional explosion of back-firing engines, the vintage cars made a juddering start one after the other. A different sort of explosion ten kilometres away had brought the festivities to a premature end.

Juvara called shortly afterwards. "Do you want me to come and get you, Commissario?"

The thought of returning to Lemignano was dispiriting, but he hoped the mist would have blanked out the ugliest parts of the district. "Alright. I'll meet you in Via Cavour, but watch out you don't crash into the Nuvolari car."

"Commissario, the days of the Mille Miglia are long past."

A few minutes later, the police Alfa Romeo flashed its lights from Via Pisacane. "These people are mad!" the inspector shouted. "They nearly ran right into me. What's going on? Is this some costume drama?"

"Nearly," the commissario laughed. "The party's been ruined and that's why they're going off their heads. Tomorrow they'll be on to the Chief about law and order and dangers to public safety. And you can be sure that blame will be laid at our door. Again."

"What party was ruined?"

"You obviously don't keep abreast of the goings-on in high society in this city! It was the wedding of the century."

"Don't tell me those cars were there for the Dall'Argine . . ."

"You see, you knew after all. You obviously read the glossies in the hairdresser's."

"You're kidding. It was in the papers today. Two whole pages."

"Instead of printing something serious . . ."

"Now I get it," Juvara said. "The Dall'Argine boy was marrying the Soncini girl and that's why they put a bomb in the Golden workshop. At about the very moment the daughter was saying 'I do'."

"Right," the commissario said.

"A terrible business," Juvara said as they got out of the car in the darkness at Lemignano, but it was not clear if he was referring to the dynamic of events or to the large black mark on the factory wall where a fire had briefly blazed, shattering the windows.

The investigating magistrate, with her blonde, flowing locks standing out in the headlights as clearly as the phosphorescent jackets of the carabinieri, arrived within minutes. Maresciallo Santurro of the carabinieri had taken charge because of the success of his detachment in making the arrest, and he directed operations like a little Napoleon. Soneri had little to do except observe what had happened and absorb any suggestions of the kind invariably prompted by a crime scene. While Marcotti went to speak to the maresciallo, the commissario turned in the direction of the Golden offices, and there he found Soncini gazing at the burn marks on the wall with the concentration with which another man might have looked at a painting.

"I was right," he muttered without turning round.

"The facts are on your side," Soneri said drily. "Thus far, at least," he added, reminding himself of the changeability he had discussed with Sbarazza. "Anyway, they've got them in custody, so you can relax . . ."

"With those people, you can never relax. They never give up and there are so many of them. This is a warning shot. Next time . . ."

"There won't be a next time."

"You should've done something when I told you they were threatening me," Soncini said angrily. "I have the right to protection. And then . . . the business . . ." Soneri could have sworn he all but said "my business".

"They'll not try again for a while. They're not that stupid," the commissario reassured him. "To change the subject, I know you came to the station to identify your car. It seems there are no doubts, is that right?"

Soncini nodded. "It's mine alright. They wanted the blame to fall on me."

"Where are your wife and daughter now?"

"Where do you think!" exclaimed Soncini arrogantly. "At the reception. They could hardly walk out on the guests!

What would the Dall'Argine family have thought? These things make a lasting impression. Even if we were the victims, mud sticks."

The commissario began to feel so exasperated with Soncini that he was tempted to give a brutal reply. What did he have to be afraid of? The wedding had taken place and it was too late for the Dall'Argine family to have second thoughts. However, he remembered his position as a public servant and merely said: "People forget very quickly."

Marcotti came over and took him aside. "Did you know the judge has refused permission to tap the phones of Iliescu's lovers? He said there were not sufficient grounds."

Soneri stretched his arms wide, all the while thinking that had he been in the judge's shoes, he too might have been cautious. There was nothing concrete to point to them as likely murderers. They had gone to bed with Nina and had left part of their hearts with her, but nothing more.

"What do you make of this bombing?" she asked Soneri.

"It's another piece in the jigsaw, but we don't know where it fits."

She laughed. "We're still pulling in the nets and something will come to the surface. However, I have to warn you that tomorrow the newspapers are going to go wild. This time somebody has trodden on the toes of the high and mighty. It's no longer just about some poor Romanian girl."

As he went back to the car with Juvara, Soneri reflected on that obscure threat. "We're going to have the questore breathing down our necks," Juvara said.

"The city demands an explanation of the disturbing events occurring all around us," Soneri said in a sing-song voice, mimicking Capuozzo and the next morning's headlines. "As long as everything's covered up they'll all sit tight, fooling themselves they're in the best little city in the world, but the moment the dirty washing appears in public, they start screaming about it all being a terrible scandal," the commissario bellowed.

Juvara said nothing until Soneri had calmed down.

"Tomorrow," Soneri said, changing tack, "pop along to that friend of yours who sells computers and make him give you Soncini's P.C. Take it home and have a good look inside it – although you'd better talk to Marcotti first. If you can't get hold of her, try to persuade that Sauro."

"Do you think there'll be anything interesting in the laptop?"

"No, but you never know."

"A couple of days ago you told me Soncini needed something for his office computer. What was wrong with it?"

"You know perfectly well I never remember these things. It must have broken down or something . . ."

"Forgive my saying so," Juvara began timidly, "but I think you should get to grips with this field. It's fundamental for our work to—"

"I know, I know," Soneri interrupted in annoyance more than anger. "But I'm too old now to learn new tricks and I'm going to carry on with the tried and tested."

"What do you mean? You're still young. You're suffering from nothing more than mental laziness. Did you know that even Capuozzo is taking a course?"

"Well I never! He should really be taking a course to raise his I.Q., but unfortunately there's no such course available."

"And it would be a good idea for you to learn some English."

"Juvara, that's enough. You're getting on my nerves. You know what you're going to do next? You're going to come with me on a visit to the Campo San Martino Romas to see if the bulls have all been rounded up."

"In this mist? And it's nearly ten o'clock," said the inspector hesitantly.

"They can have a long lie-in tomorrow."

They took the narrow roads along the Lower Valley, as they had done the time before, when it was all starting up.

"If this is a punishment, it seems to me over the top," Juvara grumbled.

"Don't talk nonsense. I want to hear what Manservisi has to say. I think we might be given the right cards by our good friends, the Italian gypsies."

"I don't follow."

"Doesn't matter. It's a coded language I learned from Sbarazza, a highly eccentric aristocrat."

Juvara made no reply. He was relieved the commissario was not angry with him.

Soneri missed the signs to the dump and the U-turn he executed brought the inspector out in a cold sweat. Nothing much had changed in the clearing apart from the fact that there was more rubbish than ever and now it was piled alongside the huge bins. The encampment was deserted and the fires almost out. All that remained were a few tongues of flame on a bed of ashes. Some televisions flickered inside caravans. The commissario parked and walked over, with Juvara at his heels. The heads of several children appeared at windows and some doors were hurriedly opened and just as hurriedly closed. A moment later Manservisi, cap on head, came to meet them with the relaxed gait of a man without a care in the world.

"Good evening," he said, drawing up in front of Soneri. In the background, the mist took on a yellowish tinge in the lights of the service area and hypermarket. There was no music playing. Perhaps the fairground had moved on.

"I take it something serious has occurred to bring you out in the mist at this time of night. Another death?" Manservisi enquired.

"We just wanted to know how Mariotto is getting on," Soneri said.

Manservisi gave a raucous laugh. "You must be joking."

"By no means."

The gypsy put on a serious face and grew tense.

"Now it's you who must be joking," Soneri said.

"Me? Mariotto has already told you all he knew. We've told you everything too. What more can you want?"

"That you don't piss me off with that story about a bull goring him. You know very well it's not true. Mariotto was beaten up."

"Commissario, in the mist people see all sorts of things that never happened. Go and ask him for yourself."

"Don't talk shit. There's no doubt he was threatened, and it was probably you who ordered him to keep his mouth shut. In addition, no judge would credit a witness who is mentally defective."

"I have not ordered anybody to do anything. I defend my community, that's all I do."

"And you think you'll defend it by not talking? Why did the Romanians rush off so suddenly? There must have been a huge row between all of you."

"This is a big world. There's room for everybody," Manservisi said, implicitly confirming what Soneri had suggested.

"Not big enough, to judge by all that's been going on. They dump a burned body in front of the encampment, one of your lot runs off after a ridiculous theft, and another one is beaten up and it's passed off as his being gored by a bull. That's a lot of coincidences."

"So what are you getting at?" Manservisi said impatiently.

"That you know much more than you've told me."

Manservisi grunted, while somewhere behind him there was a rustling sound and a snort. They must have caught one of the missing pigs and put it in a pen.

"Anyway, the carabinieri did a search of your ex-neighbours and they came up with piles of gold. A magistrate could order the same thing here," Soneri said, knowing his threat was a bluff.

"Go ahead," Manservisi said with total confidence. "We don't touch that stuff. The people here go to work and our children go to school."

"What became of the Romanians' gold?"

"How should I know? If you had valuables in your possession, what would you do with them? Not any old stuff, but stuff that had a name and address."

"Like a painting," Soneri reflected.

"But you can give gold a new identity. You can't do that with a painting."

"That's true. Gold comes in many shapes and forms."

He remained where he was for a moment while Manservisi moved off with the same self-assurance with which he had arrived. Juvara was by the fire trying to get warm.

"Let's go," Soneri called to him, as he got into the car. Juvara ran awkwardly to the car, and there was no concealing his relief that they were leaving.

"What do you think he meant by that last remark?" the commissario said as they drove through the mist.

"I think he meant that objects in gold are easily recognisable by the person they were stolen from, but they can be melted down and transformed into perfectly anonymous items."

"Well done. I see you're beginning to develop an investigator's mind. Tomorrow I want you to go to Suzzara and see if there's been a rise in the number of thefts of gold. And persuade our colleagues to tell you if there have been robberies around Cortile San Martino."

As they reached the city boundary, one of their mobiles rang. Juvara fumbled about for a while before he located the correct one. "It's yours. They both have the same ringtone," he said.

It was Marcotti. "Soneri," she began, "I've had the two bombers moved to prison. I wanted to let you know that if you plan to interrogate them, I'll be there tomorrow morning at nine."

"Are they talking?"

"No different from the other two: not a word. And they too say they've been fitted up."

"We'll have to find some way of making them talk. Maybe they could be convinced . . ."

"Forget it, commissario. I've got experience in dealing with gangs from Eastern Europe and it's not only the Italians who practice *omerta*."

"Then we have only one card to play."

"Which card is that?"

"Medioli. I invited him to cooperate, and perhaps he will. He's not one of the Roma community and doesn't subscribe to their rites. We could look on him as an infiltrator."

"And you really believe he'll help? He doesn't seem to me quite of this world."

"Let's have a go."

He dropped Juvara off at his house.

"I'll be in the office first thing tomorrow morning and I'll get to work on the internet to do the research we were discussing."

"Internet, internet! Wouldn't you be quicker going round in person to the officers responsible for investigating thefts? Their office is only two floors up. It's always better to talk face to face."

"Whatever you want, commissario, but you really are too dismissive of computer technology."

"Enough, Juvara! And don't forget your friend Sauro. You can drive each other crazy with all this talk."

The inspector made a sign that meant 'I will obey', and shut the car door. The commissario accelerated away in the direction of Angela's house. He wanted to see her and spend the night with her. He parked underneath her residence and called her, but the telephone in the house rang out. Her mobile was switched off. He sank from desire to frustration and on to unhappy thoughts, and then began to think like a policeman and assess all possible hypotheses concerning his partner's silence, coming inevitably to the worst possible conclusion. He was tired of forever banging his head against forces that refused to yield up their mystery, first in his work and now in his emotional life. Sbarazza had been right: for him it was all too much.

He decided to go home, but then could not bring himself to drive off, so he chose instead to smoke a cigar and walk off his anxiety. He went along Via D'Azeglio with the mist ahead of him and swirling at his back. From time to time groups of Arabs and Africans emerged from the nearby neighbourhoods, their raised voices cutting through the silence of the deserted street. He came to Piazza Garibaldi and crossed into Via Farini before turning into Vicolo Politi in the direction of the court. There were still cars parked in front, perhaps belonging to magistrates. Angela might be busy inside, perhaps questioning a witness. He hung about for a while, and then saw Marcotti, the chief prosecutor, Capuozzo and Maresciallo Santurro go out. There had been a meeting no-one had told him about, and that promised nothing good for him, unless the agenda had been limited to the explosion at Golden.

He went away certain that there would be trouble the following day, but he did not want to think about it. He was tired, disappointed and frustrated. He could not take any more. The moment he got home, the telephone rang.

"Were you looking for me?" Angela said.

"You talk to me as though I were president of the society of lawyers."

"Sorry. I'm out of breath. I've been working late and I'm extremely tired."

"So am I. And not only because of work."

"What does that mean?"

"That I can't stand any more of this. I can never find you, I can't reach you to talk to you, and when I do you're very cold."

"I've really got a lot of work on."

"And I'm telling you that this is no way to live. You'll have to make up your mind, Angela. One way or the other. I know you're still seeing him. You were in the wine bar with him tonight."

There was a pause. Soneri would have given anything to hear her deny it, but instead she came back at him, totally composed. "So you're playing the policeman with me again, are you?"

"You're wrong. It was pure chance. But I believe in coincidences."

"You've already said that. You'd be better to keep your imagination in check, considering the job you do."

"Angela, I'm serious. I can't go on this way. This situation is causing me too much pain."

She sighed. "I'm sorry, I don't want to hurt you, but I'm not ready to decide. I'm too confused."

He would have liked to tell her to let events take their course, as Sbarazza counselled, but he stayed quiet and it was she who murmured: "I still want to see you."

Soneri could understand nothing, but at the same time he was aware that there was nothing to understand, that there was nothing for it but to live for the moment, savour it and take everything he could from it without wondering what would happen next.

17

JUVARA HAD BEEN at work a full two hours before the commissario arrived at the office.

"You were right," Juvara told him. "There's been quite an increase in reports of thefts of gold and jewellery in recent weeks, but the really interesting facts are contained in the data provided by colleagues who investigate theft and robbery. In the area around Cortile San Martino a lot of houses have been burgled and they've lost count of the number of cars broken into in the parking area at the autostrada petrol station."

"A whole industry!"

"And another thing. They've not spared the churches either."

"The churches?"

"Four parishes have reported thefts in the last two months, and in every case sacred vessels in gold have been carried off."

"Did this happen in Suzzara as well?"

"Apparently not, but that could be because they've only been there a short time."

A few minutes passed and then the telephone on his desk rang.

"Commissario Soneri, I've got Dottor Capuozzo for you,"

announced the questore's secretary. It seemed to Soneri there could be no worse way to start the new day.

"I'm phoning about the Iliescu crime," Capuozzo began. "I'm worried about this investigation because, unless I am very much mistaken, we're not even within sight of a conclusion."

"It's a particularly complex case, Dottore. Initially the identity of the victim was unknown, and then we established we were dealing with an illegal immigrant who was using her sister's passport, and then there was the case of the old man whose body was found on the bus."

"All that is understood, but we're going from bad to worse. Now we've got bombs going off. What are we going to tell the city?"

Soneri struggled to stop himself letting out a roar. He assumed that following the uproar created by the disruption of the wedding, some local grandees had been in touch to complain. These were the people to whom his superior was accountable, certainly not the city as a whole.

"We're working on it." Soneri said. "Neither Dottoressa Marcotti nor I will rest until . . ."

"I've called a meeting with the Prefect, the Mayor and the President of the Province for this afternoon. We must send out a bulletin."

The usual comedy with a cast of bureaucrats, Soneri thought to himself. He saw cameras and notebooks clustered around two dozen authority figures, reporting the "tireless work of the security committees". Perfect for a world which thrived on appearances.

"I hope to have good news for you soon." Soneri made an effort to be diplomatic. "Sooner or later we'll draw the right card," he said, realising as he spoke how deeply that expression had lodged in his mind. As he replaced the telephone, he felt his anger and unease return. Calls from Capuozzo were utterly vacuous, but, like an alarm clock about to go off, they always induced a state of anxiety.

"Did he tell you about the meeting?" Juvara said, as he got up to go out.

"You knew about it?"

"His secretary called this morning as soon as I got to the office, but she told me there was no need to pass on a message because she'd call back. I thought it better to spare you a half hour's bad mood," the inspector explained, before hurriedly adding, "I'm on my way to see Sauro now."

Soneri signalled his approval with a wave, but without looking up. He was thinking about the meeting. He had no wish to waste time on prattle, the only purpose of which was to command some column inches in the newspapers and give the impression of what the politicians would call "putting all arms of government on an emergency footing". He decided he would absent himself once again, even if that would do nothing for his relations with Capuozzo. If he was not going to the meeting, what would he do with his afternoon? He attempted to find a motive to justify his absence, but all of a sudden he found his head empty, as though he were about to faint. The only thought that troubled him related to Angela.

He considered telephoning her, but pride and self-respect held him back. It was up to her to make the next move, although he was aware that there might well be no move at all. Everything might be frozen in the final checkmate.

And then, without knocking, Musumeci burst in, providentially bringing Soneri's mind back to the investigation. "I've got a report here from the Romanian police which arrived a couple of hours ago. Our translator has just finished working on it."

"Report on what?"

"They've found Iliescu's sister. She works in a lap-dancing club in Bucharest, and finally we know the identity of the old man who died on the coach."

"And who was he?"

"The grandfather, but there are gaps in the report. He had something to do with the Romas. In fact it seems he was one himself."

"What made him risk his life coming to Italy?"

"The sister was very worried about what might happen to Nina, because she had heard from various sources that the Roma community here were out to get her."

"Soncini explained the reasons why they were after her, but I've no way of knowing if he told me everything."

"The fact is her sister claims she spent a long time begging their grandfather to come to Italy and try to make peace and stop anything worse happening. According to what she says, she gave him a lot of cash and paid for his journey."

"He must have drunk the cash or else someone cheated him out of it. The old man was down to his last penny when he died."

"It's likely it went down his gullet. The guy was a notorious drunk. Anyway, he didn't succeed in his mission."

"Leave this report with me. I'll read it later."

"I've given you the substance of it," Musumeci said.

There was a knock at the door and a good-looking policewoman, who drew Musumeci's appreciative attention, came in.

"Today's papers, commissario," she said, placing the bundle on his desk.

"We've made great strides in the quality of our staff," Musumeci observed, but the commissario ignored him. He was already flicking through the pages to find the local news.

The reporters had gone overboard. There were four pages

devoted to the wedding and how it had been disrupted by the bomb planted at the Golden factory, followed by an array of dramatic photographs and a rosary of indignant interviews with the well-heeled of Parma society, each one "dismayed by the escalation of violence", and some requesting "whoever is in charge" to take all steps necessary to prevent "the decline of civic standards". The heads of the Dall'Argine and Martini families had declined to make any comment. They restricted themselves to showing expressions of outrage to the photographers who captured some images of them as they emerged from the Duomo. Soneri imagined they would have used their influence behind the scenes, putting pressure on senior officials and perhaps stirring up a storm in the press by telephoning the newspaper proprietors directly. Soncini alone had given an interview overflowing with righteous indignation, thereby exposing his inferior status and putting himself on the same level as councillors, chairs of committees and the city's resident intellectuals. There was also a piece devoted to the investigation in which details were given of the various leads being followed by the investigators, but making it plain between the lines that the police had no idea where next to turn.

The commissario threw the papers on the desk in a rage. He found the hypocrisy of Parma more and more nauseating. All those people preaching respect for the law and then going about their business as though they were above all reproach. He regretted the loss of the city's democratic soul, which had always shown itself ready to scoff in public at local bigwigs and bien pensants, perhaps with a biting, satirical scrawl on walls near the houses where such people lived or with a salacious slogan on the porch of the Regio theatre. In those days, Parma could kill with a jibe.

The telephone rang on a couple of occasions and each

time the commissario dashed to pick it up. He was burning inside during that impotent wait. He had already put in a request to interrogate Medioli, but it would take some time before the final authorisation came through. He had no idea how to fill his time.

Mercifully Juvara came back and took his mind off the various pieces of bad news.

"It was the hard disk," the inspector told him.

"Whatever that may be," Soneri said.

"It's the core of the computer, where all the data end up. It's a bit like our mind and memory."

"Soncini had broken its brain?"

"Not quite. It wasn't broken. In fact it was working, and perfectly."

"So?"

"Sauro told me Soncini had asked him how to go about deleting all trace of the operations executed by that machine."

"And Sauro replied that he had to change the . . . what's it called?"

"It's the only way. Everything is stored on the hard disk, and any technician worth his salt would have no problem reconstructing the life of the computer and all the operations carried out on it."

"At last, something interesting."

"You see what you can do with technology?" Juvara said enthusiastically. "You can set up whole lines of enquiry with the help of computer technology."

"Did he change the . . . whatever it's called . . . for him?" Soneri interrupted Juvara, but he was beginning to feel guilty for having underestimated his colleague's skill.

"Yes, but he told me he only changed the hard disk after a couple of days. Soncini came back to say it didn't have enough memory and he needed a more powerful computer.

In other words, he now had different requirements, and that was another reason why Sauro didn't bother too much about it."

"Did he hang onto the old dish?"

"Disk. He's afraid he threw it out. He doesn't have a lot of space, but he'll have a look and let us know."

"If he has thrown it out, we've wasted a lot of time."

"We'll know this afternoon."

"Listen, if that thing turns up and is of any use to us, I swear I'll buy myself a laptop."

The inspector smiled. "I'm sure you'll fall in love with it."

"Meantime, let me buy you lunch. I haven't eaten properly in days."

"I'm sorry, I'm on a diet," Juvara said, pulling out a plastic box containing an assortment of lettuce leaves, diced carrot, sweetcorn and slices of tomato. On the top there was a sachet of oil which had to be squeezed to produce a dressing for the whole concoction.

"That stuff would disgust even a bunny rabbit," Soneri said, staring at the transparent packet with an expression of sheer nausea.

Juvara apologised, patting his stomach to indicate *force majeure*.

When he was on Via Repubblica, the commissario felt the need of someone to talk to. It was a new sensation for him and gave him the measure of his depressed state of mind. Loneliness had never held any fear for him: in this regard, he was like a cat. Perhaps this was one of the effects of his crisis with Angela. He asked Alceste to prepare him a bit of space in the kitchen, so he could chat to him while he was doing the cooking. He enjoyed watching pots boil, waiters running about and steam forming the same shapes under the ceiling as the mist outside. It was the kind of day that called for a plate of *anolini* accompanied by a good Bonarda. He counted on the calories to set him up for an afternoon which threatened to be grim.

The warmth of the wine and the pasta, the aromas of the prosciutto and salame had the desired effect, and when he was on his way back to the police station he already felt better. The good humour lasted until he reached the piazza and saw from the clock that the time was two-thirty. He felt a lump in his throat. Angela had not called, and between her hostile silence and his proud indifference their post-lunch appointment had passed. By the time he got to the office, his foul mood had returned. Juvara avoided speaking first.

"Any news?" the commissario said.

"Nothing yet."

"Have you requested printouts for the mobile phones of Soncini and his friend Razzini?"

"I have, but you know what these companies are like. They go at their own pace. I called back this morning to ask them to get a move on. Dottoressa Marcotti called as well but . . ."

The telephone rang. Soneri feared the worst, and in fact it was Capuozzo's secretary. "The questore would like to know if you intend to be present at the meeting," she said. She had the perfect voice for cajolery.

"Tell him I'm very sorry, but no. I'm waiting for the results of a crucial line of enquiry. I can't leave the office. I have to be here just in case."

The secretary said she would pass on the message. Fortunately she made no effort to put Capuozzo on the line.

"And what will you do if Sauro doesn't come up with anything?"

"It means Capuozzo will remove me from my post, and

when all's said and done, it wouldn't really upset me. But let's hope we pull out the right card. So far, we've only been dealt the occasional face card, but you can't really believe, can you, that we could go through the whole game without getting one ace?"

"I don't know much about cards. What game are you talking about?"

"You don't even know how to play *briscola*? Every time I talk to you, you make me feel Neanderthal."

The conversation fizzled out under Juvara's embarrassment and Soneri's black mood, but the silence which fell in the office was even more oppressive. The two were like castaways on a drifting raft. The telephones remained obstinately silent. Finally impatience got the better of Soneri and he could wait no more. "Give me Sauro's number."

The inspector wrote it on a scrap of paper and handed it over.

"Hello? It's Commissario Soneri here. I was anxious to know if you'd managed to locate that hard disk," he began, pronouncing the English word impeccably. "Ah, you have? You were just going to bring it over. No need. Inspector Juvara will come and pick it up from you in Borgo Regale."

He replaced the telephone with a satisfied expression. "We'll need to play this hand right."

"I'm on my way," Juvara said

"I'm coming with you," Soneri replied, grabbing hold of his duffel coat.

While Sauro and Juvara starting combing through the memory of the hard disk, the commissario felt left out. The two communicated in computer-speak, a dialect unknown to him. The words he heard seemed to belong to a language with no verbs and with no connection to anything he understood.

"We've struck it lucky," Soneri cut in. "If you'd thrown it out . . ."

"I nearly did, you know. In fact I should have. Soncini told me to."

"What made you hold on to it?"

"A customer came in looking for a computer for his son. The new models were too expensive so he asked me if I had a second-hand one lying about. It was then I thought about recycling the hard disk. It wouldn't cost me a thing. I know it wasn't strictly correct, but I've only just started up and the debts are mounting."

Soneri burst out laughing. He thought of Sbarazza and his theory that chance offers us thousands of opportunities every day: the problem was to know how to recognise them.

"If we ever get to the bottom of this story, it'll be all due to coincidences and chance," he said with a smile, addressing Juvara.

Sauro looked at both men without understanding. He decided it did not matter and turned back to the computer.

Soneri watched the two of them intently. On the screen, sequences of numbers, questions and windows with lists began to appear. Every so often Sauro and Juvara would exchange phrases which were incomprehensible to him. After half an hour, boredom forced him to start walking up and down the room, but then it began to seem too narrow and he felt himself suffocating. He needed to get out.

"Call me when you come up with something," he said.

Once outside he lit a cigar and began walking around the *borgo* between Via Farini and Via Repubblica, already cloaked in the gathering dusk. He realised that for the first time in his career he was reliant on the work of a younger colleague. Until now, Nanetti and his forensic colleagues had always seen to the scientific part of any investigation, but he was a contemporary and he could take that from him. Juvara was of a generation light years younger, and belonged to a world alien to him. He wondered if he should indeed learn a little English, especially now that even Capuozzo was going on a computer course. Never had he felt so completely washed up as at that moment. A hardened peasant, by-passed by time, an old coin forgotten in a piggy bank.

Such was his gloomy frame of mind that when Juvara called from the shop, he did not even react to his good news. "Commissario, we've made some very interesting discoveries. I told you computers—"

"I'm being converted," Soneri said.

"Soncini has done a bit of surfing, using different search engines."

"What do you mean, engines? Juvara, talk clearly. For me engines are things that drive cars."

"Search engines are used to find information on particular subjects, and in general you consult them via a key word."

"Like the one you used to access the terminal?"

"Nearly. With search engines, a key word is used to find texts which contain that word."

"What words did Soncini use?"

"Oh, he used a lot, but for half a dozen searches the key words were 'woman', 'burned', 'autostrada'. Speaks for itself, doesn't it?"

Soneri shook off his gloom.

"It certainly does. When was he doing these searches?"

"In the days immediately following the murder," the inspector said, choosing his words with care.

"Juvara, you've won your bet. Tell Sauro that one of these days I'll be over to invest in one of these devices. I trust you'll give me advice about which one to choose."

"I'll be your consultant and I'll teach you how to use it. Then you'll be able to reply to Capuozzo when he sends you an e-mail."

The commissario mumbled something intended as light-hearted. "Pick up the disk and let's go to the questura."

As he turned away, he thought again about what had been found in the computer, and his initial enthusiasm waned.

"There's no way Soncini can wriggle out of this, Commissario," Juvara repeated several times once they were back in the office.

"It's only a clue," Soneri cautioned. "Don't forget that Nina was Soncini's lover and she was an illegal immigrant. It wouldn't have been possible to do a search through official channels, so he had to use his internet to find out if a local paper had carried some report."

"Then there's the car . . ."

"Stolen by the Romanians." The commissario shook his head. "On the basis of the information we have, both the Roma revenge theory and what we've just uncovered remain possibilities," he concluded. Juvara weighed up this verdict with evident disappointment.

"Maybe the printouts will tell us which lead to follow," Soneri said.

"I'll be sure to get them tomorrow morning, even if I have to present myself in person at the office of the telephone company," Juvara said grimly.

"You need to be patient. Reality is extremely complex. Computers are so fast because they deal with numbers, not human beings."

"This seems to me a really barbaric story. Is anyone going to be saved out of all this?"

"Have we ever had an edifying story to deal with?"

"This one seems more savage than any other."

"I'd save only Nina. She was one of life's unfortunates, doing her uttermost to escape from poverty and from the miseries of those around her."

18

HE STAYED ON in his office pretending to work until
Juvara too started making preparations to leave, not before
asking hesitantly: "If there's anything you need, Commissario . . ."

"On you go," Soneri said, with a grateful smile, but the
moment he was on his own he grew dispirited at the prospect
of the empty evening ahead of him. He decided not to go out
until later when there would be fewer people about, apart
from some lonely souls like him.

He went into the wine bar without seeing the people he
feared. He ordered from Bruno a portion of Parmesan shavings and some slices of *coppa*, then he made for home, taking
the long way round. On winter evenings, in spite of all the
vandalism which had been wreaked on its inner spirit, Parma
seemed to him simply beautiful. Its straw-coloured patina
survived intact, indifferent to the torrent of vulgarity which
threatened to drown it. Soneri still carried inside himself
the city he had once known and attempted to locate it in the
doorways, in the façades and in the irregularly shaped attics
in the roofs on the far side of the river. He descended slowly
into that malaise called memory, while simultaneously keeping a tight grip on his mobile in the hope of receiving a call
in the present. But perhaps, as Angela's persistent silence on

the future of their relationship implied, she too would soon belong to the realm of memory.

He walked in the direction of Piazzale della Pace where, in days that now seemed far off, he had taken the call from Juvara that had initiated the investigation. He thought back to that moment before his life had fallen apart, as it had now. He was reliving that situation when his mobile, in a curious reprise of the other occasion, rang again. It was Musumeci, wanting to update him on the developments concerning the rapist. The woman who had driven Candiani out of his wits *was* Nina.

"Commissario, this woman was a real demon with men!" the inspector exclaimed. Soneri thought about the more colourful expressions he would have employed with his fellow officers. "To keep up with her, they had to be forever snorting some substance or other."

He had never thought of it in those terms. Many of her lovers were cocaine addicts, but that was not altogether unusual in the circles of wealthy men in search of new emotions. Everything was becoming complicated again. There were too many men who wanted that girl and too many who ended up frustrated. He quickened his pace. Once again, there was nothing for it but to let events take their course.

And the following morning they did, in fact, take their course. The printouts of the calls made by Soncini and Razzini on the night of the murder were at long last delivered. Soncini had switched off his mobile around 22.00 and had turned it back on about two hours later. The mast to which his phone received the signal was the one at Cortile San Martino, while the last call had been routed through the transmitter station near Lodi. Razzini, on the other hand, had received half a dozen calls and texts via a mast somewhere south of Lake Como. Soncini's alibi would not stand up. It was clear he had been with his friend until a certain time, and then they had gone their separate ways.

"That ties it all up," Juvara said. "And this too is down to electronics," he let fall after a moment's silence.

Soneri did not immediately reply. "There's still something that doesn't add up. In this whole business, every time you seem to be getting to the heart of things, new doubts jump out at you and you're back to where you started."

"I was sure we'd found the ace this time. At least I hoped we had," Juvara said.

"The car. That's what doesn't add up. The stolen B.M.W."

"Commissario, that's all based on the evidence of a drunk."

"Yes, but he's also a fanatic who knows all there is to know about cars."

"It could've been another car of the same make."

"You're forgetting the horse on the side."

"The symbol of the Cerreto equestrian club."

"Did you get a membership list? Have a look and see if one of the members has a B.M.W. like Soncini's."

The commissario got up and went over to Juvara's desk and picked up the folder with the documents. He began flicking through them.

"Can I help you?" Juvara said.

"I'm looking for the Cerreto number. Call that bar on Lake Como where Soncini claimed he spent the evening with his friend and ask the owner how Razzini got home."

"In what sense?"

"If he left in his own car or if he got a lift from someone else."

Without waiting for an answer, Soneri took hold of the telephone and dialled a number. Juvara watched him act with the determination he showed at his best and assumed he must have formulated a precise theory, but then he noticed that, on the contrary, he was calling Nanetti.

"Listen, what model was the B.M.W. stolen from Soncini? What was that? A turbo diesel 520, year of make 2005?"

Next, without even replacing the receiver on the cradle, he dialled another number. "Hello? Is that the Vehicles Registration Office? This is Commissario Soneri. Could I speak to Ronchini, please? . . . Ciao, how are things, Eugenio? Listen, I need you to do me a favour. Could you run a check on all the cars owned by Arnaldo Razzini? That's the one, the lawyer."

As he waited, he turned to look at Juvara but saw that he too was on the telephone. A few minutes later, he called Ronchini back. "What's that? A Fiat Punto and a B.M.W. turbo diesel 520 convertible? Thank you. That's a great help."

Soneri and Juvara hung up at the same time, but before the inspector had time to open his mouth the commissario picked up the phone again. "Musumeci, go and find Razzini, in his office or at his home. Have a good look at his B.M.W. It's a black turbo diesel 520 convertible. What I want you to do is check if it has a sticker with a galloping horse attached to one side. Let me know right away."

"Commissario, do you suspect . . ." Juvara stuttered.

Soneri nodded. "I suspect that Nina's burned body was not dumped from Soncini's car but from his friend's. They're identical, and that would mean that Mariotto was not mistaken."

"At the joint on Como they told me Razzini went home with an acquaintance. He was a bit tipsy and was seen getting into a car with this other man, an habitué of the place."

Soneri confirmed this version. "In fact Razzini must have had a lift, because that evening Soncini took his B.M.W."

"This time you can't say there are any doubts."

"We've reached the first solid point in the whole story," the commissario conceded, "but there are still doubts. Bear in mind that there's never any closure except in a judicial sense, but that'll do us."

Their satisfaction lasted no longer than the delivery of the newspapers which fired off a fresh round of accusations, aimed equally at the police and the civic authorities. The prefect was quoted as saying he was "on the side of the people" for the "restoration of law disrupted by recent events".

"A bunch of arseholes," Soneri yelled. He was heartily sick of such drivel in a city given to preaching, as if the much-vaunted "civil society" was made up of saints. "They go around shitting in the streets like their pet dogs and then complain about there being dirt everywhere," he shouted, banging the papers down on the desk. To make matters worse, he had heard that Capuozzo was furious with Soneri for deserting his post the day before.

"Don't get too worried," Marcotti tried to calm him down over the phone. "Until somebody decides otherwise, I'm coordinating this investigation and I'll decide who to put in charge of the case. Capuozzo can jump up and down all he likes."

Here at last was a woman who dispensed reassurance, the commissario thought to himself, reflecting again that she was the one he would have chosen to marry.

"I would like a warrant to search Signor Razzini's car. I have reason to believe it was the one used for the murder."

"Could you give me the background?"

"Soncini carried out some internet searches with com-promising key words at a time when very few people could have known about the murder. In addition, Razzini owns a car identical to Soncini's, with, as I believe, the same emblem on the side. We've learned from the owner of the bar where Soncini and Razzini say they spent the evening when Iliescu was murdered that Razzini was given a lift home by an acquaintance. Am I making sense?"

"Perfect sense. In this regard, I meant to tell you that the head of the Romas arrested at Suzzara in connection with the theft of gold has admitted that the boys driving the car have nothing to do with this case, and said he'll provide the proof soon."

"So let's wait a bit. Dottoressa, will you take it on yourself to inform Capuozzo? Right at this moment, our relations are not of the best."

"Certainly. I'll see to it," she said. The commissario would have liked to kiss her.

At last he felt at peace. He looked up at Juvara and saw him looking in his direction. "This is the moment to put the noose round Soncini's neck," Juvara said.

Soneri's mood darkened once more. "But what made him do it?"

The motive, one of the fundamental elements in a murder case, escaped him. Did Nina want to leave him? She had had so many other relationships. Or did he plan to leave her only to find he could not get rid of her? But she was not the type of woman to entertain regret, even if accompanied by threats of blackmail. No matter from which angle he examined the question, he could not make out what had led Soncini to kill her.

Musumeci's call disturbed his reflections. "Commissario, I can confirm that the B.M.W. has the emblem of the equestrian club on its side."

"Stay where you are. I'll send Nanetti over to join you."

"But we need a warrant."

"You'll get one."

He called Marcotti immediately. "Dottoressa, there is a horse on Razzini's car as well."

"Carry on. I'll sign the warrant at once."

He then telephoned Nanetti, who said to him: "You sound in good form. That means that everything is coming to a head."

"I might have found the person who murdered Nina."

"Is that all? I thought it was something else entirely. That's just routine for you."

He would have liked to tell him to go to hell, but the moment was not right.

Two hours later, the first results came in. Traces of petrol were found in the boot of the car, perhaps spilled from the container of petrol used to set fire to the body. In addition, luminol had shown up traces of blood on the rugs, even though it was evident that the car had been valeted with immense care. Tests would establish whether the blood was Nina's.

While having a sandwich in a bar in the city centre with Soneri and Nanetti, who had spent the morning working on Razzini's car, Dottoressa Marcotti set out her own conclusions. "It's clear to me that the proof is overwhelming, but I have to warn you that in the present situation that proof is only circumstantial. That's sufficient for me to lock him up, but it will be a different kettle of fish when the case comes to court."

The commissario was the first to share her doubts and feel dissatisfied. He thought he had had Soncini in his grasp, but instead he only had him by the hem of his coat. The affair still looked murky. It stank, but like something which spreads foul air all around without anyone being able to determine its source.

"If you want my advice," she said, shaking her magnificent blonde hair, "don't stop working on this case. We haven't got to the bottom of it yet. Anyway, you know what the next step is."

"Soncini," Soneri said.

"Come to my office and I'll sign a warrant for his arrest here and now."

It seemed as though he had been waiting. Possibly Razzini had managed to make a call before the police arrived, but Soncini had the complexion of a man who had been ill. His face no longer showed that world-weary look which the commissario had found so unsettling. Two days' growth on his chin, greasy hair straggling around a head which suddenly appeared small and pointed, wrinkles in the leather-coloured skin of his cheeks, all combined to give the impression of a man who had grown old overnight. The combative manner which the commissario had been confronted by in the first interviews was gone, and he now looked like a man resigned to letting himself go without even the slightest attempt to fight back.

"This is not a happy situation," Soneri said, after a silence in which he pretended to be reading through some documents. In fact, he knew every word by heart, yet took his time so as to keep his adversary on tenterhooks. He expected Soncini to deny the charge or seek some way out but against all expectation he murmured: "Yes, I know."

The lawyer who had accompanied him, a young man about Soncini's daughter's age, was also surprisingly reticent.

The commissario took that meekness as a sign of assent,

and went straight to the heart of the matter. "Why did you kill her?"

"I didn't mean to. It was an accident," Soncini said, in a whisper.

"Bollocks!" Soneri threw back at him in an explosion of anger which surprised even himself. The figure of Nina pregnant appeared in front of him, with once again the memory of his wife superimposed.

"It was obviously premeditated," he said, trying to control the words which were tumbling out of him in real fury. "You borrowed the car from your friend Razzini so that you could incriminate whoever had stolen yours. Maybe that was because you knew exactly who *had* stolen it."

"It all happened by sheer chance," Soncini protested. "Razzini was drunk. Nina had called to ask if we could meet as soon as possible. That was why I borrowed my friend's car, and anyway he was in no state to drive. Do you really think I'd have planned to use a car the same as my own?"

"It was the best way to ward off suspicion."

"It was an accident, I tell you. I left the place on Lake Como before ten o'clock. I don't deny that. Nina was pestering me with calls, so I arranged to meet her in Parma in a bar not far from the toll booth on the autostrada, and after a short while I switched off my mobile. She sounded extremely agitated and kept on saying she had something very important to tell me."

"Agitated in what sense? Terrified?"

"No, no. Highly emotional. Excited. She seemed happy and afraid at the same time. When we met, she threw herself into my arms, like a teenager, and told me . . . well, she told me she was expecting a baby. She'd just got the results from one of those kits you can buy in the pharmacy."

"And you were none too pleased."

Soncini looked at him with the ghostliest of smiles. "No, I didn't take it well at all. You can understand that. I'm a married man."

"That doesn't seem to have stopped you playing about," Soneri said bluntly.

"No, but there were no babies involved."

"You mean there was always a clear agreement?"

"Nina had always told me there would be no problems. And then with the life she led . . . I couldn't even be sure it was mine," he said indignantly.

"So, you could take any liberty you wished, provided your affairs remained out of sight. It's a sad old story, a little bit of philandering on the side. Even your wife went along with it, I imagine. From what I've picked up, there was nothing much between you."

Soncini nodded slowly. "The fact is that Nina wanted to keep it," he burst out as though this was the greatest monstrosity imaginable.

Once more Soneri had to make an effort to contain himself. The interview was touching more than one open sore, and he was tempted to punch Soncini's face. "Do you think it's easier for a woman to have an abortion than to keep the baby? For a woman like Iliescu, I mean, with the life she was leading?"

"She wanted us to get married. She wanted me to throw everything up," Soncini sobbed. That too seemed an outrage in his eyes, that she would ask him to give up exclusive clubs, luxury holidays, moneyed friends.

"So you made up your mind to be done with it all, mother and child in one fell swoop," Soneri cried, cutting the air with his hand like a guillotine falling.

"No, I keep telling you it was all an accident," Soncini protested. Even the lawyer began to show signs of impatience.

Soneri made a sign to both of them to remain calm. "Explain to me how it happened."

"We'd been talking a long time and it got quite heated. Nina would not budge. She said she was tired of living that way, that she was young and wanted a normal life. I told her she had cheated me and that it took two to produce a child. Then she started insulting me, saying that I'd taken advantage of her, that I had a good life while she was struggling to get by. We both lost our tempers and people in the bar started giving us funny looks. Next thing we got into the car and drove around a bit until we found an out-of-the-way place, not far from Lemignano. I gave her an ultimatum: either she had an abortion or else it was all over between us. She could say the child's father was one of the other men she'd been seeing, or else she could say, for instance, she'd been raped by Candiani. What did it matter to her? She could take him to court and make herself a bit of money. Everybody knew she'd been seeing him. But she wouldn't have it. She wanted me. She wanted to ruin me. Well, I started hitting her, not too hard, just enough to keep her under control and make her see sense. But she jumped out of the car and started running away, shouting in the mist that the whole city would find out because she was going to tell everybody. She seemed to have gone off her rocker. I ran after her. I thought I'd never catch her, but next thing I found myself on top of her. We had both run into a fence which you couldn't see in the mist. She kneed me in the balls, and I lost it. I won't deny that I went too far that evening. It was pure instinct and maybe I lost it. The fact is I landed a punch on her, the sort of punch you would give a man, and she seemed to fly backwards, as though she'd been carried away by the wind. I'd got her full on, under the chin. She fell with her neck against an iron railing. It had all happened so quickly that when I stopped to draw breath it seemed unbelievable, in the stagnant mist, the utter silence . . . I knew right away she was dead. I was scared out my wits. I had a couple of grains of powder with me and I took them. What did it matter any more? I was done for. There was no hope. However, the cocaine cleared my head and I started to think. I dragged the body into a field. Then I went to the workshop and got a container used for solvents and a sheet of canvas used for packing. I filled the container with petrol at a self-service garage, and went back to get Nina. After about a quarter of an hour I bundled her into the boot of the car. I returned to the workshop and went round to the yard at the back. It gives onto a ditch there where they often light fires to burn the crates used by a transport company. I had an hour before the arrival of the night guards on their midnight round. The petrol makes quick work of everything. It flares up quickly, burns a few minutes and then dies down. With all that mist around, there wasn't much chance of anyone seeing me. I waited for the corpse to cool down before I could wrap it up in the canvas again. That didn't take long with the temperature what it was. I laid the body on the back seat and drove onto the autostrada. I knew there was an encampment of Romanian gypsies at Cortile San Martino, and since Nina was an illegal, I thought of leaving the body there. An autostrada is the most anonymous place in the world. The whole world uses the autostrada! However, I couldn't have foreseen that there would be a pile-up at exactly that point. But for that, the body wouldn't have been discovered for ages."

Soncini collapsed on a chair as though he were on the point of fainting. He appeared more distraught and unnerved than before. Soneri allowed the silence to emphasise the gravity of the confession, but his mind went back to the farce played out in front of him a few days previously by Soncini, his wife and daughter, and his fury increased. In comparison,

Nina, no matter how casual with men, seemed to him like a lost soul trying to stay afloat in a sea of filth. The thought of her helped him nurture a little hope that he would not sink into that slime.

"It would have been better for you to keep the baby and pretend to be a caring partner. Perhaps even, for the first time in your life, you would have assumed responsibility for something. And you wouldn't be where you are now."

"Please," the lawyer intervened, "avoid making judgments. It's not your role."

The commissario threw a contemptuous look in his direction. "You're quite right. It's up to the judge to do that." He turned once more to Soncini. "You forgot to add one thing."

Soncini looked up, giving him a quizzical look.

"You'd have had to resign your position as a kept man." Soncini bowed his head again and said nothing.

19

AFTER HE HAD signed his confession, they took him away. Soneri watched him being led off by two officers followed by the lawyer, done up like a mannequin, and wondered why at that stage murderers appeared to him always so banal, so bereft of all pride, even of the pride of malice. He invariably found himself confronting unremarkable faces or insignificant people who were nothing out of the ordinary. It was impossible to see them in the role of killers. He recalled substantial mafiosi who looked like pensioners, serial killers with the appearance of admin staff, rapists who could have passed for seminarians and pitiless female poisoners with the features of a doll. Never had there been one with the surly expression of a cut-throat, the menacing eyes of a basking shark or the insolence of arrogance.

As he reflected on this, he felt his disquiet grow. There was something artificial in Soncini's submissiveness. He might have been playing a part. If it all went well for him, he might indeed be able to show it had been an accident and perhaps even get off with a sentence of a couple of years' imprisonment. He might claim he had acted under the influence of cocaine, and that burning the body had been a reaction of fear produced by the drugs.

All these doubts were swept aside for the time being by a

flood of congratulations, starting with those of Capuozzo, who knew that this way he was guarding his back against public opinion and laying the groundwork for the parade of the following morning's press conference. The newspapers were guaranteed to write that the investigators had done their job, and the political bigwigs would express their renewed faith in justice. Even Esposito phoned him from his car: "Well done, Commissario. We've pulled it off. You're the pick of the bunch."

Soneri was pleased, but he found it hard to show his satisfaction in public. He was uncomfortable with compliments because he never knew what to say. Fortunately the investigating magistrate, Marcotti, who was very like him in this way, restricted herself to a vigorous handshake and an eloquent look which said it all. The thought occurred yet again to him that if they had been contemporaries, he could easily have fallen in love with her. Juvara, who had been gazing into the middle distance for a while, apparently wrapped in thought, attempted to bring him back to earth. "Don't forget your promise, commissario."

"What promise?"

"The computer, remember? If we've solved the case, it was all down to the hard disk."

"It was down to chance. And self-interest. Young Sauro thought he could make a bit of money from a machine he should have put out. He did it because some guy had asked for a computer at a giveaway price, so he was acting in his own interests."

"That's a very reductive analysis. Sauro could have kept quiet, told us he'd thrown everything out and fitted the hard disk to another computer," Juvara objected.

"He had just opened up and needed customers. He might have decided it's always a good idea to stay on good terms with the police. Anyway, what did he care about Soncini? You're a much better customer."

The inspector surrendered. "You're always too pessimistic. Anyway, the case is solved and that's what matters."

"Solved? Mmm . . . You know what bothers me? That note, the one at Nina's house, covered with insults. Whoever wrote that must have known Nina's intentions regarding Soncini, and presumably before finding out about the baby."

Not knowing how to reply, Juvara threw up his hands helplessly, but at that moment the telephone on Soneri's desk rang.

"Commissario, Dottor Capuozzo has called a press conference for tomorrow morning at ten and would like to invite you to come along," the usual secretary announced.

"Unfortunately I can't be there. Please give the questore my apologies," Soneri said perfunctorily.

The secretary was by now accustomed to Soneri's refusals, and acting almost mechanically she assured him she would tell her superior.

"I'm going out for a breath of fresh air," he told Juvara.

He wandered about in the city centre and dropped in to a couple of tobacconists to buy cigars and the wooden matches he continued to use in preference to a lighter. He detested those bright little implements which produced fire with no smoke, these being two elements which should always go together. He made his way back to the questura, but when he was in the courtyard under the fir trees, he realised he had no wish to shut himself up in an office, so he got into his car. He had a vague idea of where he would like to go. He would like to drive across the plain towards the first of the Apennine slopes and from there climb above the mist. On the road towards the hills, the skies would gradually clear, the sun would begin to peep out, but then he would briefly plunge once more into the last of the white mist before everything would finally brighten and the world would change. At times it was only a matter of a couple of metres. He would be happy to warm his bones over lunch in a trattoria on a hillside, looking down at the plain under its sheet of chilly mist.

Such thoughts were in his mind as he got to Via Spezia but instead of proceeding in the direction of Cisa, he turned at Lemignano towards the industrial zone. He did not know what had made him abandon the idea of an outing to the hills, but he soon understood as he parked in front of Golden. He was missing Angela. Once in the hills, he would be reminded of their days away from the city, and that was what had made him turn back. He had no wish to invite pain. Better to face the hostility of Giulia Martini, who was even now staring resentfully at him. The commissario preferred to tussle with another person rather than with himself.

"Did you manage to visit your husband in jail?" he said.

"No, and I don't care to. As far as I am concerned, you can keep him. That man has been my ruination."

"You could have left him, if you hadn't been slaves to a *bella figura*."

"All my life I've had to put up with his affairs. The man is an inveterate womaniser," she said, without restraint. "After a while, I told myself I didn't care about him anymore and he could do what he liked. Once my daughter had grown up, she understood. However, I could not tolerate the idea of him breeding a litter of bastards. There is a limit."

"Don't go any further. That unborn baby had very little to do with it. What mattered was your self-interest. You're not defending respectability, just business."

The woman seemed about to assault him. The commissario savoured his own mordant lucidity and was indifferent to any offence he gave. He stood in front of her, throwing down the gauntlet with words she had never wanted to hear, words which stripped her naked.

"For years the two of you were happy to play the part of the united couple, just so long as it kept the business turning over. It was of no concern to you if your husband went after other women in nightclubs, because the thing that mattered was to put on a brave front for the people who placed the orders, the ecclesiastical curias. A fine marriage, a flourishing company, a daughter who marries into the Dall'Argine family, a veneer of dutiful Catholicism . . . a model family," he said sarcastically. "And all to display an irreproachable image, a guarantee for the bishops and traditionalist clients who buy the gold and jewellery from you. And then a Romanian girl turns up and it all gets serious. She wants a family. You know perfectly well she'll not back off and so you threaten her, you send her threatening letters, but the girl holds fast. At that point, you take to blackmailing your husband: either you stop seeing her or I'll cut off your allowance. No more *dolce vita* as kept man, no more women, no more clubs and expensive cars. And when you find out she's expecting a child, you deliver your ultimatum. He's got his back to the wall, forced to choose between the playboy life and giving up Nina, and he opts for the second, but he didn't reckon with her sheer grit. She really did want an ordinary life with the man she loved most of all of them. So she had to be got rid of. After all, what was she but an illegal immigrant from Romania? Who's going to go looking for her? And in fact nobody did go looking for her, except one old grandparent who set out for Italy to act as peacemaker between the girl and the gypsy community, but the bus journey finished him off. End of story." By the end of his story, Soneri found himself trembling with rage.

"You're a visionary!" Martini screamed, hissing like a

cobra. "You can believe anything you like, but she was no more than a common whore. She gave herself to one and all, and I'll tell you something else. She had a great talent for getting men all worked up. She knew how to appeal to their weaker side, playing each one in a different way. She sniffed them out like a snake, and then drew them into her trap. I can't help laughing at your portrait of her as a victim. A vulgar prostitute! A slut!" She was yelling at the top of her voice, all pretence at being *una vera signora* cast aside.

Soneri stared at her in consternation. At that moment for the first time he grasped just how venomous to each other women can be, and to a degree unimaginable in a man. Her eyes expressed infinite ferocity, and her snarling mouth twisted by hatred could have torn off chunks of meat with a single bite. The commissario took a step back when she screamed at him to get out of the office. He felt sick, and as he left he was glad once again to breathe in great, reviving gulps of fresh air. He felt himself growing lighter and lighter, less bound to life and for this reason more pitiless in his judgments of it.

He sat behind the wheel of his car and when he got to the turn-off for Via Spezia he contemplated for a moment which direction to take, Cisa or the city. He remembered it was time for lunch and thought it would be a waste of time to go looking for the sun when the sky would already be taking on the colours of dusk. In the mountains in winter, only morning counts.

When it was almost two o'clock, anxiety began to take hold of him again. He was still hoping for some communication from Angela, but he sensed that she would not call that day. He decided to go to Alceste's, once again looking for refuge in food and drink. With a wry smile, he recognised that there was not much else available to him.

There were not many people there, but Sbarazza had had the luck to find one table which apparently three women had just left.

"You've chosen a place where there's not much for you to eat," Soneri said, coming up behind the Marchese.

"Man does not live by bread alone," Sbarazza replied. "I was very taken by the lady who was seated here."

The outline of her lips had been imprinted on the serviette in crimson, and Sbarazza gazed longingly at that trace of femininity. "I can smell her perfume and the seat still has the warmth and the very form of her body," he said, as if in a dream.

The commissario smiled. The old man was one of the few people with whom at that moment he was happy to spend the afternoon. There was something profound and consoling in his conversation.

"I hear you've solved the case of that unfortunate Romanian girl," Sbarazza said. "So did you finally draw the right card from the pack?"

"It did finally emerge, although I was on the point of despair."

"You see? Never give up. Never lose faith."

"For the last few days I had been thinking I would never get a good hand."

"It's when it seems that nothing can happen that chance does its work for us. Even at this moment while we're here eating, absorbed with nothing more than flavours and scents, perhaps something which concerns us is occurring. A billiard ball rolling into a pocket can be the result of a thousand cannons," the Marchese chuckled.

"Maybe you're right," Soneri said as a plate of *tortelli di zucca* arrived at the table. "Maybe something will cannon off something else in my path this afternoon and change the prospects for me. This morning . . ." He tasted the first *tortello*.

"What happened to you this morning?"

"I was making for the hills when, on an impulse, I changed direction. I made a choice, there and then. If I'd gone the way I first intended, I'd have spent the morning quite differently. For a start I wouldn't be here talking to you, and instead of having a plate of *tortelli di zucca* I'd be having a plate of *gnocchi ai funghi*."

Sbarazza made a sign to him to stop. "Don't go down that path. It'd be an infinite process and finish up in complete nonsense or with the conclusion that everything you do is wrong because there's always a more promising possibility."

"So? Is that not true to life?"

"I prefer to believe that if a choice has been made, there's a reason for it. You could call it providence, or determinism, but in both cases our will is only in part responsible. The rest is something obscure that we are not permitted to know, whether it's transcendent or immanent," the Marchese declared, in philosophical mood.

"I deal with much more banal but all too human causes: money, sex and the passions which spring from them."

"Those are only effects. Don't muddle them. If you think about it, that obscure, pre-eminent cause which directs our lives conducts itself in such a way that killing or loving are, when all is said and done, on the same level of potentiality, but then, in time, the balls cannon off each other in a certain way and produce now one outcome, now the other, or both."

The commissario savoured another *tortello*, and then muttered his dissent: "Do you know why I enjoy your company? You make me feel an optimist. I can't resign myself to the thought that we're all machines controlled from long range. Neither one of us can rule out the possibility that we might become murderers, but the fact is that we are not. The majority of people are not."

"From fear, only from fear. For a minority there's also an element of awareness."

"What is this awareness? Morality?"

"A conquest, a point of arrival. When someone in thought or deed falls to the very lowest point of humanity, he begins to be aware. Then and only then, after dabbling in evil, can he choose. Other people draw back from fear of the reaction which wickedness arouses, but life with its limitless sequence of possibilities could entice them to say yes to even the most nefarious acts."

"Are you one of the fellowship of the aware?"

"Don't you know I've done all sorts of things? And you too are a member of the fraternity, after all you've seen."

The commissario smiled and got up. "I do see so much that is appalling," he said, thinking of his most recent meeting. "And I see no end of it."

"Seize every opportunity. You know what to do."

"Well . . ." Soneri said. "I'll go and face whatever the afternoon brings."

The first thing was the authorisation to interview Medioli. Soneri arranged to see him in the evening, and hoped he had decided to talk. He was seeking some enlightenment on the world of the Romas. All those years spent in the caravans could not have been in vain.

The second thing to arrive was news brought by the beguiling policewoman who had made such an impression on Musumeci.

"There's someone here who wants to talk to you. Looks like a gypsy," she told him.

In the commissario's mind, the Roma camp and the man asking to see him fused into one.

"Send him in."

The man was dressed like the old peasants in the Apennines, in the modest but dignified elegance seen in ageing prints. He said his name was Floriu and he must have been in Italy for some time, for his Italian was fluent.

"You've come from Suzzara?"

The man nodded. "From the camp."

"If it's about the gold, you'll have to go and talk to the carabinieri."

"I know, but that's not why I'm here. I've come about those two boys."

"The ones in the B.M.W. stolen from Soncini?"

He nodded once again. "I wanted to tell you they had nothing to do with it. They were just showing off."

"Are you the father of one of them?"

"No, but I'll take responsibility for what has happened. I stole the car. I came to give myself up, provided you let the boys go free."

"I doubt if it really was you who carried out the theft, and anyway the legal system does not allow exchanges of that sort."

"They had nothing to do with it," the man repeated forcefully. "The car was in the camp to be dismantled and sent off to Romania. There are lots of our people going there and back. They would have reassembled it over there. It's the safest way, but those two pinched the keys and went out for a run. That's all there is to it."

"Are you telling me this to get revenge on some family enemy? Why otherwise would you give me a tip-off like this? To save two boys who'd be let out soon in any case?"

Floriu straightened up, betraying his embarrassment. "No

vengeance, and no tip-off. It's the first car we've handled. I know others do it, traffic in cars, but in our camp it's the first time it's happened."

"Why should that be? You've decided to branch out?"

"No," the old man stammered. "There'll be no trafficking in cars."

"Well then, explain yourself more clearly." Soneri was growing impatient. "None of what you've said so far makes any sense to me."

"It was those four. They did it."

"Which four?"

"The ones who were involved in stealing the gold. They took the car, even if they've never done it before. I don't know why. One night they came back with it. There are honest and dishonest people among us. Like among you Italians."

"Now you're making more sense," the commissario said. "The four found by the carabinieri with the gold are the same ones who stole the B.M.W. Is that what you're saying?"

The Romanian nodded, but without much conviction.

"But you insist you've never stolen a car?"

"No, never."

Soneri said nothing for a few moments. He was trying to understand, but the whole matter was beyond him.

"In your opinion, why did it happen?"

The man shrugged. "I don't know. You'll have to ask them."

Floriu's attitude had changed, and now he seemed keen to get away. Perhaps he was disappointed at the way the interview had gone.

"You do know why it all happened," Soneri insisted.

"I'm here to state that those boys had nothing to do with it, but if you don't believe me, I have nothing more to add." He stopped there. It seemed as though a shutter had been pulled down. The Romanian's grim expression was distrustful, so much so that when he had gone, Soneri felt he had not been up to the challenge. Perhaps subconsciously he had believed the case was all but closed and he had failed to pick up the signals the Romanian was giving him. He had not remained open to every possibility, as Sbarazza would have said.

"Juvara, do you remember that text relayed from the mast at Cortile San Martino, the one to Nina saying that everything was ready?"

"Yes, from the stolen mobile."

"What do you think it meant?"

"I haven't a clue," the inspector said. "On the other hand we have found something interesting among Soncini's papers."

"What's that?"

"There was money deposited in a current account in Iliescu's name at the Savings Bank."

"What's so extraordinary about that?"

"That she had 750,000 euros in that account."

"Do you think the money was hers?"

"No. Aimi has access to the account as well."

"The accountant?"

"Commissario, if there's one thing in this whole story I just don't get, it's the bomb at Golden. Everything up to that point has a logic of its own, but not that explosion. And now there's this account."

"I know. If only these Romanians would talk. The guy who came today seemed to want to tell me something."

"They're releasing the two teenagers. This morning they were let out of the Young Offenders prison and now they're with Marcotti at the magistrate's office."

Soneri jumped to his feet at once, as though his desk was

on fire. Juvara watched him walk briskly across the courtyard in the direction of Via Repubblica and disappear through the gate.

Ten minutes later he was in the investigating magistrate's office. The young men had the same hostile expression as before.

"Commissario, don't waste your breath. These two have made up their minds not to speak. They must have been ordered on pain of death to keep their mouths shut," Marcotti said.

The commissario pulled up a chair and sat facing them. "We know you didn't kill the girl, and we know the B.M.W. was stolen by other people, in fact by the four men arrested at Suzzara," he began.

The two exchanged glances and for a moment it seemed their hostility softened a little. "You'll be out in a short while. All I want to know is why you took the car when you knew that the men who had stolen it planned to send it to Romania bit by bit to make some money on it. You knew that you risked being stopped and that would wreck the whole scheme."

The two said nothing, staring straight ahead with the same impassive expression.

"Isn't it odd?" Soneri said to Marcotti. "There's a car which is really hot and two boys with no licence take it out for a ride. They say they were framed, but they framed themselves. A right pair of idiots, amateurs."

The last words struck home with the pair, who were apparently unwilling to be taken as fools in what they considered their line of work.

"That car no stolen," the older of the two burst out. "That car given."

Soneri continued to look at Marcotti. "Given by whom?"

"By Italian man. No know name."

"Soncini?"

"No know name," the Romanian repeated, raising his voice slightly.

The peremptory tone indicated that there would be no further dialogue. After a few minutes more, Marcotti cut proceedings short. "Let's take it slowly," she said, handing the two boys over to the officers who would take them back to the Suzzara camp.

"Commissario, you should be pleased," the magistrate said. "You've learned one important thing. It seems the car was not stolen as Soncini claimed."

"Do you think they're telling the truth?"

"Do you think someone who does my job could risk putting her hand in the fire? But if you really want my opinion, I do believe it," she said, winking at Soneri. "Why should they make up a story? People only do that when they have some reason for it, but in this case they've nothing to fear, don't you agree?"

The commissario nodded. "That means the Romas and Soncini were in business together."

"Cocaine?"

"I thought of that," the commissario said. "But in that case, what are we to make of the bomb at Golden?"

"Maybe it was directed at Soncini."

"If you're in business with somebody, you know nearly all about them. Anybody doing business with Soncini must have known that he and his wife wielded quite different levels of economic power," Soneri said.

"And who's to say, in spite of that, that they were not united when it came to business?"

He was about to reply, but he stopped himself. Marcotti's hypothesis suddenly shed a new light on the case.

"Who knows? You might be right."

When he emerged from the magistrate's office, night was falling and he had still not seen Medioli. He was grateful for the fact that this man who had lived in exile from the world had been caught up in the whirlwind of events. "Our infiltrator", Soneri had called him as he took his leave from Marcotti.

"I'd put my money on him," she had replied, winking at him once more.

20

AS HE DROVE along Via Mantova in the direction of the prison, he felt like Fabrizio del Dongo fleeing towards the Po, on the same road and perhaps in the same state of mind. His instinct was that this was the final round and there would be no second chance, whatever Sbarazza might think. Capuozzo had made him a lengthy speech, in his customary woolly style, strewn with vague suggestions. The murderer was behind bars, the motive was clear enough, Nina's relatives would soon forget and public opinion was pacified. Why waste more time? There was no shortage of work in the questura, and anyway digging too deep often resulted in bringing to the surface questions no-one really wanted spend even more time confronting.

Nonetheless, Soneri pressed on. He was aghast at the prospect of dealing with bureaucratic matters, signing papers or pursuing half-witted drug addicts who had held up tobacconists with a dirty syringe. And of contemplating life without Angela. The reasons for deciding to persevere with Medioli were professional pride and curiosity, but also vanity with regard to Angela. For some days, his name had been on the front pages of the papers she read. It was his way of keeping his profile up, even if there was only one reader who interested him.

He was escorted through a dozen doors and gates before he got to the interview room. Nothing had changed – same rattling locks, same low ceiling, same stifling atmosphere, same off-white paint. However, Medioli appeared in better shape, more healthy and more at peace with himself than when they had last met.

"I've been expecting you," was his promising opening. "But I was beginning to think that you didn't care anymore to hear what I had to say. As the days went by, I was more and more convinced that the law wasn't interested in probing too far beneath the surface. I presumed that extended to me. I thought of sending a message to the magistrate saying that I was ready to cooperate, but I never got round to it. I'm fine here. I've a good relationship with everybody and I've been teaching these unfortunate lads in here how to fix engines. I gave them hope and I've found a purpose in life. That helps, doesn't it?"

Soneri nodded gravely, but he preferred to get away from this subject. "I should have come sooner. I had the explanation to so many things within reach."

"I don't know about 'so many', but some, yes. From what I read in the papers, you're already very well informed."

"No, not 'very'. For instance, I don't know what kind of deal the Romas and Soncini had with each other."

"Soncini?" Medioli started to snigger, but immediately pulled himself together. "You know that in a camp there are all kinds, honest and dishonest, the same as anywhere else. But you must also know that the Romas have a weakness for gold."

Several different thoughts coalesced in Soneri's mind to form one unbroken thread – Golden, Soncini's deals, the

Romas' gold and Marcotti's idea that Nina's murderer and Soncini's wife were partners in business and not only to keep up appearances.

"Are you saying that Golden used gold stolen by the Romas and that Soncini was the go-between?"

"You're missing one item: Nina Iliescu."

"She was an intermediary?"

"What I reckon is that at the beginning she was put under pressure by her fellow countrymen, used as a means of recycling all that gold. With the Romas as with everybody else, nothing is like it used to be. They're as greedy for money as the next man. There was a gang in the camp who could never get enough to keep them satisfied. They even started robbing churches, and that's when the friction broke out. There are some things you just don't touch, and in their world tradition still counts. That's why the Romanians moved out, because the feuding was turning into an ethnic war."

"So Iliescu was caught in a web?" Soneri said. He still clung to the belief that Nina was a victim of the clan.

"In my opinion, yes. Don't forget that her family was related to the Romas."

"In the end they hated her. Maybe she had managed to crawl out of the dunghill?"

"Maybe that's what happened, maybe she was already condemned, but from the night of the accident, when you arrested me, I don't know anything more."

"What about Mariotto? Why did they beat him up?"

"Because in spite of the alcohol, he'd seen what really happened. The B.M.W., I mean. Without that information, you'd have had a hard job of it, wouldn't you?"

"Razzini's B.M.W., the same model as Soncini's," the commissario said, as though talking to himself.

"I don't know who this Razzini is," Medioli said. "What

I do know is that Soncini dumped the body there that night because it was the safest place. Nobody ever climbs down the slope beside an autostrada, and the Romas were there to guard it. But with all he'd been up to beforehand, it all back-fired on him."

"But Nina really was one of them . . . ?"

"You said it yourself. In the final stages they hated her. There were nasty rumours circulating about her."

"Why?"

"I think she'd breached some code. Or as you were imply-ing, probably she wanted to get out, which in the eyes of the community came to the same thing. I believe the Romas had agreed to eliminate her, and I wouldn't be at all surprised if one of them was there on the night of the murder. Business was going well with Soncini, if you see what I mean. Nina was a loose cannon and knew too much."

"So it wasn't just about the baby?"

"That was a matter for her lover's wife, but Signora Martini herself didn't do too badly out of the arrangement: access to cheap gold, you understand? And if Soncini hadn't been such a brainless cocaine addict, it'd all have gone smoothly. Mariotto was beaten up because he blurted every-thing out and that was no good to anybody, but it was really meant as a warning to Manservisi. He hates the Romanians like poison and told you what Mariotto had seen. He wanted to give you a tip-off, but he couldn't say too much because he was afraid."

"But then Soncini, when he reported the theft of his car, tried to double-cross the Romanians . . ."

"No, not at all! As I just said, Soncini is a moron who fucked up even his own swindles. His wife used to pass him the cash to pay off the Romas for the gold, but he pocketed it to feed his cocaine habit. When they came looking for their money, he had to hand over his car to keep them quiet. Then his wife found out, and I suppose she went crazy. She ordered him to report the theft to the police. Just imagine what would've happened if a B.M.W., property of Golden, had turned up in a Roma camp with no report submitted! That car was hot! So a deal was struck with the Romas. The vehicle would be theirs, but they would make it disappear when the time was right, perhaps by taking it apart. And that's not all. Soncini, to keep up appearances, got hold of another car of the same kind from some friend he'd made while they were snorting together. So you see, Soncini was the weak link in the whole chain."

"In other words, Soncini had no wish to put the blame on the Romanians. He did use that car for the murder, but he'd been driving about in it for a while, and he was doing so so as not to arouse suspicions about his gold deals," the commissario reflected, thinking that once again the coincidences were multiplying.

"Apart from anything else, it's a very fashionable car in their world. He would never have had the guts to dupe the Romanians. He's too much of a coward. You're attributing to him a bigger brain than he has. He simply got himself entangled in his own lies, in the games a prick like him gets up to and in his craving for cocaine. When you act like that, you're on a slippery slide and there's no way back."

When Medioli fell silent, he and the commissario sat staring at each other. "You don't look convinced," Medioli said.

"I see everything from a new perspective. I'd better get used to that."

"Reality has many faces. We get accustomed to one and think that's all there is to it. Maybe it's just laziness, but the others seem unbelievable. It happened to me when I entered the Roma world, and my previous life just melted away."

"Now I too . . ." the commissario began, but he stopped because he was beginning to think about Angela again.

"What a shit heap!" Medioli said. "Get out while you can, or you'll end up stinking as well."

"I'm more likely to go mad," Soneri corrected him as he was about to leave.

"Commissario, do you think what I've told you will be enough to get me some time off my sentence?"

"I'll do my best," he assured him.

It was only when he was walking to his car, in the centre of a square covered with a mist which made the lamplights seem to quiver slightly, that he realised how utterly he had lost his bearings. Reality kept losing its outlines in spite of all his efforts to impose some shape on it. Soncini was unquestionably a killer, but he was also a victim – his wife appeared to be in charge, but she was overwhelmed by unhappiness. The Romas suffered a life of exploitation while searching for prosperity; Nina's lovers seemed to be winners but ended up losers; and Nina? She was the only one who had lost everything, dead in her early twenties while pursuing the dream of a normal life.

As he drove, he gripped the steering wheel tightly and trembled with rage. To calm himself down, he took out his mobile and dialled Marcotti's number.

"That Martini woman is in it up to her neck," he said. "She was turning out jewellery and sacred vessels with gold stolen, even from churches, by a gang of Romas."

For a few moments the investigating magistrate made no reply, and the commissario imagined her shaking her blonde mane in indignation.

"We'll have to pay a visit to the Signora," she said finally.

"It won't be easy to find anything at this late stage, but it's worth a try."

His next call was to Juvara. "Get in touch with Musumeci. Organise a search at Golden. Maybe Martini will move from being a plaster-cast saint to a she-devil."

"What are we looking for there?"

"They'll have got rid of anything compromising. Get hold of balance sheets, order forms, movements into and out of the warehouse, and pay special attention to deliveries to the various curias."

Juvara tried to say something, but Soneri cut him off. "See if you can find a member of staff who's willing to speak. There might be an employee who's got a grudge against Martini, somebody who got sacked. Talk to the trade union. With a temperament like hers, she must have made a fair number of enemies."

All of a sudden he felt tired and a little afraid. He would have liked to stop and end the investigation there because he feared he had not yet got to the bottom of it. Every probe took him one more step further down.

He drove aimlessly around the city streets without knowing where he wanted to go, but when he was advised that the search was already under way he made for Lemignano. He avoided Signora Martini, fuming with rage inside Musumeci's car together with her daughter, who was just back from her honeymoon and was in all probability, after the clamour of recent days, facing an early divorce. It was unlikely in the extreme that the Dall'Argine dynasty would tolerate their new daughter-in-law figuring so prominently in such a scandal.

He went into the now familiar office and found Juvara

standing under the portrait of the Pope. The inspector was examining the sacred vessels one by one. Soneri joined him, and when he saw him pick up a chalice, he smiled contentedly.

"Commissario, I noticed this one because it seemed so out of place. When I took a closer look, it reminded me of something."

"You're improving all the time," the commissario told him, still smiling. "I'd have started from there myself. Very often clues are so obvious that it's easy to overlook them."

"No, I'm being serious. This chalice reminds me of an object I saw in the office on a website featuring reproductions of stolen goods. You see the engraved image of Christ? It's strange because it's a clean-shaven Christ, whereas normally he has long hair and a beard."

Soneri turned serious. "Where was it stolen from?"

"From the parish church at Pedrignano."

"Is there a parish priest there still?"

"No, but an aunt of mine who lives nearby says that the priest from Sorbolo goes there to say mass."

"Bring the chalice. We'll go now."

They drove again through the mist, with Juvara clutching his seat belt, scared out of his wits by Soneri's carefree driving and by all the plane trees looming suddenly and menacingly out of the mist.

The parish priest, Don Mario Baldini, was having dinner, and the housekeeper was taken aback when the two men told her they were police officers. The priest himself, a napkin still tucked into his collar, came to the kitchen door.

"We've got something for you," Soneri said, handing him the chalice.

Don Mario took it in his hand with respectful delicacy, walked over to a sideboard and put on his glasses to examine the object. After a very few moments examining it, he said: "It's the one that was stolen."

The commissario and Juvara let out a sigh of relief. A priest had just handed down a sentence on the Martinis, mother and daughter. Perhaps the prison chaplain would give them absolution.

On his return, Soneri called Marcotti and told her about the chalice and its identification.

"See if you can get in touch with Musumeci," he suggested. "He can carry out the arrests."

"This story's got everything, hasn't it? The only thing missing was a chalice used for holy Mass but manufactured in mortal sin," the magistrate chortled.

"For once I'm going to take Capuozzo's advice. I'm going no further with this case."

"We'll have to see about that, Commissario. Don't forget that I'm the one who makes the decisions on investigations."

Soneri drove Juvara back to the office, and decided he had done enough for the day. Hunger was calling him to the wine bar. Bruno laid out a mixed plate of *torta fritta*, *spalla cotta*, *coppa* and *prosciutto*, together with shavings of Parmesan and a bottle of Bonarda. This was his psycho-medicine of choice, and he was confident he would feel a new man after downing such delicacies. When his feelings of euphoria were at their height and the wine had quite gone to his head, his mobile rang.

"Commissario . . ."

"Angela!"

The tone of both voices was already reconciliation enough.

"If you're calling to give me bad news, you couldn't have

chosen a better moment. I've still got half a bottle of Bonarda on the table in front of me . . ." Soneri babbled.

"I can't say if it's good or bad news, but I was wondering if you'd like to come round."

The commissario hesitated.

"Assuming you've no other commitments, work or whatever . . ." Angela went on.

"You can't be serious."

"No, never more serious. But you'd be fully entitled to . . ."

"I'll be there in ten minutes."

He left half his meal on the table and ran out. Bruno, unaware of what was happening, shouted after him: "Man labours for food, but if man doesn't eat . . ." But Soneri was well on his way and did not hear him.

Once they were face to face, they gazed at each other intensely. Neither knew where to start, both deeply embarrassed, Angela restrained by a sense of guilt and Soneri by a feeling of insecurity. The relationship they hoped to rekindle appeared to both of them fragile, and each feared rupturing it with an ill-judged word or move. As often happened between them, they communicated by looks while their rambling words served to ease tension.

"You've done brilliantly," Angela said.

The commissario picked up in her tone of voice something more than a compliment. They were indirectly exchanging words of love, while pretending to speak of other things.

"The poor girl!" Soneri said. "All she wanted was to enjoy life like anyone else. She wanted a partner to spend her life with, but all she found were wealthy men on the prowl."

Angela looked at him affectionately and tenderly. "Are you sure that's the way it was?" she asked, laughing warmly as she spoke. "If there's one thing I like about you and have never found in any other man, it's that you manage to combine the naivety of a boy with the cynical pessimism of an old man."

"Everyone has their contradictions."

She shook her head. "That's not the point. You see the vilest aspects of this world and you accept them with pragmatic resignation, but you never give up thinking like a dreamer. Or a child. In spite of everything, there is a spring of hope in you. It's this quality that makes me love you."

Soneri was thoroughly confused. Angela had left him naked to the point where he had no idea what to say. He felt defenceless but happy to be so in front of this woman who, he now felt sure, was deeply attached to him.

"And that's why you're so wrong about Iliescu," Angela said.

He might have succeeded in finding the culprits, but he had not understood anything. He felt inept. His partner's words were both wounding and confusing.

"Are you determined to extinguish the hope that remains in me?"

"No. I've just said it's the thing I most admire in you. But that girl really was a pernicious person."

"How do you know?"

"You won't lose your temper if I tell you?"

The commissario shook his head.

"The other man, the one . . ."

"I understand."

"Well, he's defending Candiani . . ."

". . . who can now say anything he likes."

"No, there's only one version. The other man knows all about the cocaine deals."

"And what does all this have to do with Nina?"

"Quite a lot," Angela assured him. "The other man convinced Candiani to come clean, and in a couple of days he's going to hand over a memorandum to his defence team in which he'll detail all the various moves in the cocaine trade. Nina was more than a pawn."

Everything was falling apart around Soneri. His reality was evaporating into the mists.

"She worked for Aimi, and the Cerreto club was one of the distribution centres for 'snow' in Parma. She even had an account which was used to transfer the money raised by the drug deals. She took a percentage on the quantities ordered and she got a cut on any new clients she recruited."

Soneri turned a quizzical look on her, while the outlines of the affair shifted yet again, sinking to ever lower depths.

"Franco, it's the truth!" she smiled. "Iliescu was no more than a whore – a high-class whore, if you like, but a whore nevertheless. Her role was to seduce men who had money to burn. Or bored, empty-minded people searching for excitement. She had a real gift for that. Once she'd ensnared them, she talked them into taking a little of the stuff until she made them users. And you thought she was a victim?"

"She was. After all, she was murdered," Soneri insisted.

"She went too far. The Romas saw her as a traitor because she bowed out of the gold deals. They probably threatened her, and she thought she was in a stronger position than she actually was. She most likely threatened to blow the whistle, and so the Romas, Soncini and his wife decided to do away with her. But even with Aimi, according to Candiani, she carried on raising the stakes. She was pretty, she had them all at her feet, but there was no satisfying her. Greed is so often a factor."

"All this could well stand up, but what about the baby?" Soneri objected, thinking of his dead wife and his own sorrows. These were matters which had perhaps confused him all throughout the investigation.

"You have no idea what some women are like. Passion can go hand in hand with cynicism and calculation with emotion. Just possibly Iliescu really was in love with Soncini, maybe she did want to have that baby. She wanted the lot, but when you no longer experience hunger, you risk contracting indigestion. She wanted money and a comfortable life as well as a man and children. She never had time to bring all her hopes together and put them in order. She wanted them all, right away, in one go."

"I could go along with that as an investigator, but I'm still a very poor psychologist."

"That's not the point," Angela said. "It's that you are a better person than the people you have to deal with. And I'm not just talking about down-and-out criminals, but about the wealthy middle class of this city. That's where you find *real* criminals."

"You're speaking like a woman in love." Soneri tried to make light of the situation, but Angela took him seriously and nodded.

"Yes, I am," she said.

They embraced with raw urgency, like two old comrades-in-arms.

"I had given you up for lost, but now you're back," Soneri whispered. "I don't know how this has happened."

"I needed time to reflect. I knew I was hurting you badly, because I know you love me, but there were a lot of things going on. Let's say it's all down to Providence," Angela said with a touch of irony.

"You're not the first person to be lecturing me about that. I've been stumbling over it for some time now."

"We all trip over it. We try to make plans, but often

something turns up that blows us off course, like scraps of paper in the wind."

"And what blew you off course?"

"Life with you was too routine, that was the first thing. Then the other man came along and made me feel desired once again."

"You liked him, that's all there was to it. And perhaps you still do."

Angela did not deny it. "I never considered leaving you. Maybe if it had all worked out with the other man, I'd have had to choose. But, I don't know how to say this . . ."

"In what way did it not work out? Tell me who I have to thank?"

"Chance, providence," Angela said with a laugh. "A couple of days ago I bumped into a colleague I hadn't seen for ages. It just so happened that both of us were due to have trials before different courts, but both trials collapsed. What sort of coincidence was that? We found ourselves having a coffee in the same bar. In the course of the conversation, gossiping about mutual friends, the talk turned to the other man. She didn't know what had been going on between me and him, but she let slip that last month he had been courting her insistently. In other words, he was trying it on with both of us at the same time."

"So I should send a bouquet to your colleague."

"Maybe it would all have ended in any case," Angela said, without much conviction.

"I doubt it. You were fond of him, and if he hadn't slipped up, which you found out about by pure chance, you'd be with him still and you'd have left me," Soneri groaned.

"At some stage, I'd have had to make up my mind."

"You'd have chosen him. He excited you, you were elated."

"He made me feel important."

Soneri fell silent. He was gripped by anxiety over what might have been. "You had effectively left me. You were about to tell me so when something made you turn back. I was already an ex."

"But now we're here," she said.

"By pure chance."

"We are light, unbearably light, made of nothing. We can only seize the moment, but we can't claim there is any continuity in what we are, nor can we make plans that are anything more than vague desires. In a flash something can change the unstable formula of our attachments. It's an infinite round of waltz steps. Life produces saints and killers, monks and pimps, thieves and honest men."

"Now it has produced the two of us, and has allowed us once more to walk a little way together. It's no good thinking too far ahead," Angela said.

"Alright. Let's take full advantage of this opportunity your other man has offered us," Soneri said, taking out his mobile to call the investigating magistrate.

"Dottoressa, do you have a moment? It appears to be the case that Nina was a link in a chain for the distribution of cocaine, centred on the Cerreto club. In the next couple of days, you'll have in your hands a memorandum written by Candiani for his defence. That Aimi needs more attention as well."

As they spoke he could hear in her voice annoyance and disappointment over that human betrayal of his. "But, forgive me, why are you telling me this? I entrusted the case to you."

"We're talking about drugs now, something for the narcotics squad to look into. For the rest, no need to look any further than Musumeci, who took care of Candiani."

"Look here, and I'm saying this for your sake, it seems

they want to take the case out of your hands. I don't get it," she said.

"Capuozzo was right. It's as well to stop at a certain point. I have no desire to sink any deeper into this shit."

Valerio Varesi

RIVER OF SHADOWS

Translated from the Italian by Joseph Farrell

A relentless deluge lashes the Po Valley, and the river itself swells beyond its limits. A barge breaks free of its moorings and drifts erratically downstream; when it finally runs aground its seasoned pilot is nowhere to be found. The following day, an elderly man of the same surname falls from thewindow of a nearby hospital. Commissario Soneri, scornful of his superiors' scepticism, is convinced the two incidents are linked. Stonewalled by the bargemen who make their living along the riverbank, he scours the floodplain for clues. As the waters begin to ebb, the river yields up its secrets: tales of past brutality, bitter rivalry and revenge.

MACLEHOSE PRESS

www.maclehosepress.com

Subscribe to our quarterly newsletter

Valerio Varesi

THE DARK VALLEY

Translated from the Italian by Joseph Farrell

Commissario Soneri returns to his roots for a hard-earned holiday, a few days mushrooming on the slopes of Montelupo. The isolated village of his birth relies on a salame factory founded by Palmiro Rodolfi, and now run by his son, Paride. On arrival, Soneri is greeted by anxious rumours about the factory's solvency and the younger Rodolfi's whereabouts. Soon afterwards, a body is found in the woods. In the shadow of Montelupo, the carabinieri prepare to apprehend their chief suspect – an ageing woodsman who defended the same mountains from the S.S. during the war.

MACLEHOSE PRESS

www.maclehosepress.com
Subscribe to our quarterly newsletter